ONE BAD TURN

EMMA SALISBURY

Copyright © 2016 Emma Salisbury
All rights reserved.

No part of this publication may be reproduced or transmitted in any form or by any means without permission of the author.
All the characters in this book are fictitious and any resemblance to actual persons living or dead is purely coincidental.
Although real place names and surveillance operations are referred to in this book the storyline relating to them is completely fictitious.

Book cover design by Aimee Coveney
Typeset by Coinlea Services in Garamond

ACKNOWLEDGEMENTS

Thanks to the folk who have pointed out the rubbish bits, made me lose the prologue when I was umbilically attached to it, and flagged up a character halfway through the book that hadn't got a mention anywhere else. You know who you are.

I got the idea for this story while reading James Bannon's *Running with the Firm* on holiday, an account of the violence which permeated football back in the '90s. I'm planning to read a book on anxiety management on my next trip so who knows what Coupland's next storyline will be…

Saving the best until last my biggest thanks go out to my readers, yes, YOU, for choosing this book and continuing to support me. And for those of you who go on to post reviews, well, you're all fan-bloody-tastic.

CHAPTER 1

A proper little fighter this one. Didn't even scream when he jumped out behind her, just shoved him with both hands, sent him flying backwards while she tried to make a run for it. She had some speed on her, he'd give her that; shame about the heels holding her back. That was her biggest mistake, he reckoned, not taking them off before she tried to leg it. She'll pay for that, he smirked, just as her ankle gave way. He might not be athletic but he could outrun a fit woman in heels any day. He grinned as he began to catch up with her, grabbing her by the hair before pulling her into the bushes. She hit him then, a punch rather than a girly slap, and the shock of it sent him off balance. 'You can't win this,' he sneered as he righted himself, dragging her down onto the gravel path. He straddled her, yet still she struggled, as though there was any other way this was going to pan out. A pile of rocks were within arm's reach, looked big enough to do the job. He lifted one, felt the weight of it, cold in his hand. He held the rock above her head, staring at her features in the moonlight. He hadn't realised what a looker she was. 'Shame about that,' he whispered as he brought the rock down.

Coupland bounded through Manchester Airport, Lynn and Amy flanking him, a grin plastered across his face despite the flight's arrival being delayed by an hour. 'I tell you what,' he observed as they'd taken the green route through customs, 'that lot wouldn't dare search through my case, not without their bloody latex gloves, all the rich food we've been having.' He seemed disappointed no one had paid them any attention on their return journey.

'Kevin,' Lynn rolled her eyes at the back of his head as she tried to keep up with his cigarette starved pace, 'it's just routine when you go through security now, they were only doing their job.' Even though two weeks had passed since he'd suffered the indignity Coupland was having none of it.

'You were giving them dirty looks, Dad,' Amy piped up between texting God knows who at this hour to say she was back and raring to show off her tan.

'I wasn't giving them dirty looks, it was my tired face.' Coupland reasoned. 'I just wanted to park myself down in the lounge and get some shut eye, which, might I add was impossible once they'd gone through my suitcase with a fine tooth comb. You'd think they'd offer to pack it back for you but no, you're on your own for that part.'

Lynn pursed her lips. 'There was no need to make such a song and dance about it though; we only just made it to the boarding gate on time.'

Coupland pulled a face. 'We were only late because Her Nibs wanted a bloody manicure she could have had on any number of the days she's not in college but no, it has to be this season's latest bloody colour.' His eyes widened as he said it. 'Have you two heard what you've done to me?' he spluttered. 'You've turned me into Gok bloody Wan.' Even as he said it his chest filled with the sheer pleasure of moaning about normal things, inconsequential things that were no longer related to life or death. Or cancer. He caught Lynn's eye and smiled. 'All I'm saying is it's funny how they're not so eager to search through my scuddies now.'

Lynn stared him down. 'I do your washing Kevin,'

she pointed out. 'I wouldn't wish that on anyone.' Two strides and they were through the exit, joining the cluster of nicotine addicts lighting up and sucking on cigarettes as though their lives depended on it. Coupland unzipped his rucksack, tore the cellophane wrapper from a pack of 200 Marlboroughs he'd bought in duty free. 'Why don't you have one of your electronic cigarettes, Kev?' Lynn cajoled.

He shook his head like a crazy horse because he could do that and inhale at the same time. 'Are you serious?' he spluttered after the first hit reached his lungs. 'Ten hours suspended mid-air with nothing beneath you but a bloody great ocean, only the real McCoy'll do the trick right now, thanks very much.' Coupland held the first mouthful of smoke down in his lungs before slowly releasing it into the air.

'Does it not bother you, Dad,' Amy piped up, her attention momentarily distracted from her phone as she studied him, 'the horrible photos, all the stuff printed on those packets, showing the harm it can do?'

Coupland stared into the distance, thought of the countless cases he'd worked on, the crime scene photos depicting the numerous ways each victim had met their untimely death. A cigarette didn't feature in any of them. He gave silent thanks that in Amy's world the greatest threat to his life was smoking, rather than the killers he came in contact with more times than he cared to ponder. The cocoon he'd created around his family remained intact; they worried about his lungs and his diet like they were a normal little unit. Like he was a bus driver or a teacher, rather than a detective sergeant in Salford Precinct's murder squad. He downplayed his role on every case that he'd worked on, did all he could to put their minds at rest. Amy's question told him it worked. 'It'll take more than a packet of cigarettes to finish me off, Ames,' he quipped. 'I'm like Wolverine, me, bloody indestructible.'

'You've got the werewolf bit right,' Lynn observed, brushing her hand across his unshaven face. The familiar buzz in his pocket took the edge off his mood. Pulling his mobile phone from his jacket he pulled a sorry face at Lynn as he barked his name into the phone. He hadn't switched it on more than two minutes since and already he was needed. His face darkened as he listened to the person on the other end, grunting a response before slipping the phone into his pocket. 'I'll walk you to the taxi rank.' He took Lynn's case from her and wheeled it with his own, his mood sombre. 'Something's come up.'

Leaving the airport and driving along the slip road that would take him onto the M56 Coupland turned on the radio. More bad news about the refugee crisis, people trapped in a collapsed building in India. At least on the radio you were safe from the graphic images, the tragic photos and videos bandied about the internet like disaster porn. It didn't make sense why people clicked onto these sites, why folk would choose to look horror in the eye, experience close up someone else's tragedy. Coupland pulled the e-cigarette Lynn had bought him out of his pocket, eyeing it with suspicion. 'It's time you started to cut down, Kev,' she'd wheedled. It wasn't the first time she'd said this, but there was a steely look in her eye when she'd spoken, as though he wasn't going to get off as lightly this time around. 'Especially now you're getting to that age.'

He'd bristled at that. 'I'm at the top of my game,' he'd objected, but they both knew that wasn't true. His bulk was genetic, a bullying father who only stopped knocking seven bells out of him once he'd outgrown him. He'd never played sport, was an avid spectator though, rugby, football, pretty much anything that could be broadcast via Sky into his local. The pies and pints had taken their toll; his bulky frame was starting to soften. Lynn had put them both on a low-fat diet, and to be fair he was feeling the benefit. He might not be able to take on Usain Bolt in a sprint but he could still hold his own in a dark alleyway if the situation called for it. There was a place for healthy living, he was sure of it, but didn't you have to believe the future was worth it? Coupland pushed the mawkish thoughts to the back of his mind; the jet lag had made him maudlin, his holiday already receding into the past. He took a puff on his vapour stick out of loyalty to Lynn. To think she worried about his health after all she'd been through... he puffed some more.

Coupland parked his car, shivering as he climbed out of it, whether from the change in temperature now he was back in Salford or from what he was about to see he wasn't sure. He stepped towards the cordoned off area where a uniformed officer stood guard. The officer nodded, lifted the cordon to let him pass. The information he'd gleaned from the earlier call had been sketchy, a body had been found in an area of woodland along the perimeter of a recreation park in Worsley. By the level of activity going on it had been discovered a couple of hours ago; that and the number of press cars circling the area like vultures smelling carrion.

The crime scene manager leaned against the driver's

door of his car as he made a call. He nodded at Coupland, watching as the detective took a pair of shoe protectors from the open car boot and slipped them on. He clamped his hand over the phone, 'Didn't know you were back,' he tutted, 'no bugger tells me anything.'

Coupland grunted. 'A bit of shut eye would have been nice.'

A blond haired, slim built man appeared through a clearing, signalled for Coupland to make his way over. 'Good holiday?' DCI Mallender asked as a courtesy, already turning and heading towards the locus before Coupland had time to answer. Coupland grunted once more, his mouth forming a grim line. It never got easier, observing the dead. Especially when their exit had been violent. 'Looks like she was taken by surprise,' was all Mallender said before they stepped through the inner cordon. 'There's a bus stop a hundred yards or so further up, at a guess I'd say her attacker grabbed her from behind and dragged her into the bushes.' A tent had been erected to protect the body from prying eyes; it would also keep the rats at bay while the forensic team went about the business of collecting hair and fibre samples.

Coupland stepped into the tent, nodded at the photographer setting up a tripod in the furthest corner. 'Can you give us a minute?' He waited while the man put down his equipment noisily before stomping out into the cool night air. We've all got bloody work to do, his body language seemed to say, but he'd been on the wrong side of the fat sergeant before and was in no hurry to repeat that mistake. Mallender stayed by the tent's entrance; he didn't need or want to survey the body a second time. Coupland let out a slow breath. There was no easy way to do this.

When he was a kid he used to sneak in to the local cinema to see horror flicks all the time, his big build making it easier for him to be let into the 18-rated screens. If there was a bit that was too gruesome he could cover his eyes, wait for the camera to move onto a different scene. He wished he could do that now, shield himself against the worst bits, the bits that would come back to haunt him in the early hours. He let his gaze move over the victim's body. The woman was in her twenties. Black. Slim but not skinny, wearing a fitted business suit. Her skirt had ridden up over her thighs; her tights were torn in several places. Coupland turned to Mallender, eyebrows raised. The DCI answered his silent question. 'Her underwear's still on, so I'm guessing she's not been sexually assaulted.'

'Maybe not for the want of trying...' Coupland observed.

'Her bag was found beside her too,' Mallender added, 'a good one, by the look of it. Her mobile was inside it; along with a purse containing fifty pounds in cash, so the motive isn't likely to be a robbery is it?' The question was rhetorical; he'd already turned his gaze away from the tent's interior.

'What's her name?' Coupland asked.

'Sharon Mathers.'

Coupland had put it off long enough; he leaned over the woman's body to get a closer look, allowing his gaze to travel upwards. A halo of scarlet pooled around what remained of her head. Something foul tasting caught in his throat. The public seemed to think this part got easier, the more dead bodies you saw on the job the more immune you became to the sorrow but there was no truth in that. This woman had been loved, was still loved,

Coupland may even have crossed paths with her at some point, sat beside her at the dentist, made small talk with her in a supermarket queue, she'd lived and breathed and cared for someone, yet had been discarded like a broken doll. It was the eyes that always did for him, the last fearful moments reflected in each victim's stare. Their faces were never at peace: they were shocked, frightened, or just plain sad. It was a palpable sorrow, one that weighed heavy on his shoulders every time. 'Jesus, have you seen what he's done to her face?' he whispered. There was a crater in the front of her skull; one eye socket was no longer visible. It seemed grotesque that the make up on the other half of her face was intact. From what remained Coupland thought she might have been pretty.

Once.

'Look at her hands,' Mallender prompted, and Coupland got down on his haunches to study them. Red painted nails were unbroken but her knuckles were swollen.

'She managed to get a punch in then,' Coupland muttered. All that fight yet it had still come to this. Coupland felt his hackles rise. He had a wife, a daughter, how often had he told them just to run away, put their energy into escaping rather than screaming for help, and failing that kick the bastard where it hurts and then run. But the truth was men were stronger than women, and a bastard hell-bent on doing harm was nigh on unstoppable. Coupland stepped out of the tent, he'd seen enough. This young woman had literally fought for her life and lost in the worst possible way. He pitied the poor sod who'd stumbled upon her. He locked eyes with Mallender. 'Who found her?' he asked.

The DCI pulled a face. 'Boyfriend. Been living together for the past three years. She was late home from drinks after work. He'd started to get worried when she didn't answer his calls. Walked along the route she'd normally take when she got off the bus. Kept dialling her phone as he looked for her when eventually he heard a ring tone he recognised coming from the clearing.'

'Poor bugger.' Coupland muttered. He looked at his watch then realised he hadn't changed it back to Greenwich Mean Time. He pulled his mobile from his pocket. It was 3am. No wonder he was knackered. 'So the boyfriend found her about 1am?' Mallender nodded. The bus service was pretty regular until midnight, which wasn't a late night by many standards. Most people only considered cabs once the buses stopped running. Coupland ran a hand over his face. His euphoria on landing in one piece had long since evaporated; he felt like the walking dead.

'How did the boyfriend seem?' Coupland was referring to the defence wounds on the victim's hands. By the state of her knuckles her punches had found their target. Whoever killed her won't be looking too pretty by morning.

'He's clean by the look of it. No black eyes or bruises emerging but we'll carry out a full check on him.'

'Where is he now?'

Mallender inclined his head in the direction of a small development of houses beyond the bus stop. 'Back home, he's been assigned an FLO. I want you to go over there first thing. Get as much out of him as you can. Obviously until we get the all clear he's our key suspect.' Coupland knew the drill, not that it made it any easier. The fact remained that every week two women in the UK were murdered by their partners, so the process of elimination followed by the police during a murder investigation was not without just cause. 'I'll finish up here,' Mallender offered, 'Curtis will want a preliminary report on his desk first thing and you look ready to drop.'

Coupland nodded, grateful to be making his way back to his car. He'd intended to go home to grab a couple of hours sleep but found himself driving on autopilot, arriving at Salford Precinct station some fifteen minutes later. A bit like Coupland, from the outside the station seemed barely to have changed since it was built in the seventies, although the interior had had a major refurb over the last five years, firstly to bring the building in line with modern safety regulations, secondly to reduce heating and lighting costs, make it run more efficiently. Apart from five years spent at Stretford which he'd rather forget, Coupland had spent his entire career stationed here. Starting out as a young cop on the beat, in the days when that meant pounding the streets alone, never certain of what was round the next corner. Some of his contemporaries looked back on that time with nostalgia, reckoned it was better back then, safer, the public held the police in high esteem. Coupland wasn't so sure. Hard faced men had stared him in the eye for as long as he could remember, all that had changed were the fashions, not the attitude.

Coupland enjoyed one last cigarette before leaving the car. Yes, he was tired, he could sleep on a clothes line given the chance, but two hours kip wouldn't even make a dent in it. Might as well work through his exhaustion. They'd be setting up an incident room by now and he had a chance to read through the early statements that had been taken, get some momentum going under this investigation before he called it a night.

Or day, depending how you looked at it.

CHAPTER 2

Coupland's desk was scattered with files, biscuit crumbs and reports needing sign-off but he'd seen worse. The lack of paperwork didn't reassure him; his inbox would be full to bursting with circulars from HR he wouldn't bother reading and incident updates he'd been copied into in the general arse covering way that the senior ranks preferred, all marked 'High Importance,' making it impossible to prioritise. There was a card on his desk from Alex Moreton, thanking the team for baby Todd's gifts with a post script which read: 'The nipple cream you sent has really come in handy.' She'd added a smiley face after that bit. Coupland looked around the night shift officers setting up a dedicated incident area for Sharon Mathers' murder, holding the card aloft in his hand, 'And who was the joker?' He demanded, 'I thought I'd checked everything we'd bought from the whip round before it got posted?' Coupland stared at the men around him half-heartedly, time was when he'd have been the instigator, sending a rubber ring or cabbage leaves to the new mother, but what was once harmless fun between colleagues was now seen as harassment. Mallender would be all over him like a rash in an STI clinic if he got wind of this. He returned the card to his desk. He wasn't going to make a big deal of it, the team knew he was displeased and that would have to do for now.

DC Turnbull had been pushing a desk from one end

of the room to the other. He stopped, raised his hand sheepishly. 'It was me, Sarge,' he pulled a face, 'I just wanted to lighten the mood a bit, you know, after everything...'

How could any of them forget the murder of a young DC on their watch? It had hit everyone hard, including Alex, who'd named her new baby after him. 'Fair enough,' Coupland grunted, locking his drawer, 'but best not to draw attention to it, though, just to be on the safe side.'

'Good holiday?' DC Robinson called over, preparing the incident wall with the photograph and scant details of the victim they'd gathered to date.

'Not too shabby at all,' Coupland responded, trying but failing to suppress a grin. 'Lynn took to Blackjack like a duck to water, and I had my first ever full body massage in a spa. Thank Christ for the twin centre holiday.'

'And Amy?'

'She spent all her money shopping in Vegas then all her time on the beach texting some lad from college.'

'Expensive,' Robinson sympathised.

'You don't know the bloody half of it,' Coupland grumbled but his eyes told a different story. Turnbull and Robinson returned to setting up the incident room; a harmless enough duo, they could be relied upon to carry out tasks assigned to them. Both detectives had worked together so frequently they appeared to Coupland as a single unit, like the Chuckle Brothers, or Ant and Dec.

'Has Alex's maternity cover come through?' Coupland enquired.

'You mean you've not been keeping up with your emails while you were away, Sarge?' Turnbull laughed, 'Shame on you. Nice threads by the way.'

19

Coupland looked down at himself, remembered he had responded to the call straight from the airport. He was wearing light coloured chinos and a flowery shirt the girls had bought him teamed with a creased linen jacket. The man from Del Monte meets Hawaii Five O. At least he'd not made the mistake of wearing his flip flops on the plane; he had on brown loafers Lynn had bought for his last birthday that he'd never worn before and his tan was so deep he'd gone without socks. There was a time when a get up like this would have made him feel self-conscious but the good people of Antigua hadn't batted an eyelid. Lynn had certainly been complimentary. That was one of the many differences between men and women, he mused, when a man found himself a wife he didn't want her to change while a woman saw a husband as a work in progress, as though the clothes he wore and the way he cut his hair were just trial runs until she took over. Having said that, the tan combined with the holiday wardrobe he had cultivated over the last couple of weeks did make him feel like a million dollars. 'You can joke,' Coupland countered, puffing up his chest. 'I might start dressing this way every day.'

A couple of the officers snorted. 'You'll be moving into a houseboat and getting an alligator as a pet next,' Robinson panted as he leaned into a filing cabinet to nudge it along the wall a bit.

'You'll have to explain to the children,' Coupland responded, glancing at the officers under forty who were looking at Robinson perplexed.

Leaving the DC to explain the merits of Miami Vice to the Matrix generation Coupland made his way over to Turnbull. 'Seriously, have we got enough cover for this?'

With Alex on maternity leave they were one man down but no one'd give a toss about that when they were looking at the unit's clear up rates. A murder on his first day back. A logistical nightmare when they weren't working at full strength. Coupland reminded himself it was no walk in the park for Sharon Mathers' family either.

Turnbull nodded. 'He started last Friday. Transferred from The Met by all accounts, left under a cloud if rumours are anything to go by.' In Coupland's experience there was a grain of truth in all gossip, far more than in the official spin often meted out in an attempt to deter it. *'Relocation to be near family,'* was just the bull people churned out to save face after a demotion.

'So, he thinks he's a big fish in a small pond, does he?' Coupland grinned; he wasn't averse to bringing some jumped-up southerner down to size. 'What's he like then?'

Turnbull hesitated; a pained look came over him though it could have been trapped wind. 'Looks a lot like that Luther fella on the telly,' he managed. The room fell silent. Coupland could feel the collective discomfort around him.

'He means I'm black.' The gravelly voice came from behind Coupland forcing him to turn.

'I can see that,' he shrugged dismissively. 'Ignore Turnbull, you'll get used to his lack of detail after a while, just don't ask him to put together an E-fit or you'll find yourself trawling the city looking for stick men.'

The detective studied Coupland before holding out his hand. 'DC Chris Ashcroft, Sarge, I've been looking forward to meeting you.'

'DC?' Coupland repeated, sliding a glance over at Turnbull who'd sloped off back to pushing furniture around. 'You came back for family reasons then?' His eye had a sly gleam to it.

'Something like that,' Ashcroft murmured. He was taller than Coupland, around six foot two, with a waistline that suggested abs rather than paunch.

The men weighed each other up. 'Don't be taken in by my Tweedle Dum exterior,' Coupland warned him, 'in my spare time I have been known to run into burning buildings and rescue small children.'

'I was admiring your jacket,' Ashcroft replied. 'Ralph Lauren if I'm not mistaken.'

Coupland shrugged. 'My missus shops at TK Maxx, can't resist a bargain. I feel sorry for her at times, can't seem to help getting ideas above her station. Goes to sleep dreaming of Daniel Craig and wakes up staring at Johnny Vegas. Mind you, she hasn't changed the locks yet so I must be doing something right.' Coupland eyed Ashcroft suspiciously. 'You're early for the day shift.'

Ashcroft shrugged. 'Couldn't sleep so I had the radio on. News report said a body had been found. Thought I might be more use here. Anyway, what's your excuse?'

'Me? When I finally sleep it'll be the sleep of the dead. Might as well work up a head of steam before that happens.'

Mallender passed by the window looking into CID. Did a double-take when he saw Coupland talking to the new DC. 'I thought I'd told you to call it a night,' he chided, putting his head around the door.

'No point.' Coupland rubbed the back of his neck. 'Besides, I'd rather crack on.' He also didn't fancy his chances of getting any shut eye with Sharon Mathers' injuries etched into his brain.

Mallender nodded. 'Have you got a minute, then?' Indicating that this was something he wanted to say in private.

Coupland turned to Ashcroft. 'Make yourself useful, start reading through the notes taken so far relating to the boyfriend, bring me up to speed on anything worth pursuing first thing. Oh, and get me something out of the drinks machine.' With that he followed Mallender out of the room.

'What do you want, Sarge?' Ashcroft called after him.

Coupland shrugged. 'I'm not bothered, as long as it's warm and wet.'

'Sugar?'

'I'd prefer it if you called me Sarge until I know you better,' he chided, before shaking his head in answer. 'No, I've got sweeteners…' A hush descended on the CID room followed by sniggering. He could feel the collective mickey taking that would be triggered by this new revelation. 'Lynn's finally got me to pack in sugar, so what?' he said defensively. Friends were already saying he looked better for it but this lot would never say anything nice now everyone knew the effort he was making. Christ, what the hell would they do when they found him in possession of a vapour stick? Where the hell was Alex Moreton when he needed her? 'Neanderthals, the lot o' you…' he hissed under his breath.

Mallender's office was tidy but not obnoxiously so. His working life was bogged down with preparing reports for the Chief Super and the ever growing burden of making sure crimes had been recorded accurately, though it was a constant battle. Victims of robbery were often assaulted, but the Information Commission had found that several forces were recording data differently, resulting in bun fights further up the food chain and as the saying goes shit only ever runs downhill. Mallender's role was a sticky one, Coupland didn't envy it, but at least the DCI didn't have to interview a grieving partner on little to no shut eye and not nearly enough caffeine to see him through.

They sat down either side of Mallender's desk. Coupland, resisting the urge to drum his fingers, waited him out. Mallender shuffled a few papers and cleared his throat. 'Superintendent Curtis…' he began, letting Coupland know as subtly as he could that he didn't endorse the statement he was about to make, '…feels the murder should be treated as a Hate crime.'

Coupland blew out his cheeks. 'I suspected he might,' he said glibly, 'though it's too early to call in my view, I mean it's not like there's ever any love lost between a killer and his victim.' Coupland disagreed with the way top brass wanted every case classified the moment it came in. It was no wonder there were so many errors. Officers were expected to make snap decisions before all the facts had been gathered. 'We've only just found her, Guv,' he added, 'no disrespect, but the body's hardly had a chance to get cold. I've not seen anything yet that makes me think this killing is the result of the woman's race or religion or anything else for that matter.'

'Me neither,' Mallender's voice lowered a notch as he said this, 'but the Super's paranoid about being caught with his trousers down if something comes up later. Better to treat it as such at the outset.' There had been a flurry of outcry a couple of years before that the five categories used to record hate crimes: race, religion, disability, sexual orientation or transgender identity –

were not enough, and in 2013 Greater Manchester Police expanded the classifications to record offences against members of alternative subcultures – Goths, Emos, Punks, and Metallers. You really couldn't please all the people all the time.

Coupland gave in and drummed his fingers on the desk impatiently. He wanted to be sure they weren't being hasty, closing down lines of enquiry before they'd even begun. Worse still, going down blind alleys. 'But that means trawling through local neo Nazi cells, BNP splinter groups, anyone with an axe to grind.'

Mallender nodded. It took all of Coupland's strength not to sigh. If he wanted to run the investigation the way he felt was appropriate as well as take this route he'd need double the resources and there was no point asking. The staffing situation was dire, thousands of jobs gone nationwide after the last spending review. They had to make do with what they'd got. 'But we still interview and eliminate the boyfriend?' he clarified, already allocating caseloads in his head.

Mallender nodded once more. 'Better to get him out of the way as soon as possible,' he agreed, 'at least that way he can get on with the process of grieving.'

By the time Coupland returned to his desk his drink was already tepid. He pulled a face as he swallowed the bitter coffee, deciding not to bother with his sweeteners; the liquid wasn't hot enough to dissolve them. 'Cheers,' he called over half-heartedly to Ashcroft but the DC didn't reply. Coupland fished his phone from his jacket pocket and sent a text to Lynn telling her he wouldn't be back until the end of his proper shift. She replied straight away: **Any excuse to get out of the washing, Kev...**

Typical Lynn, no matter what time they returned from holiday she never went to bed until the final pile of dirty washing had been loaded into the machine. It was her thing. Just like his was crashing on top of the duvet in his clothes, snoring and passing wind until she brought him a coffee when she finally came to bed.

Coupland looked at his watch, remembered he needed to reset the time now he was back in the UK, so slipped it off his wrist, admiring the white strip of skin. 'You ever been to the Caribbean?' he called out to Ashcroft.

The DC's shoulders set and he clenched his jaw a couple of times before answering. 'Can't say I have, Sarge, no.'

'Just back from Antigua, beautiful place,' Coupland beamed, 'never gone further than Spain before, but the Missus had her heart set on it. Mind you, we started in Vegas first, always fancied going since that George Clooney film.' He slipped his watch back on his wrist. 'Dayshift starts in about an hour. Fancy getting us a couple o' bacon rolls before we go through what you've been reading?'

'Not hungry, Sarge.'

Coupland looked up, 'My treat?' he coaxed. The DC shook his head.

Turnbull, slumping on a nearby desk, sat up Meerkat-like. 'I'll have one if you're feeling flush, Sarge,' he called out getting to his feet, hand outstretched for Coupland's money.

'Go on then,' Coupland grumbled, 'and get me a latte with an extra shot.' A murder and a temperamental new DC on his first day back. It was going to be a long day.

Ashcroft began filling Coupland in on Sharon Mathers

and her boyfriend. She was twenty five; the boyfriend – James Grimshaw – was a year older. They'd been living together for three years, had been going out together since they met at work five years ago.

'Why wasn't he on the night out then?' Coupland asked.

'He'd moved jobs, got a more senior position at a rival firm. Didn't think the bosses would have been too happy if he'd tried tagging along.'

'Her colleagues make a habit of going out midweek?'

Ashcroft shook his head. 'They went out every payday, a few drinks rather than a bender.'

'Any previous?'

'Both clean as a whistle.'

'History of domestic violence?'

Ashcroft shook his head once more.

Just then Turnbull returned with Coupland's bacon roll and latte. 'No change?' Coupland asked, eyeing Turnbull as he bit into his own roll appreciatively.

He wiped his mouth with the back of his hand before replying. 'Bumped into Robinson,' he smiled, 'and I knew you wouldn't want him to think you had a favourite.'

Coupland looked back at Ashcroft. 'You hear that? Insubordination everywhere I turn.' He took the lid off his latte and with lightning speed clicked three sweeteners into it. Tucking the serviette that came with the bacon roll into his shirt collar he bit into his roll. He always returned to work after a holiday slightly more domesticated than when he left. He'd spent the last fourteen days in the company of his two favourite women; their clean ways of living were bound to rub off. He studied Ashcroft, narrowing his eyes, 'The last lad that was here was a vegetarian, you're not one of those are you?'

'No.' Ashcroft leaned back in his chair, his nose twitching at the smell of crispy bacon. 'Just not hungry, that's all,' though his stomach gave a rumble that said otherwise. He folded his hands across his body.

'I want you to come with me when I speak to the boyfriend,' Coupland said between mouthfuls.

Ashcroft, instead of being pleased Coupland was willing to involve him so quickly, seemed to bristle. 'Wouldn't you rather take one of the others?' he demanded, pushing himself up in his chair.

'I'd have asked them, if I did,' Coupland eyed him carefully, 'but my partner's on maternity leave and you are her cover. Am I missing something here?'

'No,' but the set of Ashcroft's face as he turned back to his desk said otherwise.

The room set up for Sharon Mathers' murder was packed as day and night shift overlapped to attend the briefing. DCI Mallender updated both teams with the details as he knew them, including the extent of her injuries. 'This was an angry, vicious attack, borne out by the degree of damage to the victim's face.'

One of the nightshift DCs raised his hand, 'Could it be a domestic gone too far?' he offered. 'Boyfriend might have found her in the woods with another fella?'

Mallender shook his head. 'We'll know more later but initial forensic reports state there was no sexual activity – either wanted or unwanted – prior to her death. DS Coupland will be interviewing James Grimshaw, the victim's boyfriend, first thing.' Mallender paused. 'The incident is to be treated as a Hate crime for the time being. I want no stone unturned for us to either prove or disprove this theory.' He waited while Coupland allocated actions relating to checking out local right wing organisations and their members, also any known offenders who may have previously been working their way up to murder. 'I want this carried out swiftly and robustly, and paper trails to reflect that.' Mallender added.

Coupland bit back a response, Curtis really had put the fear of God into him, he mused. Though to be fair, if this did turn out to be a racially motivated crime the press would be all over them if it looked like they'd missed something.

Ashcroft was quiet as they climbed into the pool car. Coupland offered to drive them since the DC didn't know his way around yet and the satnav had a mind of its own. He turned to his passenger. 'Should only take us fifteen minutes.' At least it would give them time to get to know each other better, it was always a bit awkward the first few times you worked with someone new, the sooner they worked out a common wavelength the better.

Ashcroft said nothing, looked out of the passenger window like a tourist on a road trip. We're not in Kansas anymore, Coupland thought sourly, wishing Alex would hurry up and come back. He never thought he'd hear himself admit it but he missed her fussing and the way she nit-picked over everything he did; both at work and home he'd long since resigned himself to women pecking his head.

He took a sidelong glance at Ashcroft and formed his mouth into a smile. 'So, you a Chelsea fan then? Or Spurs?' he ventured.

'West Ham actually,' Ashcroft responded, 'You?'

Coupland shrugged. 'More of a telly addict now,'

he confessed, 'can't think when I last went to a game.' Coupland scratched his head. 'Used to take Amy to Old Trafford when she was a nipper, me and Lynn used to have season tickets but they got way too pricey.' Ashcroft was only half listening. 'How you getting on with the team?' Coupland prodded.

'Fine,' he shrugged, 'they seem OK, it's not easy walking into a dead man's shoes.' Coupland clenched his jaw, blinked away an image of the young DC who had been murdered by a local gang several months before.

'I'm sorry!' Ashcroft said suddenly, turning to look at him, 'I didn't mean to sound so crass.'

Coupland swatted his words away, 'He hadn't been with us long. None of us really got to know him all that well but he was a good kid. He didn't deserve…' The lights had changed to red and Coupland found himself gripping the steering wheel. '…we let him down,' he said quietly.

Ashcroft let out a long slow breath. 'It's never easy when something like that happens, and then I turn up and you've got to start from the beginning all over again.'

As the lights changed to green Coupland broached something that had been playing on his mind. 'You seemed put out earlier, when I asked you to come with me to question Sharon's boyfriend. Is there a problem?'

Ashcroft moved his head so he was looking out of the window once more.

'You have to see how it looks from my point of view,' he said. 'For the last week I've been dealing with burglaries and assault, doing the grunt work no one else wants, then a black woman is murdered and I'm riding shotgun with you.'

Coupland cocked his head as he considered the man's words. 'Sorry,' he moved his head from side to side, 'I'm not with you.' He glanced at Ashcroft who was starting to look uncomfortable. 'Firstly, as I said earlier, you are replacing DS Moreton who partnered me regularly, so I would expect you to come along. Secondly, when you joined the team you were given the opportunity to find your feet by not being thrown in the deep end and as I understand it the good people of Salford managed not to kill each other last week so you had a reprieve, and finally, DC Ashcroft, as your senior officer I don't have to see anything from your point of view. Are we clear?'

Coupland had never had to say that last part to anyone before; most of the officers who knew him thought twice about getting on his wrong side because he was well known for flying off the handle. He felt quite pleased with himself that he'd been able to articulate things so well. Certainly without having to resort to swearing. Maybe it wasn't just his waistline going soft around the middle.

Ashcroft sighed, but it was petulant, the sound of a teenager made to do something against their will. Coupland tried not to let his irritation show in his voice. 'It might help if you tell me what's got you so bent out of shape, starting with why you actually left the Met. I always thought you had to grow an extra set of bollocks to work there,' he added to lighten the mood, 'what with you all being from the Alpha gene pool.'

The DC shook his head. 'Don't,' he squirmed, looking down at his hands.

'Why?'

'Because you're not wrong,' Ashcroft admitted. 'I

guess I did think I was the big I Am, but I also did a good job. Unblemished ten-year record.'

'Quite the mover and shaker,' Coupland countered. In his experience everyone ended up with a reprimand at some point in time, some sort of bollocking recorded on file to keep you in the career sticky stuff. Your whole time in the job was one long assessment process; he'd be suspicious of anyone with a clean slate. Never mind blemishes, Coupland's own personnel file was full blown acne ridden. He didn't have a diplomatic bone in his body, didn't like to see the way the force was going. There were too many coming into the service didn't want to put in the graft, were all too happy to let someone else put their neck on the line. All wanting a fast track out of the front line and into somewhere much less accountable.

'Look.' Ashcroft spoke slowly, as though trying to make sense of his words before he said them. 'The Met's desperate about its reputation, especially in the wake of Mark Duggan.' He was referring to the black man shot twice in Tottenham, north London, in 2011 after specialist firearms officers stopped the minicab he was in on suspicion that he had an illegal firearm. No gun was found on him. His death had sparked riots in cities and towns across England.

Coupland said nothing. He hadn't been there, he didn't know the full story, but he'd needed DCI Mallender to explain the Inquiry's verdict to him, and even he'd admitted to being confused and he'd gone to university.

'Bottom line is top brass said I was ready for promotion.' Ashcroft's face took on a sour look. 'Only the boroughs they offered to me were, what's the politically correct phrase… all ethnically diverse.'

'And to quote Groucho Marx you didn't want to be a member of a club that accepted you as a member.'

Ashcroft's brow creased. 'I guess not.'

Coupland shot him a look. 'Why not?' he challenged. 'Promotion's promotion.'

'What? And have half the division think I didn't get there on merit? And the other half sneer at the patch I'd been given.'

'Did you deserve the promotion?'

Ashcroft nodded. 'I think so, but I'd been given a limited choice, unlike my fairer skinned colleagues.'

'Be careful where you go round saying that.' There was a tinge of warning in Coupland's voice. 'Nobody likes a sour puss.'

'Does that go for you?'

Coupland laughed. 'I don't give a toss what race, religion or shoe size you are, or whether you dress in your girlfriend's underwear on your days off – or even if you have a girlfriend, for that matter. I mistrust everyone until they prove themselves. You'll get no favours from me, but you will get the same treatment I mete out to everyone else, are we clear?'

Ashcroft's shoulder visibly relaxed. 'Yes, Sarge.'

Coupland pulled up outside a row of terraced houses. He switched off the ignition and regarded Ashcroft once more. 'Are we good, now? Because if I send you for a coffee you need to understand there's no other agenda than I want a bloody coffee?'

Ashcroft nodded. 'Loud and clear, Sarge,' he replied, 'loud and clear.'

The Family Liaison Officer answered the door to them, ushering them through a narrow hallway to the living room where James Grimshaw had decamped since returning to the home he shared with Sharon Mathers after discovering her body. 'He hasn't slept,' the WPC said in an undertone.

'I know how he feels,' Coupland muttered.

James was sat on a three-seater sofa, a pillow and folded duvet beside him. He was white, with short fair hair that Coupland suspected was usually worn spiky with gel. Today it hung lank. Bloodshot eyes peered up under swollen eyelids. He looked like a man who had had his soul ripped right out of him. Coupland took a step forward. 'James, I'm Detective Sergeant Coupland and this is my colleague Detective Constable Ashcroft. I'm sorry for your loss.' Coupland put out a hand and waited, asking, 'Can we sit down?' when nothing was proffered.

James nodded, regarding Coupland with dazed, languid eyes. Mis-timing it he put out his arm to shake the hand Coupland had offered moments earlier causing Coupland to raise himself from his chair to take the man's outstretched hand. Grimshaw's movements were slow, as though he was still trying to work out what the hell he'd stumbled upon. An untouched mug of tea had been placed on a low table in front of him. In the corner of the room the TV had been left on mute, a reporter interviewing refugees fleeing another war-torn city.

Both detectives perched on the sofa opposite. A side table had a pile of travel brochures on top of it, a post-it note marking one of the pages. The FLO regarded her captive audience and plastered on a smile. 'That's better!' she trilled. A chirpy woman in her thirties, she'd been trying too hard to cajole James into talking. She crinkled her eyes at Coupland before picking up a cold mug and returning to the kitchen to make more tea.

'She means well,' Coupland leaned forward in his chair so James could hear him, 'but she's got one of those voices that makes me want to—'

'—she brought me a quilt down,' James gestured towards the bedding beside him on the settee, 'said sleep would do me some good, but it won't bring Shaz back, will it?' Coupland's shoulders sagged. Not for the first time he wondered what it was like to have a happy job, one that brought nothing but pleasure to the people you came into contact with. There weren't many occupations with the happiness factor guaranteed, he supposed, but working for the National Lottery must be one of them, nothing but life changing – in a good way – news to impart all day long.

'I need to ask you some questions, James, do you think you are up to that?'

'And if I say no?' James responded bitterly. 'Will you go away?'

Coupland shook his head. The living room was small and tidy, little by way of ornaments: a metal figurine of a floppy eared hare on the window sill, Coupland recognised it from the *Guess how much I love you* book he used to read to Amy when she was knee high. A wood burning stove was a central feature in the room, a basket of logs beside it, the kind you can buy from petrol station forecourts. There were several framed photographs on the feature wall, James and Sharon standing in front of various foreign backdrops, The Eiffel Tower, The Empire State Building, Edinburgh Castle. She was a looker alright. Coupland cast a glance at James, wished to hell he hadn't been the one to find her, see his beautiful girlfriend with her face undone. He wondered how long it would take for that memory to recede, wondered if it ever would. He stood, moved towards the photographs to get a better look. In one the couple were standing in front of the Bellagio. 'Vegas, eh? Just come back from there, myself.' Coupland pointed to the picture. 'Only stayed a couple of nights, mind, policeman's salary and all. Was a bit of a special occasion for us.'

James looked up. 'We were going to get married,' he said, 'you know, in the Elvis chapel, but when we got there we decided we couldn't do that to our families, deny them their special day.'

Coupland nodded. If his Amy ever did something like that he'd… He dragged his thoughts back to the photo. Didn't pay to dwell on all life's possibilities.

'We decided to blow our money on the slot machines instead.'

'Any luck?' Coupland asked.

'Nah, there's only ever one winner with stuff like that, isn't there?' James seemed to visibly deflate, then in a blink his head reared up. 'I just don't get it! She was always so confident. Said she'd never let anyone get the better of her. Always reckoned she could handle herself. We used to watch the news, reports where women had been abducted and killed. "Swear to God, Jamie," she'd say, "anyone tries to have a go at me and they'll need A&E by the time I've finished..."'

'She was feisty then?'

A nod. 'Hard as nails. She's got three brothers; she knew how to defend herself.'

The FLO returned with a tray laden with a teapot, milk jug and four mugs. She was about to start pouring when

Coupland cleared his throat. 'Biscuits might be nice,' he suggested, reluctant to let anything stop James now he'd started talking.

'I don't think there are any in the cupboard...' she began, before it dawned on her she was in the way. 'I'll pop over to the corner shop,' she offered, 'any requests?'

'Take your time,' Coupland muttered into his chest. Once the front door closed behind her he resumed their conversation. 'Sharon get on alright with her brothers?'

James nodded. 'Now the two older ones have stopped treating her like a china doll, yeah, there's a younger one too, just started uni, she tends to make a fuss of him.'

'They a close family?'

'Yeah, normal you know, had their ups and downs, they were always kind to me.'

'And what was your relationship like?'

'With Shaz?'

Coupland nodded.

'Good, in fact it was great. She was gorgeous, funny, she liked my mates and didn't mind me playing on the X-box.'

By modern standards she sounded an ideal partner, Coupland agreed. 'And were you as perfect?' he asked, 'What would Sharon say if she had to describe you?'

James's face soured. 'That I was moody, sulked when I didn't get my own way, and that the reason we worked so well together was because she was happy to be the one that always gave in.'

Coupland frowned. The same could be said of his own marriage, Lynn was definitely the grown up in their relationship. 'Were you often moody then?' Coupland pressed. 'Were you prone to losing your temper with

Sharon?'

James's already drawn face clouded over. 'Hang on a minute, if you're asking did I ever hurt her… Christ, you're asking if I killed her, aren't you?' He looked about helplessly, flapping his hands around him on the settee like a drowning man trying to stay afloat.

Coupland's voice was quiet but firm: 'These are routine questions James, it's normal in these… situations to question the person who found the body *and* the victim's partner, and you happen to be one and the same.'

'So next time I find a body I should run for the hills, is that what you're saying?'

Coupland shook his head. 'I'm not saying that at all.'

DC Ashcroft leaned forward in his chair, spoke for the first time. 'What do you do for a living, James?'

James's brow creased as he regarded the DC. 'I'm a financial analyst.'

Ashcroft was unfazed by his answer. 'So you deal with a lot of numbers, right?' James nodded. 'And you what, predict where people should put their money?'

'Well, in the crudest sense, yes.'

'And how do you get to those conclusions?'

James creased his brow, 'I don't quite see the point—'

'Just humour me, yeah?'

James shrugged. 'We look at the fund in question's past performance, some sectors or industries have certain characteristics that make them more prone to risk, say, than others, for example a pharmaceutical company faces a constant threat from protesters sabotaging its products.'

'OK,' Ashcroft said agreeably, 'well, policing is similar to that. We start each murder investigation with a process which has been informed by data collected over a great number of years, which gives us a set of certain characteristics, such as most murders are committed by someone known to the victim, and top of that list is their partner.'

'Wait a minute…'

'Wouldn't you agree that it's in the interests of this investigation to follow that procedure, to eliminate you from our enquiries as soon as we possibly can, so that all our resources and energy can be spent finding the person who did this?'

James lowered his head. 'I suppose so,' he agreed.

Coupland nodded appreciatively at Ashcroft and continued with his questions. By the time the FLO had returned with two packets of biscuits – 'Everyone likes chocolate digestives but you can't beat Hobnobs for dunking' – the tea had gone cold and Ashcroft had just finished reading James's statement back to him. Shoulders sagging, James rubbed shaking hands over the stubble on his chin. 'I wish to Christ we'd got married now,' he said sadly, 'grabbed our moment when we had it, but you never know it's your only chance at the time, do you?'

*

They drove in silence for a while. 'Poor sod.' Coupland said.

'Yeah,' agreed Ashcroft.

Still, you could never be too careful. 'Check out their bank balances,' Coupland instructed, 'did he owe anyone any money? How was he really doing at work? What were their life assurance arrangements, had he recently set up a new policy?'

Ashcroft nodded; pulling out a small pad he jotted down a few notes. 'I'll go to his work and check what his colleagues have to say about him.'

'Agreed,' nodded Coupland, 'and find out whether he's been putting it about.' Coupland sighed, it brought no pleasure always thinking the worst of people, but at least his opinion could only improve.

They parked outside Donald Gillespie, the firm of accountants where Sharon had worked for five years. The office was situated on Barton Road, a two storey red brick building with a beauty salon upstairs. It was just past nine o'clock. Coupland watched someone open the blinds, sipping from a mug one-handed as they carried on a conversation with a colleague behind them. They then moved on to unbolting the door. 'Ever fancied a nice nine to five?' Coupland asked, 'Get home to the missus the same time every night, only dealing with your clients during the day?' Greater Manchester Police's clientele tended not to respect business hours.

'Chance'd be a fine thing.' Ashcroft sighed, 'too late for me now though, I'm no good for anything else.'

Coupland nodded glumly; like most cops he was entrenched in the chain of command, work involved following orders or giving them out. He wasn't quite sure how it worked in civvy street, didn't think he'd be too successful *negotiating*. 'So is there a missus, then?' Coupland asked, 'Or even a mister?' he added, mindful of the equality and diversity course he'd been sent on six months ago, a punishment from Curtis for addressing female civilians as 'love'. The women hadn't minded, but the newly promoted Superintendent had taken exception on their behalf. Flexing his muscles, likely as not.

'There's never been a mister,' Ashcroft replied, 'and no missus to speak of either, not anymore. It was a woman that drew me into the Met, only that's where the fairy-tale ended. We were both from up north originally but she had a bee in her bonnet about moving to London. She'd have happily left if I hadn't gone with her, same as she stayed put when I decided I'd had enough. She's a DCI now.'

'Doesn't always work, both of you being in the job, especially if you want different things.'

Ashcroft pulled a face. 'She said I lacked ambition.'

'Nice.'

A girl in her late teens hurried up the road carrying a carton of milk. She entered the accountants in a flurry, shaking her head and waving her hands as though saying the bus was late wasn't enough, the story needing embellishing somehow. Coupland glanced at Ashcroft. 'They've had long enough to enjoy normality. Let's go and break the bad news.'

'Can I help you?' The receptionist asked. It was the girl who'd arrived late; Coupland noticed her mobile semi hidden beneath a file on her desk. Not two minutes through the door and already she was texting someone, probably to tell them she was late again and what she'd had for breakfast.

'Can I see the boss, love?' Coupland replied, reaching in his jacket for his warrant card.

'Show them through Cara,' a voice behind her called out. A man in a dark grey suit and checked shirt stood at the far end of the main office. He looked at Coupland as though he knew what he was, didn't need his warrant card to prove it. Coupland felt different in his holiday clothes but the set of his face must have given him away for the man said nothing further, just watched as Cara lifted the counter hatch to let both detectives enter, his eyes never leaving them as they made their way through several desks scattered around the room, all occupied by clerical staff tapping away onto computers, some of them wearing headsets.

It was as though the mood of the two men in their midst was contagious, everyone pausing their work to glance at them before frowning and throwing curious looks at each other. The man had moved to stand in the doorway to his office, his eyes searching Coupland's face for some sort of clue as to the purpose of their visit. There was an office beside his; through the open blinds Coupland could see a desk and chair, a filing cabinet. The door to this office was closed. 'That's my deputy's office,' the man said, following Coupland's gaze. 'Sharon Mathers, she's normally in by now,' he said furrowing his brow, 'was it her you wanted to speak with?'

'I think you'll need to sit down for this,' Coupland said quietly.

CHAPTER 3

Afternoon briefing, Wednesday

Coupland stood beside Mallender as he read from the notes he and Ashcroft had taken during the morning. 'Ten people work at Donald Gillespie; all but two went out for a drink on Tuesday evening. The PA couldn't get a babysitter and the office junior didn't have any money although it was more likely she wanted to spend the evening with a new boyfriend. They went to the pub up the road from the office – The Dog and Duck – stayed there until people started heading home just before last orders. The next day was a work day so no one was on a bender. Sharon caught the bus with a couple of colleagues; she was the last to get off. The others don't remember anyone paying Sharon particular attention but then by their own admission they were all a little bit tipsy.'

Mallender nodded. 'Have we requested CCTV from the bus company?'

'We're already on it, Guv.' Coupland turned back to his notes. 'Her boss, Gordon Gillespie, had nothing but good things to say about her, I got the impression he meant it too, not just the lip service that's often meted out after a tragedy. I don't think there was anything going on between them, either; though that's not to say the boyfriend didn't have a jealous streak. They were closing up as we left, Gillespie was sending everyone home. "No one's going to get any work done anyway; we need time to process it all," was pretty much how he summed it up.'

The DCI considered this. 'No petty jealousies, then? She wasn't up for a promotion someone else felt more entitled to?'

Coupland shook his head. 'It doesn't fit.' The attack was too violent for an angry colleague, Sharon's work mates weren't particularly burly, there was more chance of one of them jabbing her with a letter opener in a fit of pique than smashing her skull with a rock.

Mallender addressed Turnbull: 'How about the Neo Nazi groups?'

Turnbull shuddered. 'Went to the Salford headquarters of the British Defence League and persuaded them to show me their membership list. No recent additions, no one transferred into the area, same crackpots there's always been… They claim they don't advocate violence, that anyone even remotely showing violent tendencies would be reported to us anyway.'

'You believe that?'

'No… but Sharon Mathers' murder is an extreme step. I had a look at their events diary on their website and there haven't been any members' meetings recently, their last rally was in March, so there's been nothing to stir anyone up or put fresh ideas into a potential wacko's head.'

'So it could be a standalone extremist?'

Several pairs of eyes locked onto Turnbull as he shrugged. 'Could be… I've trawled through the national crime database to identify racially motivated offenders going back over the last five years, discounting those who are already enjoying a break courtesy of Her Majesty, a couple are now dead… Natural causes,' he added.

'A real loss to the gene pool that is,' Coupland threw in. Several grunts of agreement followed.

'Some have moved out of the area,' Turnbull added, 'but that still leaves sixty-five names that need to be traced, interviewed and eliminated.'

Mallender turned to Robinson. 'You able to give him a hand?'

Robinson nodded. 'I've completed background checks on both the victim and her boyfriend; apart from their mortgage they didn't have any outstanding debt. No county court judgements, not even an outstanding parking fine. Neighbours said they both seemed happy together, no obvious signs of domestic problems, Sharon had just started helping out with the local Girl Guide unit.'

Mallender nodded, satisfied. 'What did she do at this firm?'

'Account Executive.' Coupland pulled a face to show he wasn't sure what that meant.

'She had her own list of clients that she gave financial advice to,' Ashcroft answered, already anticipating the DCI's next question.

'Have we contacted—?'

'—I'm working through a printout of her client list now, sir.'

Mallender smiled, 'OK, good work, let's see if we can narrow it down to something tangible we can take to a press conference.'

Coupland regarded Mallender. 'Are we not going to get James to do an appeal anyway?'

The DCI shook his head. 'Superintendent Curtis feels we need to have a clear line of direction with regard to the investigation before we appeal for the public's help.' Which roughly translated meant Curtis wanted to keep his distance until the correct classification of this crime had been determined.

*

'Stand by your beds,' Coupland called out as he let himself into the three bedroomed semi he shared with Lynn. The house was quiet, no washing machine hum or Amy's music blaring from upstairs, no *'He said, she said,'* phone calls punctuated by exclamations of *'No way!'* or *'OMG!'* He placed his car keys on the hall table and made his way through to the kitchen where his taste buds were awoken by a mouth-watering aroma that seemed strangely familiar. Lynn smiled as he made his way over to her and kissed her on the lips. Amy had her back to them so Coupland let the kiss linger a little longer than normal. Any public displays of affection tended to be greeted with screeches of *'ewwww, get a room…'*

'Tough day?' Lynn lifted a pot of something delicious smelling out of the oven before giving it a stir and putting it back. 'I thought I'd make that dish we liked on holiday.'

Coupland's spirits lifted. 'The one with the chicken in?'

'I couldn't find all the same spices mind, but I thought it would be a nice way to ease us back.'

'Can't argue with that.'

Amy had been texting someone but slipped her phone into the pocket of her skinny jeans before turning round. 'We heard about the woman who was murdered on the news, Dad, is that why you were called away last night?'

Coupland grunted a yes while taking off his jacket and placing it over the back of a kitchen chair. He didn't like bringing his work home with him, wanted to keep the four walls of his home an untainted place. Lynn understood his reluctance to talk but Amy thought working for the murder squad both fascinating and gross in equal measure.

He washed his hands at the sink, making sure he didn't dry them on the wrong towel; he didn't want to get in Lynn's bad books when she'd gone to such trouble with dinner. First night back from holiday was normally fish and chips because neither of them could be motivated to buy food in so he appreciated the effort it had taken. 'Hang on a minute.' He studied Amy as she put out the place mats on the table. 'Are you feeling alright?'

She threw him the look that said she wasn't going to rise to it but he carried on anyway. 'I mean, since when do you give your mum a hand without being enticed by money or a lift? Or is that it – are you off somewhere afterwards and need a taxi?'

'Ha, ha you're hilarious,' she muttered, moving to the cutlery drawer where she exchanged a worried glance with Lynn. Something was afoot.

'Amy,' Coupland continued, 'why are you setting four places? Oh, don't tell me, I am a detective after all. Is it this mystery lad you've been texting while we were away? He's going to grace us with his presence, is that it?' He winked at Lynn, 'He must be keen.' He paused, eyeing her with caution, 'You're not pregnant are you?' he asked before he could stop himself.

'Dad!' Amy's neck and face turned red as she turned to her mother, eyes pleading, 'Mum, tell him…'

'Kevin,' Lynn said on an outward breath, the way she did when he'd committed some awful faux pas. Just then the doorbell rang.

'I'll get it!' Amy shrieked but Coupland was already one step ahead of her, beating her into the hall,

'I'll get it sweetheart,' he grinned, 'it'll be my absolute pleasure.'

'Arright, Kev.'

The man on the doorstep looked oddly familiar for all the wrong reasons. The face rang a bell, a very big bell, but everything else about him was different. The clothes were clean, freshly ironed, the hair longer than he remembered. But still… Coupland's gaze fell upon the open collar which gave it away. The tattoo on the neck that if he wasn't mistaken spelled *Pussy*. Vincent Underwood. How the hell did this toe rag find his address? Coupland kept his face impassive. 'Well, well, well. You're not getting the hang of this are you, Vinny? When you've done your time you get out of jail and keep walking, go back living under whatever stone you crawled out from. You don't drop in on the guy that put you away,' Coupland laughed, 'that's not how it works, son, bound to ruffle a few feathers if you start making house calls on the local constabulary.' The toe rag's eyes twinkled. Behind Coupland Amy's footsteps cantered along the hallway.

'Vin!' she gushed in a sing song voice, 'Mum's made a special dinner, come on in.'

Coupland blinked. 'Hang on,' confused now, 'what the hell's going on here?' He looked at Amy's flushed face, then back at Vinny's smug one, 'Don't tell me you were waiting for this scumbag?'

Amy bristled, but Vinny's grin just got wider. 'Dad!' she hissed, 'Can you not do this?'

Coupland regarded her with suspicion. 'Do what?'

Her eyes darted in Vinny's direction. 'Be such a cop about everything…'

'I am a bloody cop, Amy!' His tone sharper than intended. 'This scrote's been inside,' he added, 'I know because I bloody nicked him.' He sighed, irritated Amy had put him in this position. 'Look, it's dead simple, I don't want him in my house, and I sure as hell won't sit round the table having dinner with him.'

'Well it's your choice,' Amy moaned, 'but Mum's gone to a lot of trouble for Vinny, she won't be pleased if it's all for nothing.'

She went to a lot of trouble for *me*, Coupland thought, his face sour.

'Dinner's ready!' Lynn called from the kitchen.

Coupland wondered how much she knew, whether Amy had got her on side and the two of them had plotted how to butter him up. But Lynn knew him better than that. Surely if she'd been in on this she'd have given him advance warning? He stood back to let Amy step into the kitchen. Vinny made to follow her but not before Coupland grabbed his arm, squeezing as tight as he could before leaning in so close to an outsider it looked like he was planting a kiss. 'This isn't over,' he growled into his ear before letting him go.

They managed to survive the meal. Lynn had raised her eyebrows at Vinny's tattoo as he walked into the kitchen but recovered her composure quick enough. He was a few years older than Amy, something Coupland knew Lynn wouldn't be comfortable with. He caught her eye as she ladled out the casserole onto everyone's plates; she gave a slight shrug as if to say wait and see. The conversation was stilted, mainly because Coupland refused to join in. He ate his meal in silence, glaring at Vinny who seemed to be doing his utmost to charm Lynn who was warming to him by the second. 'So you're at college with Amy?' she asked.

'I work there, *Lynn*,' he explained, sliding a look over at Coupland. 'I work in the maintenance team. Any repairs that need doing on campus, I'm your man.'

'But you're doing some online classes, aren't you?' Amy prompted, her voice chattering over everyone as though it was important to fill in any gaps. She hadn't looked at Coupland once since they'd sat round the table. So, his daughter was dating the odd job man, one with a criminal record to boot.

Coupland ground his teeth as he pushed his food round his plate. Lynn looked over at him anxiously, 'How's your chicken, love?' she enquired.

'Fine,' he nodded.

'Seconds?' She lifted the ladle resting in the serving dish, smiling as Vinny held his plate up for more.

'Not for me,' Coupland said, the sauce too sour for his liking.

Coupland made a start on washing the pans while Lynn loaded the dishwasher. Boy wonder had offered but Coupland had insisted he didn't need his help. When Vinny announced he was leaving Amy walked him to the door and after five minutes the front door slammed. Five minutes of Coupland shushing Lynn so he could listen through the kitchen door, five minutes of wondering what the hell the scrote was up to when he couldn't hear their voices. 'Finally,' he muttered through gritted teeth, taking his anger out on the caked-on food that stuck stubbornly to the bottom of the pan.

'What's wrong?' Lynn closed the dishwasher, pressing the eco cycle. She was smiling because she thought he was jealous, that his mood was nothing more than having his nose put out of joint by some young buck.

'Did you know he's been inside?' he hissed, turning to her so he could check her reaction. Stop, a voice in his head warned, you're not at work now.

'What?' Lynn screwed her eyes up in confusion, 'How do you know?'

'Pur-lease,' he looked at her as though she were simple, 'how do you think I know? I put the bugger away!' He rinsed the dish and placed it upside down on the drainer. 'Amy!' he yelled, moving towards the kitchen door so his voice would carry upstairs, even if she'd put her earphones in. 'Get down here now!'

'Don't have a go at her,' Lynn warned, 'she might not know,'

'She knows alright!' Coupland countered. He could feel his blood coursing through his veins. 'I asked her in the hallway and she acted like it was no big deal.'

Amy walked into the kitchen, her face a sullen mask. 'Putting Mum off him now, are you?' she spat. 'Why do you have to spoil everything?'

Coupland stared at his daughter. 'Amy, he was sent down for GBH last year. He's only been out a couple of months, if that.'

Lynn moved to Coupland's side. 'Did you know he'd been to jail?' she prompted.

Amy's face looked like it could curdle milk. 'Well of course I knew! We don't keep secrets from each other.'

'So he told you what he did then?' Coupland raised his voice so he could be heard above the racket, but it wasn't a shout, not yet. The women quietened and turned to him, he had their full attention. 'He assaulted a bloke in a bar—'

'—The guy had been laughing at him,' Amy argued, 'he just lost his temper and pushed him. Once.'

'And that's okay, is it? He spent the next week in an induced coma with a clot on his brain,' Coupland informed her.

'He didn't mean it!' Amy yelled back. 'Besides, hasn't he paid his debt to society or whatever you want to call it?' She leaned back against the kitchen worktop, wrapping her arms around her as she looked about the kitchen. Her shoulders had dropped, along with the temperature in the room. 'Surely he should be allowed to do whatever he wants, now.'

'With the exception of going out with my daughter, yes.'

Amy turned to Lynn. 'Mum, can you tell him?'

Lynn chewed her bottom lip. 'I'm not sure that I can,' she said evenly. 'You should have told us about his past before you invited him here.'

'WHY?' Amy shouted. 'So you could try and stop me from seeing him?' She swiped at her face with the heel of her hand, smudging her eye-liner. Moving a step towards them, she lowered her voice as she looked up at them both. 'I wanted you to meet him first, so you could make your own mind up about him, then I would have told you what he'd done, I promise.'

'What about your Dad?' Lynn countered. 'How was that ever going to work? He recognised him straight away.'

'Well it's not like Dad's here for most meals,' she said sourly before stomping out of the room, 'what were the chances of tonight being any different?'

*

Thursday morning briefing, Salford Precinct Station
Coupland gave an account of the meeting he'd had with Sharon Mathers' boyfriend the previous day and reported that for the moment he was not a person of interest – though until all avenues had been explored they should keep an open mind. Ashcroft confirmed he'd made contact with Sharon Mathers' clients – all checked out. There had been no unnecessary contact, no 'extra' services provided, all were very happy with her professionalism and shocked to hear of her murder. None could think of any enemies she might have. He also reported that according to the bus CCTV no one else got off at Sharon's stop, although two passengers had got off the bus one stop before. A poster and social media appeal had gone out asking for all the passengers on the bus to contact the incident room number. Respondents would be cross referenced against their image on screen and anyone who hadn't come forward in 72 hours would be actively pursued.

Mallender snapped his attention to Turnbull and Robinson. 'how did you get on with our resident Neo Nazis?'

'Down to the last ten,' Turnbull replied, 'the majority of them had low level schoolboy misdemeanours from way back when, most are married now, holding down jobs, quite a few were embarrassed to be reminded of their past.'

'Not all though?'

'No, there were some real die-hards, but even they

checked out, they'd kept their nose clean most of the time, frequented the more notorious pubs, caught on camera chanting at football matches, went on to be banned from Old Trafford and Etihad Stadiums.' Mallender nodded impatiently. 'All had alibis for Tuesday that checked out,' Turnbull concluded.

'And the last ten, you say, what's the hold up?'

Turnbull and Robinson exchanged glances. There'd been no hold up, the reason they'd managed to eliminate so many names from the list was because they worked through the night, turning up at addresses in the arse end of nowhere to check for themselves that claims made could be verified.

'They're pulling out all the stops here, boss,' Coupland spoke up in their defence, though he knew the real person who needed to hear this was Superintendent Curtis and he wasn't even present. Mind you, his handicap must be single figures by now.

Mallender raised his hands in mitigation. 'Don't shoot the messenger,' he pleaded. 'I just want to know we're going down all the right avenues. Step by step we should be closing in on this bastard. Kevin, can you allocate the workload giving priority to concluding the Hate crime actions by close of play? I've an update to prepare.'

Coupland nodded, delegating tasks before asking Ashcroft if he could cover for him for an hour, there was something he had to do. Before he had time to change his mind he drove to Amy's college, careful not to leave his car in the public car park where she might see it but in the car park allocated to staff, with a card he placed on the dashboard stating he was on police business. He followed the signs into the main reception area and flashed his warrant card at the woman behind the desk.

'I'd like to speak with the principal, love. Now.'

CHAPTER 4

DCs Turnbull and Robinson pulled up outside the King Jimmy on Walkden Road and looked at each other. The pub attracted little attention from its drab exterior, but the back room was notorious for being the meeting place of a chapter of Neo Nazis since it went under new management ten years before. 'Do you think we should call for back up?' Turnbull asked, glancing up and down the street as though expecting a lynch mob to arrive on the back of a jeep.

Robinson tutted. 'Don't start getting cold feet on me. It's hardly chucking out time. We go in, ask a few questions, bugger off out again. Job done.'

The landlord was leaning on the counter rubbing the edge of a coin over a scratch card. He glanced up as the pub door opened, scowled when he caught sight of the warrant card Turnbull pushed under his nose. 'Looking for Gerrard Bundy and Charlie Deeks, through the back room I take it?'

The landlord regarded the detectives without speaking. Stubble was starting to grow through on his shaven head. A gym bunny who guzzled steroids by the look of it, either that or he had a bicycle pump out back that he used to blow up his arms, each one covered with a sleeve of tattoos. The number 8, signifying the eighth letter of the alphabet, representing Hitler's surname, had been inked on the back of his hand. He glanced over to the pub's main entrance and both detectives had the sense not to deprive him of the notion they had come alone. A couple of lone drinkers sat in the main bar, hard-up men too broke or too lazy to be fussed about the pub's usual clientele. They broke eye contact when Turnbull looked at them, as though looking away made them invisible.

'The back room?' Robinson persisted. The landlord, who'd been sipping at a coffee mug, banged it down noisily, nodding his head in the direction of a door at the far end of the bar.

'I don't want any trouble,' he said loudly, and then, louder still, 'Rozzers are in!'

Either the mug shot on the Police National Computer had been taken recently or time had been kind to Gerrard Bundy, for he still looked the same. His black goatee beard and barbed wire tattoo along the right side of his face made him easy to pick out from the half dozen men nursing their pints. The assembled punters resembled death row inmates, bare arms and necks displaying the usual range of supremacist paraphernalia: SS Lightning Bolts, Swastikas; the US confederate flag. Bundy's left arm had a home-made portrait of Hitler tattooed on it, only the dimensions were wrong so it looked more like the fat one from Laurel and Hardy. The woman beside Bundy smiled meanly and said something under her breath making him smirk.

'You must be Charlie,' Turnbull said to her, amicably, 'you've changed.' The snide look she'd greeted him with turned into a glare for time had been less kind. A bloated version of the picture held on the PNC, she wore a black beanie hat pulled down low over straggly dyed black hair. Her nylon bomber jacket was tight across her middle, a baby bump or flab Turnbull couldn't determine.

'What d'you want, copper?' Bundy sneered. He raised his pint glass to his lips before realising it was empty, undaunted he tilted his head back to swallow the frothy dregs before replacing the glass on the table beside him.

'Five minutes of your time,' Turnbull said, pulling out the stool in front of the couple without waiting to be asked. Robinson remained standing by the exit, his back to the wall in case things got nasty.

'Whatever it was, he was with me,' Charlie mocked.

Turnbull fixed her with a stare. 'What makes you think it's him I'm interested in?' The smile froze on her lips. 'You've got a history of serious assault,' he added, as though she needed reminding.

'History,' she repeated, amenable, 'that's all it is, we're a proper couple now.' She patted her belly fondly.

Turnbull eyed the cider and black in front of her, the packet of roll-ups beside them. 'Very happy for you I'm sure,' he responded. 'What were you doing after last orders on Tuesday night?'

'Eh?' Charlie scratched her right breast absentmindedly.

Her companion's face broke into a grin. 'Hang on, that's when that darkie was murdered, it's been all over the news, you trying to fit Chas up for this?'

'Good luck to 'em,' someone muttered from another table.

'Enough!' Robinson ordered, careful not to single anyone out when he glared at a group of skinheads sat around a table.

Turnbull turned towards Gerrard. 'I'd like to know your whereabouts too, as a matter of fact.'

'As a matter of fact,' Gerrard mimicked, 'I happened to be with Chas, we were down the hospital, thought she'd gone into labour but it was those pretend contractions.'

'Braxton 'icks,' Chas added knowledgeably, 'we'd gone in after the pub closed, didn't get out again 'till about four in the morning. Contact the hospital if you don't believe me.'

'I intend to,' Turnbull said evenly, getting to his feet.

*

It was a day of little progress. Turnbull and Robinson returned to the station to report that Deeks and Bundy's alibis checked out, as did the remainder of the suspects they'd tracked. 'And they don't know who's behind it either,' Turnbull added, 'some of them have lost the plot that much they'd wear it like a badge of honour if they knew.'

'So we can close the Hate crime line of enquiry,' Coupland said pointedly, darting a glance in the DCI's direction. Mallender returned Coupland's gaze before nodding. The DCI was different from Curtis; he didn't turn everything into a pissing contest. Coupland was well aware that wouldn't be the end of it, at some point Curtis would come over the hill demanding an explanation so they'd need to type up their reports in double quick time but at least the investigation could continue on the right track in the meantime.

Despite this, he couldn't shake off a nagging disappointment: the truth was they had very little to go on. Sharon's workmates had nothing bad to say about her, not unusual in itself, but people liked to rake mud, and if there'd been any hint of shenanigans between her and another colleague he'd have heard about it by now. DC Ashcroft had been tasked with carrying out background checks on the staff at Donald Gillespie and with James Grimshaw's co-workers but nothing had been flagged up so far. Mallender traipsed off to the Super's office looking like he had lead in his boots.

*

Coupland was halfway down a glass of red wine Lynn had poured them before dinner when the day took a turn for the worse. Amy slammed the kitchen door practically off its hinges as she stormed in to confront him. 'HOW COULD YOU?' she yelled, her eyes brimming with tears she tried to blink away.

'Amy, calm down.' Lynn was already on her feet, moving towards her. 'What is it?'

Amy brushed her away. 'Has he told you what he's done?' she demanded, causing Lynn to look at Coupland sharply while his heart sank into his boots. He should have come clean, told her what he'd done the moment he got home. This was going to come out all wrong now he was on the back foot.

'What's going on?'

Coupland felt his cheeks redden as Lynn eyed him suspiciously, and he'd thought the worst of the day was behind him. In a stalling tactic he blew out his cheeks. 'I went to the college today,' making it sound as though it was no big deal. Both Lynn and Amy stared at him.

'Go on!' Amy challenged. 'Tell her what you did there!'

'Kevin, out with it!' Lynn said sharply. 'You know I don't like surprises, especially if they're about to blow up, like this one by the sound of it.'

Coupland sighed. 'I went to see the principal,' he began, trying to second guess just how much Amy had been told. 'I wanted to know if he was aware there was a convicted criminal working on the college grounds.'

Lynn gasped. Coupland could see a flash of anger but out of loyalty she was reining it in in front of Amy, though he'd feel the full force of it once they were on their own.

'And what did the principal do?' Amy pushed.

Coupland lifted his chin as he answered, 'He rang through to the personnel office, who confirmed Vincent had declared his conviction on his application—'

'—Oh, there was more to it than that, Dad,' Amy butted in, 'not only does the college have full knowledge of his history; they recruited him from an offender employment programme. An assessor comes in each week to meet with his supervisor to check on his progress, so it was all above board.'

'Oh, Kevin,' Lynn groaned; there was an edge to her voice that made his toes curl. Pleased her words were having the desired effect Amy gathered pace. 'His supervisor called him in to ask why the police might be looking into him and he explained you were my dad and it was all some alpha male hang up you had with anyone I dated.'

Coupland held up his hands. 'OK, my bad,' he retorted, 'pardon me for looking out for my daughter.'

'You just don't get it do you?' Amy shot back. 'I can look out for myself, Dad, I don't need you for that now. When will you realise I'm not your little girl anymore?' She slammed out of the house.

'Oh yes you are,' he called after her.

CHAPTER 5

Here she comes, running late, apprehension pouring off her in waves. Maybe she's having second thoughts about the dress she's wearing. Maybe she's right, given the size of her. In her hurry she doesn't give the man she passes a second glance. Until he looks at her, causing her to miss a step. Is she so starved of male attention a simple smile will turn her head? 'I was nearly a gonner there,' she jokes, pausing to wave down below to the driver of a people carrier. The driver doesn't bother waving back. Instead, he executes a rather poor three point turn, heading back in the direction he came. 'Wait,' a male voice behind her says, and she stands on the stairwell, a curious look on her face but the glimmer of a smile nonetheless. 'I've got something for you,' he says, before running at her at speed.

Coupland was doing his utmost to avoid a domestic. He trailed after Lynn in the kitchen trying to second guess her every action, managing only to get under her feet. He was in the dog house, that was clear enough. Her answers to his questions were clipped, as though she were biting back the things she really wanted to say to him. Lynn had so far supported his concerns about Amy's boyfriend but his stunt at the college seemed to have pushed her towards Vinny's camp. Wine long since forgotten she opened the oven door, pulled out the grease covered shelves one by one. She must be really mad if she was cleaning the oven, it was a job both of them put off for as long as possible, saving it for times when they needed to release tension.

The last time *he'd* done it was just after Lynn's diagnosis. Following her to the sink he placed his hand over hers as she reached to turn on a tap. As a couple they were closer now than they'd ever been, the thought that bastard could interfere with that...

'He's trying his best to rebuild his life, Kevin.' Lynn chose her words carefully. 'He's been honest with his employers and with Amy about his past, we can't expect any more from him.'

'I can expect him to fuck up.' Coupland's words, as ever, came straight from the hip, 'A leopard never changes its spots.'

Lynn turned to look at him. 'You did,' she said evenly, placing a hand on his chest, pushing him slightly to put some distance between them. 'You were close to going off the rails when you were his age, you told me so yourself.'

Coupland stared at her. That she could draw any similarities between the two of them... 'Was it any wonder with my old man?' he said irritably. 'After Mum'd gone it was like he resented my existence.' Coupland had been left to fend for himself most of the time, fell in with a rough crowd that could have been his undoing if the police hadn't been recruiting the summer he turned 21. Rather than be proud he'd followed in his footsteps, his dad had responded as though he'd robbed a bank. 'Nothing I ever did was good enough.'

'Apart from marrying me,' Lynn reminded him with a gleam in her eye. 'He sent you a card, remember, he must've approved.' When Coupland had moved out of the dingy flat he'd shared with his father he'd never gone back, and the old man seemed to like it that way, living out his days wasting his police pension on drink and the betting shop. Coupland joining the police had been the final straw, and what should have brought them closer pushed them apart. It was as though his father preferred it when his life was fucked up; maybe it made him feel better about the mess he'd made of his own. Yet Coupland saw it differently, reckoned his old man felt he was stealing his thunder going into the force, the job being the one thing he'd been proud of. Coupland blinked away the memory. Lynn had a point though, he of all people should understood how easy it was to cross over onto the wrong side of the tracks, but then was it so wrong to say he didn't want that for his daughter?

He tried a different tack. 'Christ, love, we've both worked hard for what we've got, moved to a decent area with a good school, are you really saying he's what you had in mind for her?'

Lynn shook her head, 'No,' she conceded, 'but we brought Amy up to have a mind of her own.'

'That was your doing,' Coupland accused her. 'What's wrong with doing as she's bloody told?'

'Taxi for Kevin,' Lynn chided, holding an invisible phone to her ear, 'says he needs a ride back to the 1950s.'

'Thank Christ for that,' Coupland grumbled. 'I'd quite like to be king of my own bloody castle for once!'

When Lynn spoke next there was laughter in her voice, 'You wouldn't know what to do with yourself, Kev, trust me.' She was right, as she always was, so he did what he always did in that situation and said nothing. 'You're going to have to get past this,' Lynn soothed, nudging him to one side so she could get started on the metal grill. 'We both need to trust Amy's belief in him.'

He nodded, but he wasn't convinced.

*

'You couldn't sleep either?' Ashcroft called over as Coupland entered the CID room two hours before his shift was due to start. He was sitting at Alex Moreton's desk, leaning back in her chair; a smattering of pastry flakes said he'd eaten breakfast there.

'Well I'm not here for the coffee,' Coupland grumbled, glaring at the tarry substance trying to pass for a cappuccino he'd got from the vending machine.

Ashcroft flicked the pastry flakes onto the floor, the way single men did when there was no one at home to answer to. 'Area car's been out to Broadwalk a couple of times, someone reported a man behaving suspiciously, turns out he's been on the sauce all evening, was so drunk he couldn't remember his way home. Kept trying to let himself into strangers' houses, banging on the front door when his key didn't work. The last house he fell asleep on the patio.'

'Enjoying our hospitality, I take it?' Coupland enquired.

'Yup, bed and breakfast, full en-suite facilities.' He shook his head. 'Can you imagine being that out of it?'

Coupland blew out his cheeks, had to cast his mind far back, to the days before he tried behaving like a role model for Amy. 'Lucky bugger,' he muttered. What he wouldn't give to be anaesthetised right now.

The phone on his desk gave a shrill ring. He cocked an eyebrow at Ashcroft as he answered, reaching for his car keys as he pushed himself to his feet, motioning for the DC to do the same. A woman's body had been found at Salford Crescent station.

The railway station, close to the university, had two lines. Used by students and commuters alike, the commuters either working in Manchester's city centre or at the opposite end of the line – Preston, Lancaster and Blackpool. Two police vans now blocked the entrance to the station and a Police Community Support Officer was securing tape around the base of the footbridge. Another officer diverted traffic away from the roundabout on the station approach. Coupland slowed his vehicle long enough for the uniformed man to clock him and get out of his way. In his rear view mirror he saw more police vans approach, parking across any potential vehicular access to the station, including blocking off entry to the industrial site opposite. DCI Mallender's car was parked adjacent to the police vans and Coupland followed suit. Soon enough the place would be swarming with journalists; better to create as much of a barrier as possible.

The DCI's shock of blond hair stood out against the uniformed officers' flat caps. He was pointing to the other side of the bridge, waving his hands impatiently; within minutes access to the bridge from the other side of the track was cordoned off. Coupland climbed out of his vehicle. Turning to Ashcroft he pointed out a PCSO shepherding would-be commuters away from the station waiting room. 'You need to shut this place down otherwise people will be turning up here every half hour until rush hour is over. Have a word with the staff in the ticket office, no more trains to stop here until I give the all clear,' he commanded.

'Right Sarge.' Ashcroft made his way to the crowd standing by the glass fronted ticket office.

Coupland caught Mallender's eye; the DCI inclined his head, waving him over. The victim had been discovered at the base of the footbridge. She was white, early thirties.

Two rings on her wedding finger. She wasn't dressed for work, the dress she wore was flimsy, the heels suggested she wouldn't be walking far at the other end, a cab even, given the likelihood of rain. Her body lay awkwardly at the foot of the stairwell, her long hair fanned out around her. Straw coloured liquid trickled from her ears. Coupland knew that if he lifted her head the back of her skull would be shattered. He stepped closer, looked up at the bridge, for the moment keeping his thoughts to himself.

'I suppose it's possible she jumped,' Mallender suggested.

'Nobody jumps backwards,' Coupland said, 'this one was definitely pushed.'

'Forensics will confirm it.' Mallender nodded at the army of white-suited ants moving toward them. 'This one's not a robbery either.'

Coupland eyed the shoulder bag lying beside the victim, its contents spewed across the path as the DCI turned to him. 'Once it's been photographed and the contents logged I want you to go through it. Get her ID'd and let her poor family know.'

Coupland nodded at a pile of vomit two metres away from the body. 'The person who found her?' he asked.

Mallender shook his head, 'Not the person who reported it, we already checked. He's worked for the rail network for years, a ticket inspector now but back in the day drove high speed trains till he failed his medical.'

'So it's not the first dead body he's seen then.'

'Nope, though it's the first time one still had the head attached, as he was kind enough to share with me.'

Coupland moved back from the body, mindful not to

step in the puddle of sick. A sample would need to be taken for a DNA match. 'Who's the crime scene manager?'

Mallender broke eye contact. 'DC Turnbull.'

'God help us,' Coupland muttered.

'He's had the training,' Mallender reminded him, his tone sharp. 'I know two murder investigations at the same time will be a drain on our resources but we have to make the best of it.'

'Talk of the devil,' Coupland remarked as Turnbull made his way over to the crime scene, stepping tentatively on the metal plates that had been put in place to protect the locus. He had blue footwear protectors over his shoes and he carried a clipboard. Mallender made his way over to speak with him, pointing at Coupland and the woman's personal possessions that had spilled from her bag.

Ashcroft, dressed in a CSI suit, made his way over to Coupland. 'Jesus.' He stared at the victim as he approached her. He craned his neck to look up at the bridge then back down at the position of her body. 'She didn't jump, then.'

'Nope.' Coupland watched a CSI log each item beside the victim before placing it into an evidence bag.

'Two bodies in three days, could still be coincidence,' Ashcroft mooted.

Coupland laughed then, a small harsh sound that contained no mirth. 'You sound as confident as a Greek banker. Even so, we treat this as a separate investigation until we know otherwise.'

The CSI carried the evidence bag over to Turnbull who put on a pair of reading glasses before cross referencing the contents onto a pad on his clipboard. Once the items had been logged, he pushed the glasses onto the top of his head before making his way over to Coupland, asking him to sign for the contents before handing the evidence bag over to him and countersigning the form.

Coupland turned to Ashcroft. 'Better get an FLO assigned and on standby.'

Ashcroft nodded and headed towards the parked vans before pulling out his mobile. A moment later he held the phone away from him as he called over: 'There isn't anyone spare, they can assign the PC who's at Sharon Mathers' place, at least she's experienced.'

Coupland nodded. Ashcroft spoke into the phone before ending the call. Coupland took a moment to observe once more the activity going on around the body before making his way over to Ashcroft and handing him his keys. 'You can drive while I go through her belongings.'

The photographer had arrived, was setting up his equipment while the forensic team worked around him. 'Don't forget to bag the vomit,' Coupland instructed Turnbull, ignoring the scowl that flitted across the officer's face.

'You're good to go, Sarge,' Turnbull reminded him, writing 'sick' onto the itinerary on his clipboard when nobody was looking. Coupland baulked at Turnbull's words as he climbed into his car.

Good didn't come into it at all.

While Ashcroft manoeuvred the car back onto the main road Coupland pulled on a pair of plastic gloves before removing the woman's mobile and purse from the evidence bag. He opened the clasp on her purse and pulled out a debit card. 'Maria Wellbeck.' He replaced the card and looked through the other sections. 'Forty-five pounds in cash and a train ticket to Oxford Road.' He switched on her mobile. 'S'funny,' he said, after a minute or so had passed, 'no missed calls.'

Ashcroft shrugged. 'Maybe she was going away?'

'No bags or suitcases,' Coupland observed. 'Besides, she wasn't dressed for travelling, she had a flimsy dress on with tights, for a start.' Coupland swiped his finger across the smartphone. 'Good thing nobody locks their phones any more.' He tapped the screen until he found her email account which had been set up to display messages without the need to log in every time. 'Bingo,' he grinned, 'there's an email here confirming an order from Next, giving a delivery address on Fire Station Square.'

'Where's that?' Ashcroft asked, ready to tap a postcode into his phone's GPS. 'Don't bother.' Coupland pointed to a cluster of buildings beyond the roundabout. 'It's there.'

What was once the forecourt of Salford Central Fire Station was now a public space with trees and benches. The fire station itself, a red brick and terracotta building with a shaped gable featuring a clock face, had been converted by the university to accommodate its council chamber and three small boardrooms. The fire engine bays had been redesigned into meeting spaces although the firemen's poles had been retained. The properties behind the main building consisted of smart red brick terraced houses and this was where Maria Wellbeck lived.

A blink of an eye and they had pulled up outside. Ashcroft switched off the engine and waited. Coupland caught his eye as he took his time unbuckling his seat belt. 'Never gets any easier, this bit,' he sighed. Delivering the death message. The moment he walked into someone's life and fractured it.

As they approached the front door they heard a baby crying from an upstairs window that was slightly ajar. 'At least we can't get the blame for waking the child up,' Ashcroft said as he pressed the doorbell.

A harassed-looking man dressed in suit trousers and a shirt half hanging out of his waist band opened the door. He made a point of looking at his watch. 'Christ, you're a bit keen aren't you, I'll take a leaflet and we'll call it quits, eh?' he offered.

Coupland held up his warrant card; Ashcroft's was displayed on a lanyard around his neck. The reaction was immediate, the man's shoulders dropped and his face took on the look of a frightened animal. He took a step backwards, as though trying to distance himself from what was to come. 'Mr Wellbeck?' Coupland asked. The man nodded in slow motion, his mind trying to compute why two sombre looking cops had turned up at his door. 'I'm Detective Sergeant Coupland and this is Detective Constable Ashcroft, may we come in please?'

Wellbeck said nothing, but stepped back a few more paces to allow them access. As they stepped into the hallway a much older woman came down the stairs carrying an infant. The child looked no more than six months old and was grizzling, their face red and legs banging against the woman's hip. 'What's going on?' she asked as Wellbeck showed the men into a living room that had been smart once, but had since been hijacked with baby paraphernalia. 'Are the bottles ready?' the woman asked. 'Only madam here isn't as patient as her brother.' She turned to the detectives, 'twins,' she beamed, as though she hadn't got over the novelty of saying it.

'Please, Mr Wellbeck,' Coupland said, 'it might be

better if we can go somewhere private, where you can sit down.'

'I'll stand if it's all the same,' Wellbeck said gruffly, regaining some of his composure. He tucked his shirt into his waistband and held his arms out for the child.

'I really think you'd be better doing as I suggest,' Coupland persisted.

Wellbeck stared at him. 'Is this about Maria?' he demanded, causing the woman to gasp. He half turned towards her. 'They're police,' he said evenly.

'Then do as they say and sit down,' she chided him, ignoring his outstretched arms and placing the child instead into a travel cot that doubled as a playpen in the corner of the room. This time Wellbeck did as he was told. He looked at his watch once more, yet it was an automatic reaction, for every nerve ending told him the day would not pan out as he'd expected first thing. He settled his gaze upon the detectives standing before him. 'Now tell us,' he ordered. Coupland cleared his throat.

Upstairs a baby boy began to whimper.

*

'Hope you're good with kids.' Coupland said in an undertone to the FLO that arrived twenty minutes later. Wellbeck had taken the baby girl upstairs to change her nappy and the woman had gone into the children's nursery to bring her grandson down for his bottle. The twins were nine months old. Born prematurely they were small for their age but what they lacked in size their made up for in lung capacity.

The FLO pulled a face. She didn't mind kids really, but was wary of showing too much of an interest to her colleagues. She was going steady with an officer based at Eccles, she didn't want him to start thinking she was broody. 'Poor little mites,' she said instead, and set about de-cluttering the living room in anticipation of the friends and relatives that would descend as soon as word got out. She pulled the downstairs curtains closed, 'to keep out nosey parkers,' she said with authority before going into the kitchen to fill the kettle with water.

'They've got a fancy coffee machine,' Coupland told her, 'get Grandma to show you how it works, I need to get hubby on his own for a bit.' The FLO nodded, introducing herself to the older woman when she came downstairs, asking if she would show her what was what in the kitchen. The woman's eyes were red rimmed and she looked at the FLO confused. 'I need to let my husband know…' Her hand instinctively flew to her throat. 'This is going to kill him.'

'Let's do that in here, shall we?' the FLO suggested, taking the woman's arm as she guided her into the other room. Wellbeck returned; instead of an infant he carried a baby monitor. 'Asleep at last,' he grimaced, his eyes darting to the hallway and the closed kitchen door beyond. 'I've been trying her mobile but it's just ringing out.'

Behind the closed curtain the living room window looked out on to the front of the house, to Coupland's car parked on the road, with Maria's phone ringing inside an evidence bag. It was a common reaction, people expecting their loved ones to answer, prove the police had got it wrong. Coupland spoke in a quiet voice: 'We recovered Maria's phone, along with other personal items found with her bag. That's how we knew how to find you.' He let that sink in.

Wellbeck began shaking his head.

'Mr Wellbeck,' Coupland's voice remained low, 'look, would you mind if I use your first name..?' He paused, waiting for a response.

'Pete…'

'Okay Pete, can I ask why you didn't try phoning your wife when she didn't come home last night? I would have expected to see missed calls from you.'

'Maria was staying with a friend from her antenatal class, they'd arranged a night out at the theatre.' He made a sound like a tyre letting out air. 'They were really going to watch American male models take their clothes off to music,' he pulled a face, 'she thought it'd be a laugh. "It's not about the show, Pete, it's the chance of a night out, let my hair down a little," she made it sound like she was in some sort of prison.'

Coupland remembered the early months after Amy came along, Lynn's fear of taking her out shopping on her own. He'd taken a few days' annual leave when she'd arrived, well before paternity leave kicked in. The palaver of packing the changing bag then collapsing the buggy to put it into the back of the car. Timing everything around feeds and nappy changes. It was easier to stay in, Lynn would say, and she'd ring him when he was on his way home to pick up something for dinner. He didn't blame her, looking back, but he hadn't been so understanding at the time.

'Must be hard, though, with two,' he said simply.

Pete scowled. 'I told her it was too soon to start thinking about going out. It's all about going without when they're little isn't it? Putting them first… she said it was alright for me, my job takes me away for several days at a time,' he explained, 'she didn't get that it was work.'

'What is your job, Pete?' Coupland enquired.

'I'm a quality manager for a five-star hospitality group. It's my job to check that standards are maintained throughout our European chain.'

'So you get to go abroad a lot, then?'

Pete nodded enthusiastically. 'Some months my feet don't touch the ground,' he said, 'that's why when I'm home I like to chill out, only Maria's always wanting us to do something. She doesn't get that all I want to do when I'm home is kick off my shoes, have a takeaway... She'd kept in touch with the girls from her antenatal class, there were a couple of them, like her, whose husbands couldn't make it every week, and one of the women – I always thought she was a lesbian – well she could be couldn't she, these days? Anyway, she started organising nights out. Maria always looked forward to them.'

I'm not surprised, Coupland thought sourly, anything to get away from the prick she'd married. 'Were you not worried when you didn't hear from Maria? I mean, I normally check in with the missus when I'm away, not that it happens much, I expect you do the same?'

Pete looked surprised. 'No...' he said slowly. 'I don't like to disturb the twins. Once they're settled you do anything you can to keep it that way. I just assumed Maria was doing the same.'

'Can you give me the number for the friend that she was staying with?' The wheels in Coupland's mind turned slowly as he tried to work out why Maria's friend didn't ring when she hadn't arrived as planned.

Pete looked blank. 'The number will be on Maria's phone...'

Coupland nodded, reaching in his jacket pocket for a pad and pen. 'I'll find it myself later,' he said, making himself a note, 'can you let me have her name?'

Pete blinked. 'Helen Dalry, I think,' he said, 'or Dalton, I can't really remember…' He leaned forward in his chair, pressed his fists into his eye sockets, 'Oh, God…' he cried, 'how the hell did this happen?'

Coupland sat in silence for a moment; there were times when words really didn't cut it. A woman could be heard weeping through the closed kitchen door. 'At least you're not on your own,' he said feebly, 'your mother, I take it?'

Pete reared his head. 'Mother in law,' he answered in a way that Coupland felt some sympathy with. After a moment Pete lowered his hands, pressing them together as though in prayer. 'Tell me everything,' he said, leaning forward, 'because until I hear it I can't quite believe what you're saying is true.'

Coupland nodded, and while he spoke Ashcroft moved around the room, studying photographs, trying to get a lie of the land. 'It seems that Maria was fatally injured on her way out to meet with her friend. Her body was found this morning at the bottom of the station footbridge,'

Pete had been staring at Coupland's face intently, as though trying to read the words he didn't want to say. 'Are you saying she jumped? Oh, God, did she hate her life so much?' He slumped back in his seat slack jawed, his eyes taking on a glassy look.

'No,' Coupland said hurriedly, 'the way she was lying… that doesn't appear to be the case.' He let that sink in.

'So someone pushed her over the side?' there was a lift in his voice, as though it was preferable to have her taken rather than her leave them of her own accord.

Coupland remained still. 'It would appear that way.'

'No…' Pete got to his feet with such speed Coupland thought he was rushing to be sick; instead he started pacing around the room. 'She can't be dead, she can't be. She was going to meet friends.'

'Did you give her a lift to the station?'

Pete nodded. 'She couldn't walk in the daft shoes she was wearing. She'd arranged for her mother to come stay yesterday afternoon to help out, so at least I didn't need to disturb the twins while I drove her to the station and I could leave for work on time in the morning.'

'A train ticket was found in Maria's bag going to Oxford Road.'

'She was meeting the girls outside the theatre, then going back to Helen's place afterwards. They probably don't have our home number, or mine for that matter,' Pete added, 'which is why no one called me when she didn't show.' It didn't explain why there was no missed call on Maria's mobile from this Helen or one of the other girls, concerned she hadn't turned up, but Coupland would gnaw away at that later.

A shrill cry came from the baby monitor, followed by another, slightly higher pitched cry, a beat out of step with the other. The door leading to the kitchen opened and Pete's mother in law hurried up the stairs. 'I told Maria we were too young to have kids,' he scowled, 'told her we should have a few more holidays under our belt, a better car.' He looked dolefully at the people carrier parked on the driveway. 'Now look what's happened,' he said as his dead wife's mother appeared in the doorway shell shocked, a baby straddling each hip.

CHAPTER 6

On Coupland's return to the station he found a scrawled message from DC Turnbull on his desk. *Boss wants to see you.* Coupland didn't bother sitting down, went straight through to Mallender's office, stopping only for a vending machine coffee on the way. Mallender would want to get a measure of Maria Wellbeck before he ran the briefing.

Was there anyone who would want to harm her?

What was her family set up like, domestic issues, any person of interest emerging?

Two dead bodies in a week was Christmas come early for the press. They couldn't afford to look like their trousers were down by their ankles. He knocked on Mallender's door, went in without waiting for a reply. Mallender was tapping on his keyboard; he glanced up as Coupland entered the room, leaned back in his chair as though grateful for the interruption.

'How was it?' he asked.

Coupland sat in the only other chair and pulled a face. 'A young mum setting off on a rare night out with women from her antenatal group. Left behind twins and a husband who doesn't know what day of the week it is.' He didn't need to say any more, Mallender had suffered his own loss during childhood, it had made him guarded, though every now and then he'd let Coupland in.

'Anything not stack up?'

Coupland's mouth turned down at the corners. 'Not from the hubby's perspective, as far as he was concerned she was staying with a mate, which is why he opened the door to us completely oblivious, poor bugger. I'll head out after the briefing to visit her friend though, a Helen Dalton. Maria didn't arrive like they'd arranged and the woman didn't call to check she was okay. Not normal, is it?'

Mallender shook his head.

'I didn't want to make a big deal of it in front of the husband–'

'–in case the friend was covering for her—'

'Exactly, though to be honest I can't see her traipsing off to meet another fella, by the sound of it she was too knackered and stressed looking after two babies and a hubby whose lifestyle doesn't seem to have changed one little bit.'

'It has now,' Mallender said gravely.

Incident room briefing, Friday morning

The briefing was short and to the point. Due to the time the body was found, many of the officers were still at the scene or conducting preliminary house to house enquiries along the student flats and houses in close proximity to the train station. Officers present at the briefing consisted of DCs Ashcroft, Robinson and Turnbull, who had just returned from the locus. DCI Mallender joined them after an unexpected summons to Curtis's office; when he returned his poker face gave nothing away. He apologised for being late to the briefing and asked Coupland to continue.

'Maria Wellbeck was 28, married, a mother to nine-month-old twins,' he repeated for Mallender's benefit. 'I've spoken to the rail worker who found her, and the uniformed officers first on the scene – all confirm that they didn't touch the body or move any of her possessions. It was quite obvious the victim was dead as far as they were concerned so they moved into preserve scene mode. We can estimate the time of death fairly accurately: her husband dropped her off at the station in time for the 6.30pm train which she never got on yet she had on her person a ticket purchased at 6.17pm, so she was killed some time after purchasing the ticket and before she made it onto the platform.'

'Did the person in the ticket office remember serving anyone else?' Mallender asked.

Ashcroft raised his hand. 'The ticket office shuts at five, tickets bought after this time are purchased from a self-service machine outside the office.'

'How come no one found her getting off the train last night?'

Robinson, who lived in the vicinity, spoke up: 'It's mainly a commuter station, after the evening rush hour there's very few folk get off there, and depending on where they live there's every chance they wouldn't pass the body when they leave the station as there are stairs and a walkway leading in the other direction.'

'Besides,' Ashcroft continued, 'there were signalling problems last night by all accounts, a couple of trains were cancelled.'

Mallender addressed DC Turnbull: 'What about weather conditions?'

'No significant change overnight,' Turnbull replied, 'temperature dropped by five degrees, no rain.'

'Chain of evidence…'

'ID and personal belongings given to DS Coupland at the scene.'

Coupland nodded and picked up the briefing once more: 'It looks as though she's been pushed over the footbridge's barrier; now this will need to be corroborated by forensics but the way the body was found indicates she fell backwards, which as you know isn't consistent with anyone choosing to jump to their death; besides, there's a perfectly good train track she could have used if suicide was her intention. A jump from the footbridge would have been survivable from that height, she'd have had multiple fractures and her face wouldn't have been so pretty… instead she came off that bridge backwards and at speed, and in so doing suffered a major trauma to the back of her head, whether this is the cause of death or not we'll have to wait for our forensic friends to tell us in words of one syllable.'

'Husband?' Robinson asked.

'Can't see it.' Coupland shook his head.

'Two women dead in the space of forty-eight hours,' said Turnbull, 'the press are going to start scare mongering.'

'Yeah, but would they be right to?'

'There's no evidence to suggest the same person carried out both murders, is there?' Ashcroft asked. 'Jesus Christ, that'll really set Curtis among the pigeons.'

'The method of killing was different in each case,' Mallender reminded them.

'If the boss agrees I say we continue with two separate lines of enquiry, we can ascertain during the investigation whether the women were friends, or at least known to each other, but I think both husbands need to be eliminated before we go down a different path.' Coupland looked over at Mallender who was already nodding. 'You never know,' he added, 'it could be a tit for tat situation, I'll murder your missus if you do mine…' He laughed, but the sound came out hollow. His face fell serious once more. 'So how are we going to do this?' It would be normal for the family of the victim to make an appeal to the public via the press. Grief porn, but it worked. Often it was used to study the reactions of the husband or other close family members, see if there were tiny 'tells' that gave their guilt away. More usually it jarred a desensitised public into spying on their neighbour. 'I mean, do we run two press appeals, separated by an ad break?'

Mallender acknowledged his point. There was only so much bad news the public could cope with before it stopped making an impact. It was why some victims made headline news and others barely got a mention. All about timing, as though each victim were a product to be marketed.

'We either rule out the partners first and risk letting potential leads go cold if we end up having to widen the investigation…' Coupland was trying to be diplomatic, in his view it was better to do an appeal now and if it turned out the husbands were guilty then so be it. 'We've done it before,' he persisted, 'at least that way the public is geared up and ready.'

'We've never had a situation like this though,' Mallender cautioned. 'Two murders in a week will send the press into a frenzy.'

'But they're going to get wound up about two dead women anyway.' Coupland pressed his point but on this

Mallender wouldn't be swayed.

'Two appeals on the same day, or even a day apart, will lessen the impact. Let's see if we can make inroads without appealing to the public. This time tomorrow we may have a key suspect for one of the cases, and if that happens we put out an appeal on the other case.' There was logic to that; even Coupland had to concede it. He inclined his head in agreement.

After dividing the team into two small units, he allocated actions, each focussing on one particular murder, reassigning tasks where necessary. Mallender hesitated by the doorway until Coupland had finished. 'You want me, sir?' he asked before grabbing his jacket. He was about to head off with Ashcroft but something about the DCI's demeanour made him stay put. Mallender nodded awkwardly, stepping towards him. He waited until the stragglers had left, his face a mask. Ashcroft, taking the hint, made himself scarce. Coupland felt a stirring of unease. Mallender was adopting a stance he had seen often enough, usually from predecessors but the set of the jaw gave it away – he was in for a bollocking.

The DCI waited until he was sure they were alone. 'Superintendent Curtis has taken rather an odd call this morning,' he began, 'the local college principal wanting to make a complaint,' he gave Coupland a hard stare, 'about you.'

Coupland felt himself flush, his hands automatically clenching into fists at the grief Amy's toe rag boyfriend was causing him and he rocked back on his heels, preparing himself for the DCI's full force. It was inevitable, he supposed, that word would get back. He'd pissed off the college head on his own turf; it was obvious the jerk was going to return the favour. He unclenched his fists and spread his hands wide like star fish. 'I can explain—,' he began.

'—Frankly I don't want to know,' Mallender cut him off. 'I've got the gist of it already,' he added, 'from the email which followed the call, which is basically you throwing your weight about the college over a member of staff, gaining access to the principal by pretending you were there on police business,' Mallender gave Coupland a sour look, 'which you weren't.'

Coupland raised his hands in mitigation, 'I know, I know, I'm bang out of order but the muppet's—'

'I'm not interested,' Mallender cut in, 'and neither, as you can imagine, is Superintendent Curtis. Treat this as the reprimand it was intended as, stay away from the college and focus on the matters – or rather murders – in hand. Curtis is expecting an update – and by that I mean real progress – by the end of shift. Let's stay focussed, DS Coupland, okay?' Without waiting for a response he hurried out of the CID room leaving Coupland staring after him. This was the first dressing down he'd had from this DCI and the fact that it was over Vincent sodding Underwood made his blood boil.

As if he'd been hovering in the corridor eavesdropping Ashcroft wandered back into the room, carrying two coffees. 'Thought you could do with this,' he said sombrely.

'How much of that did you hear?' Coupland took his coffee gratefully. It gave him something to do with his hands, which right now he felt like placing round Vinny's neck and squeezing very hard, either that or punching the wall.

'All of it,' Ashcroft said truthfully, turning to look at the view from the windows that travelled the length of the office. The CID room looked down onto the staff car park below; a smoking shelter had been erected when health and safety refused to ignore the fire doors being wedged open when certain officers had a sly fag indoors on inclement days. Beyond the car park vehicles zipped along Belvedere Road, providing a soundtrack to the throbbing going on behind Coupland's eyes. He pinched the bridge of his nose with his index finger and thumb as he stared at the traffic.

'My daughter's going out with a knob I put away last year,' he admitted.

'Ouch,' Ashcroft sympathised, turning his attention back to Coupland. 'How did that happen?'

Coupland groaned. 'Usual story, toe rag meets girl, finds out not only is her dad a cop but the one who put him away a couple of years before, two for the price of one, really... They met at college, their eyes must have met over a blocked u-bend or something... He's not a student,' he added when a flicker of confusion flitted across Ashcroft's face, 'he was placed there through some bloody offender work programme... only I thought he'd got the job by lying about his past...'

'So you thought you'd go and enlighten his boss?' Ashcroft grinned, shaking his head.

'Something like that,' Coupland said sourly.

'What was he sent down for?'

'GBH.'

'Nice guy.'

'Amy thinks the sun shines out of his proverbial,' Coupland whined.

'That's just young love,' Ashcroft soothed, 'can't you remember that far back? Leave 'em be, she'll soon see him for what he is,' he added, 'chances are she'd have kicked him into touch sooner if you hadn't started throwing your weight about.'

Coupland baulked. 'You haven't seen the way he—'

'What? Looks at you when she isn't around? Come on, how old are you, ten? Sounds like there's a bit of horn locking, if you ask me.' He laughed, rearranging his features into a frown that matched Coupland's when he saw the detective tighten his jaw. 'Seriously though, you need to take some of that medicine that you dished out to me, I don't doubt he's an arrogant little prick but don't rise to it because it'll cost you more in the long run.'

Coupland took a step back to study Ashcroft. 'Jesus, how come you got to be so bloody smart?' he grumbled.

'It's easy to be objective when it's not my daughter we're talking about, if it were me I'd want to run the little prick out of town, but we're officers of the law and we have to rise above those urges don't we?'

Coupland lowered his head, refusing to answer.

When it came to his daughter he wasn't so sure any more.

*

Helen Dalton lived in a ramshackle semi on Newearth Road. The front garden could have done with a tidy up but Coupland had no room to talk, it was his friend Joe that he had to thank for the hydrangeas beneath his front window and the patio area out back. There was potential here, if the owners had the time, or the inclination. Overgrown rose bushes grew around the front garden's perimeter, dandelions and nettles poked through uneven paving stones. Ivy grew around the large bay window but had come loose in places. The front door was wedged open, a sign sellotaped over the doorbell read: Sleeping baby – please leave parcel in porch – AND DO NOT RING THE BELL.

Coupland raised his eyebrows at Ashcroft before stepping inside and tapping on the interior door. The wrath of a sleep deprived mother he could do without. 'Hello…'

A middle aged plump woman met him in the hallway. A baby was attached to her in some kind of sling, all that could be seen was the infant's nose and mouth poking out beneath a swathe of bright coloured material. The woman's long curly hair was tied back with a scarf. She smiled good naturedly. 'Unless you're willing to sing to this one while I go take a shower I'm not buying anything.'

'Police, love.' Coupland showed her his warrant card before introducing Ashcroft. The woman froze, planting her hand atop the hall table to steady herself.

'It's about your friend,' Coupland added quickly, 'Maria Wellbeck.'

A wave of relief flooded across the woman's face followed by shame, 'I'm sorry,' she said quickly, 'when you first said you were police I couldn't help thinking…'

'It's OK,' Coupland said amicably, 'we get that a lot, but I'm afraid it isn't good news. Can we come in, love? Probably better if you sit down…'

'You sure I can't call anyone?' Coupland asked five minutes later after telling her the bare bones of it.

Helen shook her head. 'No,' she said firmly, sinking into the armchair she'd lowered herself into on Coupland's insistence, patting the child's back rhythmically in the hope he didn't pick up his mother's distress, 'we were friends through the antenatal group, not really proper friends, if you know what I mean.' Coupland nodded. 'Of course I'm upset, but more for her little family, not enough for me to disturb my partner at work.'

'Was last night a special night out, what with Maria planning to stay at yours?'

'What?' she said distractedly. 'No, it just made it easier for her to have a drink and get a lie in the next day. That husband of hers doesn't exactly pull his weight.'

'You've met him then?'

Helen nodded, 'He came to a couple of the parenting classes, not many, always away on business I guess, but when he did turn up he was friendly enough, I think it was after the twins came along that things began to change.'

'What do you mean?'

'I don't mean to speak out of turn, and God knows he's going to have to step up to the plate now, but I got the impression he expected Maria to deal with everything involving the twins. She told me he moaned when she took more than five minutes in the shower; the babies were fine as long as they didn't impact on his life in any way. So we devised a big night out – none of us drink much anymore, I'm still breast feeding for a start, but Maria reckoned a couple of glasses followed by a lie in would do her the power of good.'

Coupland's brow creased. 'I don't understand then, why you didn't call to find out what happened when she didn't turn up?'

Helen sighed, swiping her hand across her face. 'Because she was flaky,' she sighed, 'I've been arranging these get togethers every month or so since we all sprogged and she hasn't turned up to one of them yet! She never bothers to cancel, just doesn't turn up on the evening. We waited around for her the first time, we were just getting together informally for a pizza and hung around in the wine bar we'd agreed to meet up in for over an hour but she didn't show. She sent me a text a few days later with some excuse, but it was obvious that fella of hers wasn't happy about her leaving him in charge. She gave in too easily if you ask me, but what do I know? Divorced twice with two teenagers, I didn't think I'd be changing nappies again at my time of life, not that I'm complaining mind, wouldn't be without this one now, little poppet. But I recognise when someone's having a hard time... Yet at the end of the day, no matter how much you try and help them, they have to help themselves, don't they? Each time Maria would give me a hand planning our next night out – there are ten of us, many like me with kiddies already so it's no mean feat getting everyone's diaries in sync but we managed it, and everyone made the effort, bar Maria. In the end it got to the point where we no longer bothered waiting when she didn't turn up.' Helen dropped her gaze, her shoulders shaking as she began to sob. 'We didn't even say anything last night when she didn't arrive, just looked at the time and went into the theatre.'

'Nothing you could have done to change events,' Coupland tried to reassure her, 'likely as not she was already dead by then.'

'I could've raised the alarm though, couldn't I, if I'd not been able to reach her? I could've gone round there, we could've retraced her steps...' she looked off into the distance. 'You're right,' she sniffed, 'dead is dead, I suppose.'

Back in the car Ashcroft turned to Coupland. 'So what do you make of hubby now?'

Coupland shrugged. 'He's not the first new dad guilty of not pulling his weight but that doesn't make him a killer.'

'They could have argued about her going out when he gave her a lift to the station and things got out of hand.'

Coupland's eyebrows shot up. 'What? They stop the row mid-sentence so she can go and buy a ticket before carrying on with their domestic?'

Ashcroft acknowledged Coupland's point with a grunt. 'We still bringing both husbands in, then?'

Coupland nodded. 'We need to eliminate them once and for all. Robinson's arranging to get them picked up as we speak. All entirely voluntary at this stage, given we've no evidence or motive to go on. At least he'll be more diplomatic than Turnbull.'

Ashcroft's phone rang. He answered, glancing at Coupland before speaking, 'Yes,' he said slowly, 'we're just about to—' a sigh, 'yeah, will do…' He returned his phone to his pocket and frowned at Coupland. 'That was Robinson,' he said, 'says you're not answering your phone. He was asking me to give you the heads up.'

'Go on then!' Coupland said impatiently, lifting his mobile out of his pocket. He'd turned it to silent mode before going into Helen Dalton's house. His call history showed there were several missed calls, all from Robinson. 'Get on with it…' he growled, turning the sound back on.

'The Super's on the warpath apparently, Sharon Mathers' brother has flown up from London and arrived at the station demanding answers. Turns out he's some hot shot lawyer, insisting on a meeting with the Super and DCI Mallender. He wants to know why we haven't put out a public appeal yet.'

Coupland sighed. 'We only talked about that earlier—'

'I know,' Ashcroft said, 's'not me asking though, is it? And that's not all; the brother's claiming that we're treating the case differently because the victim is black.'

Coupland rested his head on the steering wheel. 'Oh, you've got to be kidding me, tell me you're winding me up?'

'Don't shoot the messenger,' Ashcroft countered, raising his hands. 'It's not my fault Curtis wants a head on a stick. He wants you back at the station. Now. Your presence is required at the meeting.'

'I bet it is,' Coupland muttered.

No sooner had Coupland stepped through the double doors into the station than all hell let loose. Normally the desk sergeant enjoyed a bit of banter as personnel came and went; today he was red faced and definitely in no mood for jokes. He called Coupland over as he keyed in the door code to access the staff only area. 'You've got two suspects waiting in interview rooms one and two. They were brought in thirty minutes ago. We've got a suspected paedo taken into custody but nowhere to interview him, Custody Sergeant's going ape – wants you to get a wriggle on, only he didn't quite word it like that.'

'I'm sure he didn't,' Coupland sighed, turning to Ashcroft. 'You and Robinson do the honours, interview both husbands, get the names of their work colleagues and close friends, we may need to rile them a bit, see if either of them were playing away from home.'

'Doesn't make either of them a killer,' Ashcroft

observed.

'No,' Coupland conceded, 'but it might give them a reason to want their partners dead. Find out if they knew each other, or their paths had crossed anytime recently,' adding, once they were out of earshot, 'don't let anyone pressurize you into wrapping it up quickly, only let them go when you're good and ready, I daresay Sharon Mathers' brother is going to be sticking around, best to get his sister's partner processed as soon as possible – charged or eliminated, so this wise guy can go back to letting us get on with our jobs.'

Superintendent Curtis's office was on the third floor, a hallowed enclave that Coupland had never previously been invited into. Most of his bollockings came at Inspector level, so there had never been any need for him to venture to such dizzying heights. As he climbed the stairs to the Super's office Coupland's mind raced as he computed all the ways possible for him to put his foot in it during the meeting. He wasn't stupid, he hadn't been summoned to bring a distraught relative up to speed – DCI Mallender was well briefed on the progress made on Sharon Mathers' case. Something more was required. Her brother was obviously running rings around Curtis and the Super needed a sacrificial lamb. The only thing Coupland couldn't second-guess was what the hell Curtis was going to blame him for.

The door to Curtis's office opened as Coupland drew near; an angry voice could be heard shouting over the Superintendent, cutting him off mid-sentence every time he tried a new approach. DCI Mallender hurried out nearly colliding with him, his frown lifting when he saw that it was Coupland.

'Where the helluv you been?' he hissed, closing the door behind him quickly.

'You know where I've been, boss,' Coupland answered, perplexed. 'I was checking out why Maria Wellbeck's mate didn't raise the alarm when she didn't arrive at the theatre as arranged.'

'I know that!' Mallender barked back, 'but I put a call out to you half an hour ago.'

'And I'm here,' Coupland said. 'What's going on?'

Mallender looked back at the closed office door, taking several paces away from it before speaking. 'Sharon Mathers' brother arrived at the couple's home just in time to see his brother-in-law get carted off for questioning.'

Coupland bristled. 'Hardly carted, he's co-operated every step of the way,'

'Yeah, well, that's not how the brother sees it. He wants to know why we haven't put out an appeal yet.'

Coupland gave Mallender the beady eye. 'And has anyone bothered to tell him?'

'He's insistent on speaking to someone at the sharp end, as he likes to put it. Now go in there and diffuse the ticking time bomb before Curtis makes it any worse.'

The Chief Super's office was four times the size of Mallender's box room with a large desk in front of the floor to ceiling window and a board room table in the centre of it with several chairs around its perimeter. It was here that Curtis was sat across from an impeccably dressed black man wearing a pinstripe three-piece suit. The man was standing, leaning forward over the table, one hand planted on the table top to hold him steady, the other hand making a chopping motion each time he spoke, which at the moment was all the time. Mallender cleared his throat as he entered the room causing both men to look in his direction. Coupland stepped out from behind him smiling meekly. Curtis had never looked so pleased to see him; however, it was Sharon's brother that grabbed Coupland's attention. The family likeness between this man and his sister was unmistakable, the same deep forehead and almond shaped eyes, high cheekbones on a slender face. He paused as Coupland walked around the table.

'Ah, DS Coupland,' Curtis beamed, regaining his composure a little as he beckoned him into the room like a long-lost friend. Coupland did as he was told, all three men waiting while Mallender shut the door behind him.

At that moment Curtis's face fell. 'DC Ashcroft not with you?' he asked, looking behind Coupland then turning to Mallender as though the DCI was concealing him.

'I didn't realise you wanted to speak to him, Sir.' Coupland frowned, looking at Mallender to help him out.

'That won't be necessary, Sir,' Mallender trying hard but failing to keep his irritation in check. 'As you know, Mr Mathers, I am the senior investigating officer heading up the investigation into your sister's murder. DS Coupland is my second in command, and leads a team of detectives currently out gathering information from several lines of enquiry.' He turned to his head to address his next comment to Superintendent Curtis. 'I really don't think DC Ashcroft can bring anything else to this discussion.'

Ignoring the Super's pinched expression Coupland moved towards the civilian. 'DS Kevin Coupland,' he said, as the lawyer stepped forward and extended a large hand in his direction.

'Damian Mathers.' His grip was firm. His gaze, steady, unblinking. He turned his full beam onto Coupland. 'Have you found my sister's killer yet?' he demanded.

'No.' Coupland stared back. He'd found over the years relatives wanted him to be frank; their brains having suffered the most dreadful of shocks could only compute information in the simplest terms. Sharon's brother might be some hot shot lawyer in the city but he was hurting, and what he wanted was for Coupland to put him out of the misery he'd found himself in.

'I think what DS Coupland is trying to say—' Curtis cut in, his gaze darting from Coupland to Mallender, arms flapping as though trying to smooth the tension in the room.

'—I'm sorry for your loss, Mr Mathers,' Coupland added, conscious of Mallender willing him to get this right. Diplomacy had never been his strong point, but honesty was. 'From the statements we've gathered from Sharon's friends and colleagues they thought very highly of her,'

Mathers visibly relaxed, nodding as he sat down in his chair.

'By all accounts she was a strong, feisty young woman,' Coupland continued, 'not easily intimidated, and I think her murder has been all the more shocking for that—'

'—under my guidance,' Curtis cut in once more, 'the investigation was initially treated as a Hate crime—'

Mathers put his hand out to silence him. 'I asked to speak to the officers working on the case because I'm not interested in your *strategic* direction.' His tone was sharp, leaving Curtis to stare at him open mouthed. 'Did you really need to go through his bins this morning, take his rubbish away? You even took his dirty washing.' His eyes hadn't blinked in all the time he spoke.

'I agree DS Coupland is best placed to answer that,' Curtis nodded vigorously.

Coupland squared his shoulders; one way or another he was bound to pay for witnessing the snub Curtis had suffered. 'I'm sure you're familiar with the process of investigation, Mr Mathers, and I know it is insensitive to call it a process but it enables us to go about our job confident that we are pursuing every relevant line of enquiry. Eliminating Sharon's partner is part of that procedure, and no, for the record I don't think he killed her, and the forensics taken at the scene will hopefully corroborate that, but I'm sure you would rather we work on fact, not supposition.' He could hardly argue with that.

'When is the forensic report due?' Mathers asked.

'Later today.'

'And how far have you got with the Hate Crime angle?' He looked sideways at Curtis as he asked this, as though he wasn't buying into that theory either.

'Far enough for me to be certain that's not what happened here.' Coupland blew out his cheeks. 'Don't get me wrong, there are hundreds of nutters out there no doubt buoyed up by that old footage of members of the royal family making Nazi salutes going viral, but there've been no local incidents leading up to Sharon's murder and that's what normally happens in most cases. We've not found any link to lead us to what's happened to your sister and I don't think we will.'

'Do you think we should make an appeal to the press now?'

Coupland paused. It had been Mallender's call to

hold fire with the press appeal until both partners had been checked out and eliminated. Coupland had wanted the appeal to go out anyway but it made no odds now, not worth airing their difference of opinion in front of Mallender's boss. He glanced at the DCI. 'Now preliminary investigations are almost complete it would be appropriate to run an appeal,' he answered.

The brother looked satisfied, turning his attention to Curtis. 'How soon can this be arranged?'

Curtis nodded toward Mallender who glanced at the clock on the wall above Coupland's head. 'We can still make the evening news if we get a march on,' he said, 'but we do need to be mindful of a second investigation we're undertaking. DS Coupland was being tactful but I have reservations about how we do this.'

'Another murder?' Mathers asked sharply.

Mallender nodded.

'Another black woman?'

'Another woman, but Caucasian this time.'

'You said this time; do you think these murders are related?'

Mallender shook his head. 'It's far too early to say.'

Mathers looked at him sceptically. 'More procedures to follow?'

Mallender bristled, but said nothing.

'We have to follow standard procedures so we're not accused of missing something by some fancy lawyer further down the line,' Coupland chimed, ignoring warning looks from Mallender and Curtis, 'and no, at this moment in time there's no evidence to suggest that's what's happened.'

'But I think you have to make the public aware,'

Mathers persisted. 'How does the other family feel?'

Maria Wellbeck's family were still wrapped up in their bubble of grief; it was unlikely the murder that had occurred two days before had even registered. 'I think we need to be careful of not getting ahead of ourselves,' said Mallender. 'They're still in a state of shock.'

'But the public has a right to know.' The lawyer was getting fired up again; he would be unlikely to concede a second time.

Coupland looked at Mallender, positioning himself so that Curtis was no longer in his eye line. 'I can promise you we will consider it,' he said, 'but if we are to make this 6pm deadline we really need to get moving.' He got to his feet along with the DCI, waiting for Mathers, then Curtis to nod before retreating from the room.

'I think he has a point,' Coupland ventured as they hurried along the corridor, 'it is entirely possible that two men in the same town had chosen to murder their partners during the same week but without forensics there isn't a single shred of evidence to back up that theory. Besides, I've not seen anything to say their grief isn't genuine. Sir?'

Mallender stopped, dragging a hand through his normally impeccable hair. He turned to look at Coupland, who had come to a halt beside him. Mallender's jaw was clenched, Coupland was asking him to make a decision, the repercussions of which could leave a skid mark on his career. Coupland bowed his head toward Mallender as if to say 'It's your call.' The DCI nodded. 'Let's do it.' he said, grim faced.

*

6pm, Press appeal, Salford Precinct station.
The press had assembled like a pack of hyenas at feeding time. As yet the information in the public domain was that Sharon Mathers' body had been found two days before and it was easy enough to let them draw their own conclusions as to the purpose of the press call. They had no idea that Maria Wellbeck's body had been found beneath the footbridge at Salford Crescent station. Reporters for the two main local papers had been circling the cordon put around the railway station when her body had been found but had so far been fobbed off with the idea that there were no suspicious circumstances, a death had occurred through natural causes. Tragic, but nothing sinister.

During the afternoon both women's partners had been interviewed under caution by DCs Ashcroft and Robinson, and there had been a tense wait for the forensic report before the men were told they could go home. The forensic reports for each investigation cleared both of them. No DNA had been collected from the defence wounds on Sharon Mathers; she'd been fending her killer off, rather than attacking him. Some of the fibres found on her and Maria Wellbeck's clothing didn't match samples of fibres taken from the home they shared with their partners, or vice versa, for that matter, yet the same trace of clothing could be found at both murder scenes. A breakthrough at last. The same person was involved in both murders.

'Bang goes Curtis's Hate theory,' Coupland said to Mallender in an undertone, 'other than someone who hates women.'

James Grimshaw and Peter Wellbeck had been taken

home following questioning, given time to freshen in readiness for the press appeal. Pool cars were sent to collect both men at 5.30pm and they walked into the room being used for the appeal behind DCI Mallender together with family members and their shared FLO. Sharon Mathers' brother sat to the right of James, while Maria Wellbeck's husband, Pete, sat alone. He had arrived with a female colleague that Coupland had sent packing when she emerged from the car. Too young, too blonde and far too many teeth for the public to feel any compassion towards the young widower. 'You want sympathy, man, not to become the target of an internet troll,' Coupland had hissed.

'My wife's parents wanted to come but someone needs to look after the twins.'

'What about your parents?' Coupland asked him as they filed into the press room behind Mallender.

'They bought a place in France a few years back after Dad had a stroke, they are flying back tonight.'

Superintendent Curtis had insisted that Coupland and Ashcroft join Mallender, albeit not at the table with the families but standing off to the side. There may be questions they could specifically answer, the Super had said, although the invitation hadn't been extended to other members of the murder squad.

Curtis pulled his tunic straight with a firm tug and walked to the table before sitting down on the furthest away chair. A place card with his name and rank sat on the table in front of him. He held a sheet of paper in his hand. He looked out at the assembled journalists and cleared his throat. The press conference began.

CHAPTER 7

Ten minutes later, everyone filed out of the room, the victims' families being led in one direction and the press shunted in another. The press officer had called the appeal to a sudden halt after Mallender's admission that the cases may be connected for fear of the journalists concocting a serial killer angle. 'It needed saying,' Coupland had said supportively when they were away from the glare of the cameras, but he knew Mallender would be under pressure from Curtis to prove or disprove this as soon as possible before the press starting criticizing the way the investigations were being handled.

'And when exactly were you going to fucking tell me?' Curtis rounded on Mallender once he thought they were out of earshot. They were standing at the foot of the stairs, five minutes more and they would be ensconced in Curtis's office but this was a reprimand that couldn't wait. Coupland hung back in case he was needed but a discreet shake from Mallender's head told him to keep his distance.

'Sir, I—' Mallender began.

'—How do you think that made me look?' Curtis hissed; at least they were getting to the crux of it. 'I didn't want to raise the possibility of another line of enquiry until we'd eliminated both men but thanks to you the press are wetting themselves with joy...'

Coupland had heard enough. 'To be fair, Sir, those

journalists can run rings round the best of 'em…' The atmosphere in the corridor plummeted to cadaver cool. Coupland drew breath, chanced a look at Mallender who tried to silence him with a look. He ploughed on: '…We've followed due process, Sir, there's no Hate Crime angle, the partners have checked out, and forensics are waving a bloody big flag saying the cases are connected. You know as well as I do there's a leak in every force, any journalist worth his salt will be keeping up with our progress step by step. What was the boss to do? He was asked point blank could the killer be the same person, was he to deny it and make us look like liars when the journo prints a leaked email?'

Curtis looked as though his head was about to explode. 'Shut it,' he spat, 'I'm sure as hell not interested in your fucking opinion, Sergeant.'

What a difference four hours made, Coupland thought sourly, shifting his balance from one foot to the other.

Damian Mathers was standing by the station's main exit when Coupland made his getaway from Curtis's dressing down. He looked as though he was waiting for someone, raised his hand as Coupland approached. 'Can I offer you a lift?' Coupland asked politely, hoping the lawyer wasn't going to rip into him too.

'I've hired a car,' Mathers said, 'I just wanted to say thanks for what you're doing, I'm sorry if I went off on one earlier, you know, in your boss's office.'

'Only to be expected, in the circumstances,' Coupland responded. 'Besides,' he added, smiling, 'think I missed the worst of it.'

'You did.' Mathers smiled back, but then, as though remembering why he was there, his face fell in on itself.

'It's just that, me and Shaz, we were close growing up, even found time for each other through college and uni, then I moved to London and, well, suddenly it's hard to find the time.'

'She's still your sister,' Coupland said, 'whether you lived in each other's pockets or never saw each other, and you want to do what's right by her now.'

'I never expected this, though.' Mathers' broad shoulders dipped.

'Most people don't.'

'I'm not just saying that,' Mathers added quickly, 'she kept her wits about her, you know?'

Coupland nodded, 'Three brothers,' he replied, recalling an earlier conversation with Sharon's boyfriend James, 'be enough to keep any girl on her toes growing up,'

'Not just us, our dad too. He was a cop, you see. You got kids?' Coupland's heart expanded as he nodded. 'Then you'll know what it's like,' Mathers continued, 'he was on her case all the time we were growing up, about keeping safe. It was hard at times for her, being the only girl, she had to earn the freedom her brothers took for granted.'

Coupland sighed. 'No one could've accounted for this, not even your old man.' Something cold slithered around his chest as he said this. He longed to be home, on the wrong side of Amy if need be but home all the same, where he could close his front door against the world.

'Your Dad, where was he stationed?'

'Pendleton, been retired twenty years or so now though, couldn't wait to be done with it.'

Coupland could only imagine. 'I was a rookie then, what's his name?'

'Nathaniel.' Coupland cast his mind back, there wouldn't have been many black officers serving in Salford back in the day, this Nathaniel could even have been one of the first. There was an officer he'd see every once in a while, mainly when the big football matches were on and reinforcements were needed. A quiet man, measured, went about his duties with dignity, despite the insults flying around back then, and not just from the supporters. 'That's why I kicked off a bit when I got here, you see.' Damian continued, 'I remember some of the things my father used to tell me, the kind of things he'd witnessed as a serving officer, injuries sustained while in police custody, it's why I became a lawyer. The number of black suspects who misplaced their footing going down to the custody suite, you know the score.'

'No, I don't.' Coupland's tone was sharp, though the man had a point.

'You saying it doesn't happen anymore?' Mathers challenged.

'I'm saying if I ever saw anything like that I'd be up on a disciplinary charge myself because I'd damn well make sure it didn't happen a second time,' he said sourly.

'Not all like you, though,' Mathers reasoned.

'You'd be surprised.'

Mathers smiled, said no more about it, shook the sergeant's hand.

'I'll be in touch,' Coupland assured him. He watched the lawyer climb into his car, the tail lights glowing in the dim sky. His thoughts returned to Nathaniel Mathers, another cop for whom the past was not so rosy.

*

Incident room briefing, Saturday morning
The night shift had been asked to stay on. Following the previous evening's press conference both investigations were to take a significant turn. 'I'm going to merge both cases,' Mallender informed the teams assembled in the incident room. 'As you know the partners of both women have been eliminated from our enquiries and as yet questioning friends and family has drawn a blank in terms of motive – there are no lovers, no love rivals, no jealous work colleagues on our radar. We now have to consider the fact that the trace evidence found at both crime scenes means they are connected in some way.'

A time-served constable at the back of the room raised his hand. 'Traces of what?'

Mallender looked at Coupland. He'd not been stationed at Salford long, didn't know the officers as well as his sergeant. What he wanted to know was whether this man was a potential press leak and if so, what harm could this information do if it got out. Coupland had no such qualms, the pockets of the press were deep enough to turn heads at any level, and George here, if he was responsible, wouldn't do it out of spite, he was one of the most easy going men Coupland had worked with, and he wasn't looking for glory or to see something he'd overheard get into print – he didn't bother with the daily papers, he was a Racing Post man through and through; with a wife in the civil service they weren't short of a few bob either. The truth was very few culprits were found; sadder still was the fact that even if they were, someone else would be quick enough to fill their shoes, police pay being what it was. Coupland looked around the room; several faces stared at him expectantly. Mallender nodded for him to take over. 'Forensics have identified identical clothing fibres at both sites. Sadly no skin or hair, but the fibres suggest it's the same person.'

'But I thought Sharon Mathers put up a fight,' another voice called out.

Coupland nodded, 'Her injuries suggested that, but when she lashed out she didn't break the perpetrator's skin. She may have shielded her face with her hands, which would explain the damage to them if she was warding off blows from a heavy instrument. Until we get the full PM report back we're just surmising.'

'Any lead on the fibres?'

'The lab has promised to have something for us by close of play Monday, so it'd be good by then to have a suspect we can match it to.' A low murmur of agreement rippled around the room.

'These are still opportunist attacks though?' Robinson asked.

Coupland was about to answer when Mallender took over. 'They may be opportunist, but there are usually some characteristics that whittle potential victims onto the killer's shortlist,' he reminded him.

'The two women couldn't be more different, though,' Turnbull observed.

'How so?' demanded Ashcroft. 'Maybe they had the same taste in music, shopped at the same store…'

'Exactly,' Mallender cut in quickly, trying to diffuse the tension he could sense in the room. Merging teams was always tricky, a good team had a synergy, built up a head of steam far quicker than lone working ever could, but asking the officers to regroup when some were just getting into their stride could throw the investigation off course, especially when there were so many personalities to navigate. Turnbull had a tendency to speak first before engaging his brain, he wasn't malicious, but he was thoughtless.

Mallender tried to move the briefing on. 'We need to consider motive – was it a thwarted sexual attack? Just because he wasn't successful doesn't mean that's not his underlying intention. DS Coupland and DC Ashcroft, can you check out registered sex offenders in say, a ten mile radius, pay anyone who's out on licence a visit who has missed an appointment with the probation service in the last couple of months, in particular anyone whose reason for not attending doesn't stack up.'

'My pleasure,' said Coupland, 'but what about those convicted of non-sexual assault, it could be the killer just doesn't like women?'

Mallender nodded, 'Fair point. Robinson, can you look into that, including cases where charges were later dropped, it could be their earlier assaults were just a stepping stone to murder. We also need to look at what the women had in common, as DC Ashcroft suggested. Hobbies, places they drank—'

'—or used to drink, Maria Wellbeck didn't get out much since she'd had the twins, according to her mate,' Coupland cut in.

Mallender nodded, adding: 'Were they members of the same gym? Did they travel on the same bus? Had there been any work carried out at the house, could they have hired the same building firm? Had they sold anything on eBay recently? Where had they gone to school? Turnbull, can you do a full background check and flag up anything they have in common.'

Apart from being dead, of course, though Coupland kept this thought to himself.

*

Coupland and Ashcroft returned to their desks to pull up names from the sex offenders register and download offender profiles which matched violent assaults towards women. Ashcroft ploughed through the MAPPA (Multi Agency Public Protection Arrangements) database. The vast majority of MAPPA offenders were managed through one agency, with information being shared across other relevant organisations as deemed necessary. The agencies included Duty to Care agencies (DTC) such as youth offending teams, local education authorities, housing, social services, NHS and providers of electronic monitoring services (tags). The probation service identified which offenders would require MAPPA management when released into the community. Planning for these cases tended to start six months before the release date.

The case management system used by police to manage MAPPA offenders in category 1 (registered sex offenders) was ViSOR. The searches Ashcroft carried out showed that one offender had recently been assessed by Greater Manchester Police Public Protection Unit, using the Risk Matrix 2000 tool applied to all adult male offenders aged 18 and over. A red flag had been placed beside his name. 'I'm getting the same name floating to the top a couple of times,' he called over to Coupland as he brought him a file.

John Malone was a 58 year old disgraced head teacher. He'd taken over as head at Hazeldean Grammar fifteen years ago after five years as deputy at a neighbouring school. Impeccable record then two years before retirement a pupil complained he'd behaved inappropriately towards her after school. Her aunt had been on the board of governors and recalled the previous year a similar allegation had been hotly disputed by the head to the extent that the board had decided not to report the matter to the police, believing that the girl had been malicious in her claims. This time, the board member reassured her sister they would not be so lax. The following day he was arrested. During the investigation twelve ex pupils came forward alleging he'd abused them, some going back as far as 1983 when he'd been a peripatetic teacher in Eccles. He'd completed an eight-year sentence before being let out on licence, was now living in a flat in Pendlebury. Coupland skim read the file, making notes. He swivelled his chair round so that he was facing DC Turnbull's desk. 'What high schools did our victims go to?'

Turnbull's tongue poked through his lips as he consulted his notes. 'Maria Wellbeck went to Mossbank High.' He closed one file and opened another. He ran his finger down a couple of pages. 'Sharon Mathers went to Hazeldean Grammar.'

'Get your coat,' Coupland said to Ashcroft as he pushed back his chair, 'I think we've pulled.'

The flat was above a Jewish clothing store on Swinton's Pendlebury Road. A busy shopping street, several fast food restaurants and a taxi office made sure the tenants didn't get much shut eye at night. Coupland parked on double yellow lines outside, placed his 'on police business' card on the dashboard. He found himself smiling for the first time in days.

'There's nothing to connect him to Maria Wellbeck

yet,' cautioned Ashcroft.

'Nothing a little visit from us won't clarify.' Coupland shrugged. In his view desk top research could only do so much, you had to look into the whites of a suspect's eyes to see if they were spinning you a yarn, and this was the bit he enjoyed.

The name beside the buzzer on the door entry system gave little away, there was no graffiti on the wall saying paedo or pervert, just a set of initials, JM. Coupland pressed the buzzer and stepped back. 'How often does the probation service check in on him?' He craned his neck to get a look at the upstairs window.

'He has to attend their office once a week,' Ashcroft replied, 'but he missed his last two appointments.'

'And what do they do when that happens?'

'Three misses and his file goes before a specially arranged MAPPA meeting, the likely consequence is they up his appointments to daily.'

Coupland pulled a face, 'So in essence he can miss another one before anything happens, and if he turns up for the next meeting he gets his wrist slapped and they revert to carrying on as normal.'

'Seems like it.'

Coupland tutted into his chest. 'Couldn't do that job,' he moaned, 'if these jokers weren't where they were supposed to be at the allotted time I'd be hunting them down, a missed appointment wouldn't be a bloody option.' He knew it wasn't as simple as that, that the staff who attended MAPPA meetings complained of growing caseloads and cutbacks, of unrealistic target setting by faceless suits, but that pretty much described policing too, the number of murders and thefts didn't reduce in line with his budget, it was the way it was reported that did that. Lies and statistics, and all that went on in between.

Ashcroft waited for Coupland's nod before he had a go at pressing the buzzer. 'Maybe he's asleep,' he ran his hand over his close shaven hair, 'or on the toilet, or…'

'I get the picture,' Coupland cut in, 'or maybe he's just waiting for us to go away.' Coupland stepped further back on the pavement so that he was visible from the window above the shop.

'Maybe you should have kept your holiday gear on, you look a lot less threatening in linen,' Ashcroft chuckled. Coupland ignored him, held his warrant card in the air.

'Could be a library card from that distance.'

'Do I look like a librarian?' Coupland smiled in triumph when the main door clicked giving them access. The stairway was clutter free but that was about all that could be said for it. A dingy interior lit with a single light bulb, uncarpeted wooden stairs that creaked with their approach. The door at the top of the stairs opened and a stooped grey haired man stood to one side, giving them right of entry. 'Well, well, well, never actually had the pleasure, Mr Malone,' Coupland began, introducing himself and Ashcroft. 'It's my colleagues along the corridor from me in Child Exploitation who have the dubious pleasure of dealing with… men like you.'

Malone sighed as though he were about to partake in a tedious in-service meeting. His hair was long for a teacher, wispy on top like an aging Bay City Roller. The man looked older than his years, though prison often did that, a lined face with hooded brows, a Roman nose that was surprisingly intact given what he'd been sent down for. 'How is D wing these days?' Coupland smiled, 'Still get a chocolate on your pillow every night?' His eyes widened like saucers. 'What, you mean it isn't chocolate?' He turned to Ashcroft in mock surprise. 'Who knew, eh?'

'I take it this isn't a social call?' Malone began, standing his ground. Tea and biscuits obviously weren't on the cards today then.

'Sorry, are we keeping you from Fake Britain or Cash in the Attic? You must be so busy these days, must be hard to fit it all in.'

'What do you want?' Malone replied, sniffing when Ashcroft put out his hand.

'We'd really appreciate you co-operating with us, Mr M, do you mind if we sit down?'

Ignoring Ashcroft's hand Malone stomped into the living room like a sulky toddler, 'Well come through if you're coming then,' he sniped, plonking himself down on a floral cotton armchair, leaving the mismatching two seater for his guests.

'I take it your wife got all the decent stuff?' Coupland observed, looking over the chipped coffee table and over-sized rug full of coffee stains.

'Something like that,' Malone muttered.

'I heard she changed her name,' Coupland added. A shrug. 'Must've felt like your world crashed in when you lost your job,' Coupland prompted. Malone pulled at a thread on the arm of his chair, spindly fingers making a pinching motion on the cotton. 'Then you come out of jail, no wife, no house, daresay your kids aren't falling over themselves to pay you a visit.' Malone kept working at the thread. Coupland moved forward in his chair. 'Been keeping an eye on the news?' Malone looked up at the detective as though he was mad. 'Sorry,' Coupland said, 'does it get in the way of Homes under the Hammer?' He slid his buttocks to the edge of his seat, any further and he'd be on his backside. 'Only, a local woman has been murdered.' Malone stared at him. 'Two as a matter of fact, but one in particular I think you'd be interested in. Used to go to your school, as it happens. Fancy that.'

Something stirred in Malone's eyes. Coupland could see the curiosity get the better of him. 'What's her name?' he asked sharply.

Ashcroft obliged. 'Sharon Mathers.'

Double blink.

'You remember her then?' Coupland asked.

Malone turned away. 'I remember them all,' he smirked.

'She was murdered on Tuesday night,' Coupland added, then, 'we need to know what you were doing on Tuesday between—'

'You can't be serious?' Malone spluttered, coming to life. 'I mean, I know what I did was wrong, but I'm not a killer.'

'We're checking your original case notes,' Ashcroft told him, 'seeing if we can find the names of the pupils who came forward from school to corroborate your victims' claims.'

'Will we find Sharon's name there?' Coupland pressed.

Malone shook his head. 'No!'

'I can almost understand in a way,' Coupland sympathised, 'you come out of jail with nothing, your wife and family long gone and what, did you bump into Sharon in the street and she laughed at you, or worst still did she snub you? And all the while you're thinking if she hadn't come forward along with her friends or egged her friends on to report you your world would have been completely different.'

'This is unbelievable, I didn't kill her!'

'Maybe you're working your way through the list of witnesses, saving the woman who made the initial complaint until last.'

'This is preposterous!' Malone spluttered.

'Another woman was murdered on Thursday evening,' Ashcroft added, 'she went to Mossbank High though; you didn't happen to work there at any time did you?'

Malone stared ahead, his mouth a straight line.

'It won't take us too long to find out if you did, so you might want to think about saving us the trouble.'

Malone sighed. 'I was seconded there for a year when I was deputy at a high school in Eccles. Mossbank needed an acting head while their head teacher underwent radiotherapy. It was a good training opportunity.'

'I'm sure it was,' Coupland said darkly.

'Look, I don't know what makes you think I'm capable of—'

Coupland leaned back in his chair, enjoying himself. '—It's a bit of a coincidence both victims attended high schools where you were the head teacher.'

Malone's face lit up. 'I hardly think so,' he laughed, 'look at the size of the school catchment areas.'

He had a point there, Coupland conceded. 'Okay,' he said reluctantly, raising his hands in mitigation. 'You need to tell me what you were doing on Tuesday and Thursday evening.' His request was met with a Cheshire Cat grin.

'Why, I'd be glad to,' came the reply.

CHAPTER 8

Coupland let himself in to his red brick semi, cocking his head to listen to the familiar sounds that greeted him. The washing machine was coming to the end of its cycle, knocking against the unit beside it as it clicked onto a high speed spin. Lynn had left him a note on the kitchen table telling him how long to reheat his dinner for; she was on lates this week and wasn't due to get up for another couple of hours. A pile of mail addressed to him lay unopened by her note: a plea from an emergency disaster charity asking for a donation towards the Syrian crisis, his car insurance renewal, which had gone up, and a credit card bill with all the purchases he'd made on holiday and a few more he'd long since forgotten. Coupland picked up the charity letter, decided he'd give it a read while he warmed up his meal. He didn't bother putting the TV on, wanting to keep the noise down for Lynn. Tonight's dinner was lasagne, his favourite, and Lynn had stuck a post it note with a kiss on it on top of the cling film covering the dish she'd left in the fridge. Coupland smiled as he lifted the dish out, his smile widening when he spotted two cans of beer left beside it. Fate, he called it as he placed the lasagne in the microwave and pressed the symbol Lynn had drawn on her note. He could have one while his dinner warmed and one while he ate. When he and Lynn had dinner together she'd pour them both a glass of wine but Coupland found it made him sleepy.

'Beer makes you gassy,' she'd chide, 'so wine clinches it, buggerlugs.' Leaning back against the kitchen counter he lifted the can to his lips.

Then froze.

He had to blink a couple of times to make sure he wasn't seeing things, but no, his vision wasn't playing tricks on him. Vincent Underwood was making his way downstairs, happy as you please, naked apart from a pair of off-white underpants. A grin spread across his face when he eyeballed Coupland. 'Alright, Kev,' he beamed, 'tough day?' He swaggered into the kitchen, his bare chest glistening with a thin film of sweat.

'What the hell—' Coupland snarled.

'Just getting a glass of water for Amy,' Vinny answered, adjusting the waistband of his jockeys with a smirk. He sauntered to the cupboard to lift down a glass but before he had a chance to fill it Coupland slammed him against the work top. A red mist descended as he slipped his hands around Vinny's throat and all at once he understood the urge to kill, for right this minute if he could get away with it, make the little bastard disappear from the face of the earth...

'DAD!'

Amy's voice pierced its way into his consciousness making him drop Vinny like a hot potato. He stood back letting his arms fall to his sides, returning Amy's stare but instead of chastising him her eyes looked on with disappointment, like the time he'd promised to win her a teddy at the funfair and they'd come away with a goldfish. He'd refused to give up despite spending more than the toy was worth and in the end the stall holder had taken pity on him; either that or he was fed up with the angry fat man scowling for the best part of an hour, his little girl beside him casting daggers at a fish in a plastic bag.

'Why do you have to spoil EVERYTHING, Dad? He was only getting me a drink; he wasn't doing anything wrong.'

Coupland winced; he couldn't bear to think what the little runt had been doing upstairs with his daughter. 'For Chrissake, Amy...' he began, 'put some clothes on.' There was nothing wrong with what she was wearing, a pair of short pyjamas, but that wasn't the point and they both knew it.

'Mum said it was OK,' she cut in, delivering the universal slap in the face for any parent bumping their gums over something the other one had sanctioned. Coupland said nothing; he didn't want to start a row, at least not one that would bring Lynn downstairs shouting the odds at him for causing the disturbance in the first place.

'Thank you.' Amy took his silence as submission. 'Come on.' She slipped her arm around Vinny's waist. He kissed her on the mouth, then opened the fridge door and retrieved the one remaining beer can.

Coupland glared at the kitchen door as it closed on them, his hands gripping onto the counter top. His meal forgotten, he tossed the charity letter into the bin. 'Got my own bloody emergency,' he muttered before marching upstairs.

Remembering too late he was trying not to disturb Lynn, he crashed round the bedroom like a bull in a china shop. 'You bumped into the house guest then,' she observed, squinting at him with one eye as she pushed herself up onto her elbow so she could see the time on

117

the alarm clock.

Coupland's shoulders sank; Lynn wouldn't get back to sleep now he'd woken her, and her good humour about it made him feel ten times worse than if she'd given him a tongue lashing. 'Did you know he was staying?' he growled, pulling off his jacket and throwing it onto the bedroom chair that doubled as a clothes horse for things he couldn't be arsed putting away.

'If you hang your jacket the creases will drop out,' Lynn soothed, but he wouldn't be so easily distracted. He unfastened his belt and yanked off his trousers, lobbing them onto the chair as though making a point.

'You didn't answer my question.'

'Didn't know I was under interrogation,' she answered, pushing herself into a sitting position. 'At least your suspects are entitled to a lawyer being present when you question them.' Her voice had an edge to it, one that warned him he was skating on thin ice, that the way the rest of the evening panned out depended on what he said or did next. Coupland sank into the chair, the pile of clothes beneath him making an uncomfortable cushion. He was backed into a corner and he knew the chances of him coming out of it unscathed were getting slimmer by the minute. The last thing he needed was for them to fall out.

'I was shocked, that's all,' he said evenly. 'I mean, we haven't even discussed it.'

Lynn sighed. 'We have, Kevin, several times,' she said gently, 'only you stuck your fingers in your ears and went "La La La…" every time I broached the subject. You need to accept she isn't your little girl anymore.'

Something jarred inside him. 'Yes she is!' he insisted. 'She's only just started wearing a bra…'

'That was six years ago, Kevin,' Lynn smiled, 'and you cried for a week.'

Coupland huffed out a breath, scratching his belly absentmindedly as he tried to prepare his argument. 'But with that toe rag?' he whimpered. 'Of all the slime balls we let under this roof it had to be—'

'—it wouldn't have mattered who it was,' she countered. 'Prince Harry wouldn't be good enough.'

'You're damn right!' he agreed, unaware he'd just proved her point. Coupland got to his feet, gave his backside a quick scratch before climbing into bed. 'Why here though?' It felt like he was having his nose rubbed in it, and he didn't like that one little bit.

'Better under this roof than round at his place, till we know more about where he lives.'

'It's a shit-hole; I've driven by it a couple of times,' he confessed, pursing his lips as he conceded her point.

Lynn leaned across and kissed his cheek, her hand sliding across his chest. Coupland felt himself stir. 'Try to get some sleep,' she said, 'I might as well get up, got time to load the dryer before I need to head out.'

Coupland sighed. Their holiday was well and truly over.

*

Incident room, Monday morning
'The night shift has managed to trace all the passengers who used Salford Crescent station the evening Maria Wellbeck was murdered. They've been contacted and all have volunteered to come in for a DNA swab this morning.' Turnbull looked pleased with the progress made.

Coupland listened, swirling the contents of a vending machine coffee around in its cup before taking a sip. He'd added three sweeteners but couldn't tell. He paused, the cup lifted half way to his mouth. 'I'd be more interested in anyone who doesn't turn up,' he commented to Ashcroft as Turnbull left the room. Ashcroft hummed his agreement.

A young DC entered the incident room with a trio of Krispy Kreme doughnuts from the 24 hour Tesco up the road. 'Needed a sugar lift Sarge,' he said when Coupland's eyes fell on the oblong box. The DC sneaked a look at his watch; he'd not been out so long that the shifts had changed over, surely? 'Been studying the CCTV footage outside the pub where Sharon Mathers went for a drink on Tuesday night to see if she was followed in or out,' he explained, on the back foot.

'And?' Coupland raised his eyebrows but his gaze had locked onto the confectionery in the detective's hand.

'No one acting suspiciously. No known faces. Apart from the local dealers, obviously.'

Coupland looked up at him sharply. 'She didn't speak to any of them?'

The DC looked at him warily. 'Not so far. What is it, Sarge?'

Coupland locked his fingers together in front of his chest, like a minister about to deliver a sermon. 'You know, I feel it's my duty to spell out the perils of the early morning sugar rush, son; after all, it plays havoc with your figure.' He turned sideways on to show the young detective his profile. 'Take me as a case in point. I started out in this job like a whippet, not an ounce of fat on me, a bit like you.' Not a word of that was true, Coupland had always carried love handles; he was stocky by nature, gave him an advantage over his skinnier colleagues when staring down a gob shite at closing time. The DC's shoulders drooped. 'Such a waste, though, if you throw them away,' Coupland counselled, 'why don't I take one off your hands? Trust me; I'm doing you a favour in the long run. It might be too late for me but you've got your whole life ahead of you.' Reluctantly the DC offered the box to Coupland. 'Giving is good for the soul, son, remember that.' The DC tried to ignore Ashcroft sitting close by but failed miserably, they were the only three people in the room and good manners dictated that he offer the other detective a doughnut too.

'Nice one,' Ashcroft grinned, his earlier breakfast already forgotten, winking at Coupland as he took one.

Coupland felt the stirrings of guilt. 'How many more tapes have you got to get through?' he asked; he and Ashcroft were still off the clock for a while yet.

'I'm on the last two, Sarge,' the DC grumbled.

'Tell you what,' Coupland took a mouthful of sticky chocolate icing, 'why doesn't DC Ashcroft here take a look at the other one for you? Many hands and all that…'

The DC's face lit up, unlike Ashcroft's. 'No such thing as a free breakfast, you should know that,' Coupland smirked at him.

He left them to it, returning to his desk with his half eaten doughnut and semi cold coffee. At least the coffee didn't taste so bad now. He logged into his computer, saw that Sharon Mathers' post mortem report had arrived, copied into DCI Mallender. No surprises, the victim had been in good health when she was struck down by her killer. Death was caused by severe trauma to her skull.

Bruising around the Vagus nerve in her neck indicated her killer had tried to strangle her. The defensive wounds to her hands implied she'd fought hard for her life, only for the bastard to finish the job off with a blow to the head. The wound was an irregular shape, suggesting the weapon they were looking for was nothing more sophisticated than a large rock. Unless the killer wore gloves there was every chance his or her prints would be all over it. A fingertip search had been carried out where Sharon's body had been found but Coupland couldn't be sure that included the recreation park nearby, or the gardens of the houses that looked onto it. He made a note to check how extensive the initial search had been. They needed to find it before the weather turned and rain washed away the killer's ID.

Coupland sighed, looked over at Ashcroft and the Krispy Kreme DC staring at screens in front of them whilst licking icing off their fingers. He was finding it hard to concentrate; the image of Vinny coming down the stairs in his underpants was seared into his brain. That and the scornful look Amy gave him when she walked in on him with his hands around her boyfriend's throat. He blinked away the image. 'How many cameras has the footage come from?' he called out to Krispy.

'Six in all, one outside the front of the pub where Sharon had been drinking, one opposite the bus shelter where she waited with some work mates at the end of the evening and four every couple of hundred yards in between.'

'And you can track her movements from one to the other?'

The DC nodded.

'No detours?' Coupland pressed.

'No, Sarge.'

'Have we checked her mobile?'

'Yup,' Ashcroft responded, 'no incoming or outbound calls.'

Coupland got up from his chair. The sugar had made him antsy, what he needed right now was a lead that would use up the adrenaline coursing through his system since his confrontation with Vinny. 'People work their way up to murder,' he said aloud as he moved towards Ashcroft's desk. 'Unless it's a crime of passion, or a flash of anger that's impossible to control.' He thought back to his stand off in the kitchen with a shudder. What if Amy hadn't walked in on them? He'd be downstairs in the cells right now rather than up here trying to find a double killer. Lynn and Amy would be devastated. And all for someone whose name they won't even remember in six months' time. He knew Vinny was playing him. He probably wasn't that interested in Amy, just saw it as an opportunity to even the score, defile the daughter of the bloke who put him away. Even the thought of it turned his stomach. He just needed to keep his cool, play the long game. Amy couldn't be in love with this fella really, Coupland just needed to give her time to work this out for herself. He moved to stand behind Ashcroft, looking over his shoulder as he watched Tuesday evening's pedestrians weave in and out of the wine bars and restaurants that had opened at Salford's Media City since the BBC became operational there.

'Sharon's already in the pub at this point,' Ashcroft informed him. 'I'm watching to see if she comes out. We know she caught the bus home with a couple of pals from work, but it's possible someone could have followed the group, after striking up a conversation. Maybe they didn't decide who they were going to pick off until the opportunity presented itself.'

'A case of Eeny meeny miny moe…' Coupland said aloud. 'Did she smoke?' he asked Krispy.

He grunted a yes, piping up, 'She's at the bus stop with her mates on this tape, she lights up three times.' Ashcroft nodded when as if by magic Sharon emerged from the pub doorway, cigarette already in her mouth as she stepped outside.

'A girl after my own heart,' Coupland commented. 'Might as well have been a chain smoker, the way it panned out.'

'Suppose that's one way of looking at it.' Ashcroft leaned forward to get a better look at the screen. Something had caught his attention. 'Hello,' he muttered, 'looks like she's about to get some company after all.' A man had come from out of the camera's range at the bottom of the screen, making a beeline for Sharon. He held something up in his hand.

'He's after a light,' Coupland said, 'let's see what he does.' The interaction was over in seconds, Sharon furrowing her brow at first, then, as she spots the cigarette he is holding she hands him her lighter. He says something which makes her laugh then returns the lighter to her before walking back in the direction he came.

'Stop,' said Coupland, his chest missing a beat, 'rewind.' Ashcroft did as he was asked, waiting for the nod to press 'play' again.

'There!' Coupland said. 'Can you see?' His pulse quickened the way it always did when he felt the familiar stirrings of making a breakthrough on an investigation, but this time the rush he felt literally knocked him off balance. He placed a hand on Ashcroft's chair to steady himself.

'What is it?' Ashcroft asked, looking from Coupland to the screen.

'Zoom in on his face,' Coupland barked, but it didn't matter that the man's features were grainy, the 'Pussy' tattoo on his neck was as clear as day.

CHAPTER 9

'Sarge!' Ashcroft called after Coupland as he stormed out of the incident room. He made to go after him but paused in the doorway, calling out to the other DC, 'Print out a screen shot of that guy, leave it on my desk,' before hurrying out.

'Wait up, Sarge!' A keen five-a-side footballer, he had an athletic build, had no trouble catching up with Coupland and keeping pace with him but found it harder to deal with his mood. They'd reached the car park; Ashcroft wasn't keen on letting the burly sergeant out of his sight.

'What is it? Who was that guy?' he demanded, grabbing Coupland by the arm as the DS aimed his key fob at his car to unlock it.

'Just leave it,' Coupland's eyes were a dangerous mix of adrenaline and anger.

'No way, man,' Ashcroft persisted, 'whatever's going on affects me too. If you want me to cover for you, that is.'

Coupland stopped at his car and instead of opening the door he turned and leaned against it. He'd forgotten to shave that morning and rubbed his hands over uneven stubble.

'The guy on that camera is Amy's bloody boyfriend!'

Ashcroft kept his face impassive as he mulled this over. 'Okaaaay…' he moved beside Coupland, hands in pockets, avoiding eye contact by staring at his feet. He poked at a cigarette butt with the tip of his shoe.

'Okay?' Coupland rounded. 'Is that all you can say? Is that the extent of your pearls of bloody wisdom?'

Ashcroft sighed. 'So he was there, in the vicinity, talking to our victim, that makes him guilty of murder, is that what you're saying?'

'He's got previous for GBH,' Coupland reminded him, 'are you saying it doesn't?' Ashcroft could see his point, but he'd worked with hot heads before, they needed careful handling. He aimed to elicit facts. 'What about bruising? Sharon put up a fight when she was attacked, managed to get at least one good punch in going by those knuckles…'

Coupland considered this 'I didn't see any marks on his face,' he conceded, 'but she might have only caught the side of his head, depending how far she could reach.'

Ashcroft sucked air through his teeth. He wondered how Coupland's usual partner would deal with this. He tried a different tack. 'You hate him because he's going out with your daughter, and because of that you want him to be guilty.'

'No I don't!' Coupland exploded, then after a moment, 'Yes I do, but that doesn't mean I'm wrong. What's that old saying, just because you're paranoid doesn't mean some bugger isn't out to get you.'

'Fine,' a shrug, 'so what were you planning on doing? Tear arsing over to his place and threatening a confession out of him.'

'I wouldn't have done that,' Coupland muttered, but his words held no conviction. He ran a hand through his hair. 'I don't know what the hell to do, to be honest.'

Ashcroft re-played the video clip back through in his

head. 'So…we've just seen this fella, what's his name again?'

'Vincent Underwood.'

'Right, we've just seen him ask our victim for a light, but let's suppose it wasn't some random encounter. Let's suppose for one minute you're right. We need to establish a link to Maria Wellbeck as soon as possible.'

'We could go and pick him up.'

Ashcroft nodded, the way he did to people threatening to jump off bridges and tower block balconies. 'Mallender would want more than a grudge match as a reason for bringing him in,' he cautioned. Coupland pulled out a packet of cigarettes from his jacket pocket and lit one, automatically offering one to the other detective. 'Only when I'm trolleyed,' Ashcroft said, waving the pack away.

'But what about Amy?' Coupland demanded, sucking the nicotine in as far as it would go. 'How safe is she while we stumble around gathering evidence?'

'I get that you're worried about your girl, maybe you can gently warn her off him?'

'That's what I've been trying to bloody do!' Coupland could feel the blood racing through his arteries, the thump, thump, thump in his chest that occurred whenever he thought of Amy and danger in the same sentence.

'Can you not send her away for a couple of weeks, to an aunt or something?'

Coupland threw back his head and laughed, 'Christ, what is this, 1960? I can tell you don't have a teenager. See these grey hairs?' He jabbed a finger at his greying temples. 'Every bloody one represents a sleepless night I've had over her and some toe rag… or an alleyway… or drugs… or date rape…'

'Please tell me the rest of the time it's like The Waltons,' Ashcroft teased; at least while Coupland opened up there was a chance to talk him down, get him on side. Coupland stared off into the distance, beyond the traffic nose to tail on Broad Street, to a time on holiday when the three of them had laughed so much Lynn was worried she was going to wet herself, his beautiful wife and his precious girl, doubled up over something he'd said, some off the cuff comment that had them rolling around in the restaurant, getting glances from the other diners. It didn't matter that he couldn't remember what the joke was about, all that mattered was after everything they'd been through he still made them happy. He'd felt on top of the world. If he could wrap Amy up in a coat of cotton wool he would. But she'd despise him for it and that thought was like a dagger to his heart. Coupland stared at the pavement for a moment while he thought of the options available.

'We put him under surveillance,' he said, grim faced.

Mallender wasn't as easy to convince as Coupland had hoped. Both murder teams had assembled in the incident room to feed back on their enquiries. There had been no significant developments which Coupland had hoped would make Mallender receptive to his suggestion.

'What about John Malone?' Mallender responded. 'You were liking him for this the last time we spoke.'

'The pervy head teacher?' Coupland scoffed. 'Boy oh boy did he have an alibi – one that checks out as it happens.' All eyes fell on him.

'Go on then, give,' Mallender demanded.

'He's only gone and joined a photography club.' Coupland smiled to himself as several eyebrows around the room shot up.

129

'Wasn't one of the original allegations against him that he'd been taking photos of girls in the school changing rooms?' Turnbull asked.

'Indeed it was,' Coupland nodded, 'only now it seems like he wants to perfect his art. Wait for this though, it gets better. The evening classes he goes to are run in the community room at the local high school,'

'What, the one where he used to work?'

'The very same. Don't you just love his brass neck? Anyway, the classes are held every Tuesday and Thursday evening – followed by a drink in the local Mason's Arms the first Tuesday of the month. Half a dozen amateur photographers can confirm he was there. One of 'em even gave him a lift home after the pub.'

Mallender recorded this information on to his note pad for his briefing with Curtis later. 'Did he give a reason why he'd missed two meetings with his probation officer?'

Coupland nodded. 'He feels he's cured,' he sneered, raising his hand to hold back the next question before Mallender articulated it, 'and yes, I've completed a MAPPA Cause for Concern form and emailed it over to the lead coordinator.'

Mallender nodded, satisfied. The local peeping Tom taking up photography had impending disaster written all over it, they may not have the manpower to keep an eye on him but those agencies tasked with managing him while he was on licence needed to up their game by the sound of it. At least Curtis could be reassured that any mudslinging in the future wouldn't come over his wall.

'So,' Coupland prompted, eyeing the DCI hopefully, 'the surveillance I suggested?'

Mallender sat up straight in his chair, pushing his

chin out a little. 'I need more than some pissing contest between you and this fella to sign off on the overtime needed,' he said starkly. 'Curtis is like a man with deep pockets and short arms when it comes to the staffing budget.' Budget cuts meant it was too expensive to physically follow someone. Modern policing meant relying on CCTV.

'I'll do the extra hours in my own time, Guv,' Coupland offered.

Mallender sighed, 'You can't go anywhere near this guy given your relationship!' he warned. 'Any defence lawyer would have a field day.'

'Look, I'll do it,' Ashcroft intervened. 'I mean, it's not like I've got a social life since I moved here.'

Mallender hesitated. 'I'm not sure about this...'

'Cheers guv.' Coupland smiled, taking the pause as permission. 'I owe you one,' he added under his breath to Ashcroft. Moving the briefing on as quickly as possible before the DCI had a chance to change his mind, Coupland checked how extensive the search had been for the murder weapon used on Sharon Mathers.

Robinson consulted his notes. 'A fingertip search was conducted right up to the periphery of the wooded area, Sarge.'

'Did we check the gardens of the homes looking onto the field?'

Robinson made a show of scanning the file for the answer but it was written all over his face. 'I can get that organised this afternoon,' he said meekly. Coupland nodded but said nothing more. It was easy in hindsight to find fault, he'd made enough snap decisions in the heat of the moment not to point the finger at someone else for doing the same thing.

After the briefing Coupland handed Ashcroft a slip of paper. 'He drives a silver Fiesta, that's his registration number. He works full time at the college; all you need to do is eyeball that he got there, check where the car is parked so we can clock it if it moves during the day. Should be fairly low maintenance, not as though he's a travelling salesman or long distance lorry driver. We can check out where he goes at lunchtime when I've waded through the night shift reports.'

Ashcroft baulked. 'We? Which bit of the DCI's warning did you not understand about keeping the hell away from this?'

'Purely in a supervisory capacity,' Coupland explained, his look challenging Ashcroft to contradict him. Ashcroft pocketed the slip of paper and the screen shot DC Krispy had printed out for him before heading out, the slight shake of his head being the only sign of disapproval. Coupland returned to his desk. Statements had been taken from the bar staff at the Dog and Duck where Sharon Mathers had gone drinking, it was a typical mid-week evening, the majority of custom coming from office workers celebrating someone's birthday or promotion. Leaving do's tended to be at the weekend, with the sole aim of getting tanked up in record time. Two bartenders remembered serving Sharon and her group, they were a quiet crowd, took up three tables in the corner opposite the bar, made their rounds last a long time but then they had work the next day. There was no trouble that night, there didn't tend to be during the week. A doorman was only employed at weekends. Coupland moved onto the statement Sharon's partner, James, had given. He'd read though it the day before but took the opportunity to check through it a second time. James had stayed in all evening, bought a ready-made dinner for one on his way home from work. His mother rang him at 8.30pm inviting him and Sharon over for lunch the following Sunday. He lifted some weights in the spare room upstairs then surfed the internet for an hour which everyone knew meant watching porn.

Coupland closed the file and made his way over to the canteen, his stomach telling him it needed a bacon roll laced with ketchup. He made a detour via reception where a small line of people were standing around, making awkward faces at each other to show they shouldn't really be there. He raised his eyebrows at the desk sergeant. 'DNA swabs in Int. One,' the officer informed him, 'for the Maria Wellbeck murder.' Coupland nodded, made his way towards Interview Room One where the swabs were being taken.

It was the largest of the interview rooms, hadn't long been repainted, didn't have the same body odour and windy bum smell as the others. It was the business class of interview rooms, made sense not to make those who'd volunteered to come in feel they'd been treated like criminals. At least not until they found a match. DC Turnbull had set up a row of plastic tubes and cotton wool buds on a table, together with a sheet of printed labels containing each person's name and date of birth. He'd placed a chair by the table and was checking the items off on his clip board. He nodded as Coupland stepped in. 'You've got quite a queue forming out there,' Coupland observed, 'do you need someone to give you a hand?'

Turnbull was already shaking his head. 'There's no one

spare, I asked.'

'You have checked the Police National Computer to see if anyone's DNA is already on the National DNA Database?' The database stored all DNA profiles taken, so if one already existed for someone a further sample need not be taken.

Turnbull bristled. 'Of course, Sarge,' he muttered, glaring at his clip board.

'Just trying to help.' Coupland backed out of the room, but not before adding, 'remember we need two samples from each.' It was hard to trust others to do their job properly, it was one of the reasons he'd never wanted promotion, he liked to be at the coal face, needed the reassurance of seeing first hand that his instructions were being followed. The last thing he wanted was to see someone walk free because they hadn't made a strong enough case. The only way to be sure was to be in the thick of it.

In the canteen two uniformed officers were tucking in to fried egg rolls. Coupland moved over to their table, made small talk for a minute or two before sending one of them to give Turnbull a hand. He was just leaving with a bacon roll he would eat at his desk when Curtis swept along the corridor heading towards the lift. The senior man blanked him, stared straight ahead like a sprinter running for the finishing line.

Tosser.

That's the way it rolled, Coupland reminded himself, one day you're invited into the upper echelons of the building, rubbing shoulders with the A-list, the next it was like you didn't exist. He found it hard to grasp the politics that was at the heart of modern policing; there were days when just keeping hold of his stripes seemed a challenge. The lift doors opened and Coupland was tempted to step in behind Curtis, stare him down until the man deigned to speak to him, but he wasn't in the playground, had to accept that today his face didn't fit. He took the stairs.

His phone bleeped signalling an incoming text. Ashcroft. Vincent's car was parked at the college. He would hang around until he eyeballed him then would return to the station. Coupland put away his phone. Was he being ridiculous? A man convicted of GBH asks a woman who later ends up dead for a light for his cigarette. That was a strong lead, wasn't it? Or wishful thinking? Back in the incident room he stopped by Robinson's desk. 'Have we got the CCTV from the train station yet?'

Robinson shook his head. 'Faulty camera, not been working all week.'

Coupland reared his head. 'Had they reported it?'

'Yup, been given a job number and everything, the station manager was at pains to tell me. There's a new camera being installed this weekend.'

'There's a surprise.' Coupland returned to his desk, logged onto his computer. Maria Wellbeck's PM hadn't come through yet, despite him emailing the pathologist to ask him if it could be given priority now they were looking at a double murder. Coupland decided to call the man, but instead got through to his answering service. He sucked air through his teeth. He didn't do voicemail, the messages he left tended to come out wrong, sarcastic sounding or like he was making a threat. He made a note on his desk pad to call later.

No sooner had he replaced the receiver than the phone rang. *'Thank heavens for caller ID,'* the droll voice said when he answered. Harry Benson, the pathologist.

'Thanks for calling me back,' Coupland began, remembering pleasantries went a long way, especially if he was wanting his victim to jump the queue.

'Save it detective, I can read emails you know. Maria Wellbeck. I was about to start opening her up when you rang. Now if you can promise to not pester me for the next couple of hours I should get a preliminary report over to you by close of play today. Agreed?'

Coupland restrained himself. He didn't tell the pathologist to shove his scalpel up his backside directly but it was implied in the way he thanked him. He smiled to himself. See, he could do polite if he tried hard enough. He unwrapped his bacon roll and lifted it to his lips. It was cold like a cadaver. He pulled open the roll; the ketchup congealed around the bacon like a festering wound. He threw it in the bin.

Images of Amy's boyfriend flashed before him. The swagger he adopted when she wasn't around. The sneer on his face when only Coupland was looking. He needed to find a link to Maria Wellbeck before Mallender would take his suspicion seriously, and without the CCTV from Salford Crescent station that would be nigh on impossible, after all it wasn't like Maria went anywhere else. For all intents and purposes her social life had ground to a halt after the twins came along. Coupland rubbed his eyes as he sat back in his chair.

Think.

Thanks to him Vinny had a record for GBH. Prior to that he hadn't been on anyone's radar. Sometimes it happened that way, especially on a weekend, a bust up over nothing with one or both parties the worse for wear. Coupland had been the one to arrest him but to be fair he hadn't resisted or tried to flee the scene. In fact Vinny had been the one to call the ambulance. A tussle got out of hand, his defence lawyer had called it, but the other fella had come off worse, and once the CPS had settled on GBH there was a tariff in place that even the best lawyer wouldn't have been able to wriggle him out of, never mind one who only familiarised himself with his client's case notes on the way into the trial. He'd been sentenced to six years. Released in less than three. Did this mean he had the capacity to kill? Coupland didn't know the answer to that. Amy hadn't seen Vinny on the night Sharon Mathers was murdered - they'd been on a plane somewhere over the Atlantic, although there'd been a raft of texts arrive from him once they'd landed. Since they'd returned from holiday Amy and he had become virtually inseparable. If Coupland wanted to find out Vinny's whereabouts on Thursday evening when Maria was murdered, he only had to ask his daughter, but he'd need to tread carefully.

Turnbull returned to the incident room with the list of commuters who'd voluntarily given a DNA sample. He handed the list to Coupland. Everyone who had agreed to turn up had done so, which meant they could be eliminated from the enquiry once their results came back – assuming no match was found. 'How long?' Coupland asked, drumming his fingers on his desk as he scanned the names on the list.

'They're being fast-tracked, should be back tomorrow afternoon barring acts of God.'

Turnbull was on his way out of the room when Coupland, who'd reached the bottom of the list, raised his head. 'There was a fella brought into the cells overnight on Thursday – off his face on booze, lost his wallet, couldn't remember where he lived. Might be worth checking him out.'

Turnbull nodded, retrieving his clipboard from Coupland's desk, muttering something as he did so. Coupland couldn't hear it all. Clutching. Straws. He got the gist.

*

When Ashcroft returned from his morning's surveillance Coupland was still at his desk. Jaw clenched, he was trying to formulate a response to an email forwarded on by DCI Mallender from Curtis. The Super had refused to sanction his overtime request, could he provide a business case to justify the spend? How about two dead women and as yet not a single person of interest? Coupland thought sourly. Leave had already been cancelled for the foreseeable, though he'd successfully argued the case for a DC due to be married at the weekend; parents in law were letting the happy couple use their caravan in Wales for their honeymoon. 'Seriously, I don't mind,' the officer had said gallantly, when the ban had been announced, 'they were talking about driving over to stay with us for a couple of days, anyway, you'd be doing me a favour if the truth be told.' Coupland emailed the DC to tell him he'd need to cut his break short after all.

'It's no good,' he groaned as Ashcroft drew level with his desk. 'I keep hitting the delete button every time I try and type a reply. I know you're not supposed to swear in emails, but that's fifty percent of my vocabulary knackered.'

Ashcroft read the email thread over Coupland's shoulder. 'Will it make a difference?' Being new to the station he didn't know the politics of the place, but he had an idea what the answer would be. It was the same in most stations. Coupland shook his head. 'The work'll get done anyway, it would have just been, I don't know...'

'An act of goodwill or something...'

Coupland shrugged. 'Yeah, something like that.' He logged out of the computer and got to his feet, rubbing the base of his back as he did so. 'I'm going over to where Sharon Mathers was found. Get a better lie of the land. You coming?'

Ashcroft nodded. 'Maybe we can think up a tactful response to the Super on our way.' Stranger things had happened, Coupland supposed.

They were leaving the CID room when Turnbull passed them on his way in. 'The drunk brought in on Thursday night, Sarge, Edward Kershaw,' he called over. 'I've got his address; I'm on my way out there to get a DNA sample from him. I called ahead and he's happy to provide one, albeit he's a little sheepish. A night on the lash after being laid off from work.'

'Where does he live?'

'Broadway Place,'

'If it turns out he was at the train station last Thursday we need to get a full statement from him.'

Turnbull grimaced, 'He'll not remember anything if he was tanked up—'

'I don't care if we have to bloody hypnotise him, I want a sodding statement.'

The approach to the recreation park where Sharon's body had been found was still cordoned off. The area had been combed for forensic evidence, although the wider search Coupland had asked Turnbull to oversee was scheduled for that afternoon. The lone officer manning the cordon looked thoroughly bored. His face brightened when Coupland approached, lifting the cordon for the detectives to step under. 'I can't believe how many times people have asked to have a selfie taken with me with the crime scene in the background,' he grumbled, scratching his chin.

'So your ugly mug'll be doing the rounds on Facebook, then?'

'Not likely,' the officer harrumphed, 'told the ghoulish beggars to sod off.'

The detectives walked on in silence. Once the media circus moved on the public tended to forget about the realities of murder, or the devastation it caused. To them the police tape was a reminder of a bit of excitement in an otherwise dull day. To Coupland it was much more than that. He'd joined the police to keep people safe. Each crime scene made him feel as though he was fighting a losing battle. 'What was he doing here, do you reckon? Before he killed her, I mean.'

Ashcroft kicked his toe against the gravel close to where Sharon's body had been found. The inner cordon and tent had long gone, all that differentiated that area from other patches was how clean it was; no dog turds, no litter, everything that had been collected was now sitting in evidence bags at the station, or had been tested for DNA at the forensic science lab. He shrugged. 'Loitering, waiting to pick out someone suitable? Could have been as simple as he liked the look of her as she got off the bus.'

Coupland said nothing. Made a mental note to make sure that the passengers already on the bus before Sharon got on had been checked out. He knew the ones who had got on at the same stop as her and all those that followed had been checked and eliminated but it paid to be thorough. Ashcroft pushed his hands deep into his pockets. 'Maybe it really was just a random act. Waiting for anyone to step off at that bus stop.'

Coupland thought about this. 'Not such a long wait if he'd checked the bus times beforehand, I suppose.'

'So, he looks up the bus times, decides to kill the first person who gets off at this stop. What if it was a prop forward, or mixed martial arts black belt or whatever, but you get my drift. He could have done all that homework for nothing.'

'Any other passengers got off at this stop?'

'No.'

'What if he really had done his homework though? What if he'd waited here prior to Tuesday to see who got off, earlier maybe, establishing a routine?'

'So we need to check for possible sightings on the days leading up to Sharon's murder.' Coupland added that to his mental list.

'The same for Maria Wellbeck?'

Coupland nodded. 'If you're going to commit an act like murder, and assuming you don't want to get caught, you'd do some sort of reccy first, check out what the footfall is like at the time and place you intend to carry out the killing.'

'So someone might remember seeing him.'

'Maybe.'

'Do you want to go over to the train station?'

Coupland started to shake his head then changed his mind. 'He'd need a totally different type of vantage point. Here, he was disguised by the darkness and the overgrowth. I'm not so sure where the hiding places would be on the approach to the platform.'

Ashcroft shrugged. 'Let's go see.'

The cordon around the footbridge at Salford Crescent station had been removed. People still needed to travel to work; the train operator had obliged closing the place down while a forensic search had been carried out by cancelling trains in both directions for several hours but they had service level agreements with the rail network that meant within 24 hours of Maria being found normal service was resumed. A police incident vehicle had been parked at the entrance to the station with poster size photographs of her in its window and a phone number for the incident room. A uniformed officer stood talking to a member of the public beside it.

Coupland walked to the spot where Maria had been found, then pointed to the place above it from where she had fallen – or more likely been pushed – to her death. 'Can you go stand on the bridge for me?' He waited while Ashcroft obliged. Coupland then crossed the road in the direction of the roundabout, stopped, then began walking back again. He headed towards the industrial estate further along the road, stood at the entrance to the car park, looked back at Ashcroft on the bridge. He could see the DC from each point, there didn't seem to be one place any better than the other in terms of vantage point. If the killer wanted to keep out of view he could have waited inside the entrance to the industrial site's car park but then he'd have had to hot foot it over to the footbridge once he clocked his victim.

Coupland walked back to Ashcroft, joining him on the footbridge as he looked out the way he had come.

'He'd have to be some sort of sprinter to reach Maria before she made it to the platform.' He nodded towards the industrial estate. Ashcroft held onto the hand rail as he leaned over the side of the bridge and looked down. A dark stain remained on the tarmac below. A single bunch of flowers lay beside it.

'Not necessarily.' He walked back to the base of the footbridge. He wore a sweatshirt over black jeans and he tugged the hood of it up to conceal his face, then leaned back against the railings. He pulled out his phone, began tapping into it. Suddenly he became anonymous, rather than some oddball staring at women. 'How about this,' he called over to Coupland, 'he waits for Maria to pass by then follows her, pushes her as she reaches the peak of the bridge.' Likely as not she wouldn't have known what was happening. There was some blessing in that, he supposed.

Coupland's mobile rang. Turnbull: *'I'm with Edward Kershaw now,'* he began, *'I've taken a DNA sample and I'll send it away once I get back but he's confirmed he was on a train that got him into Salford Crescent half an hour before Maria's train was due – he still had the train stub in his pocket. The bender he'd been on had started at lunch, three of them had been laid off without warning. What had started out as a few pints to drown their sorrows had turned into an afternoon of Tequila Slammers. Only stopped drinking when he realised he'd lost his debit card and he was off his face by the time he caught the train home. Got off because he was going to throw up, didn't think he'd make it to the toilet. The hit of fresh air had his head swimming and he couldn't remember where he lived. We know the rest.'*

'Never mind that,' Coupland said impatiently, 'does he remember seeing anyone at the station? Does he remember seeing Maria Wellbeck?'

'Hang on.' The sound of muffled voices as Turnbull repeated the question to Kershaw. Coupland sighed as he heard the one-word answer. Turnbull could be speaking to a killer; they'd need to caution him before asking anything else. *'Can you tell me what you were doing last Tuesday evening?'* Turnbull asked, unprompted. This time the reply was longer. Coupland, who'd put his phone on loudspeaker, looked at Ashcroft.

'It was my wife's birthday, took her out to the Chinese place in Worsley,' came the reply.

'Anyone other than your wife able to verify that?' A pause.

'Two of the waiters helped me into a cab afterwards,' he said, adding, *'wife thinks I drink too much.'*

'She could have a point,' Coupland said sourly. 'Get a full statement,' he barked before ending the call. Ashcroft looked at him, 'Where to now, Sarge?'

'Back to base,' he said dolefully. Time for the arse kicking to begin.

Coupland went straight to Mallender's office on his return to the station. Might as well get it over with. The investigation was going nowhere and Curtis would be starting to twist the thumb screws on Mallender, it was only fair the DCI got the chance to do the same.

Mallender was on his feet when Coupland knocked and entered his room. 'You've saved me the trip, I was just coming to see you, wanted to ask how Ashcroft's settling in?' He leaned against the front of his desk, arms folded.

'He's fine,' Coupland acknowledged, grateful for the distraction, 'got a few demons he needs to lay to rest but then haven't we all?'

Mallender regarded him sharply. 'Anything I need to know about?'

Coupland raised an eyebrow. 'Apart from senior officers determined to make a poster boy out of him?' He was referring to Curtis wanting to parade Ashcroft in front of Sharon Mathers' brother just to appease him, that and his break from protocol invitation to attend the press conference.

'Ah,' Mallender sighed. Bollockings never travelled uphill so all he could do was make sympathetic noises.

'You do realise it would have kicked off if I'd done as I was told and summoned Ashcroft to that meeting? Even if he waited until later to bump his gums, Damian Mathers certainly wouldn't have. It was patronising to say the least. Come on boss, I might be accused of having a hide like a rhinoceros but I'm not so thick skinned I haven't made it into the twenty-first century. Seems to me Curtis needs to go on one of those diversity courses he's so hot on sending everyone else on.'

'That'll be all Sergeant,' Mallender said dismissively. It was the way he avoided Coupland's eye as he got to his feet that told Coupland he'd done it again. Dug himself a hole while still emerging from the last one. He didn't need to turn his head to know that Superintendent Curtis was standing in the doorway behind him. Coupland closed his eyes. If his face looked constipated that certainly wasn't how his bowels felt. 'I need you to get onto that right away,' Mallender added, helping him out.

Coupland stood, rearranging his features to look impassive before turning to leave the room. 'Sir,' he addressed Curtis as he stood to one side to let him pass. Coupland walked down the corridor, back straight; all the while he could feel Curtis's eyes on him.

In the CID room DC Krispy was viewing more CCTV footage. He looked up as Coupland approached. 'I got in touch with the station manager, Sarge, to double check that when he said the CCTV wasn't working he also meant the station car park. Turns out the car park belongs to the council, and the security camera above the pay and display machine was working fine.'

'Well done, son.' The kid certainly had initiative.

The DC's chest puffed out. 'I've checked seven days of tapes and drawn up two lists.' He pointed to a neatly typed sheet of paper, no chocolate smudges or coffee rings in sight. 'The first list contains the registration numbers of cars that were parked there every day during the week leading up to Maria's murder, the second list consists of cars that were left in the car park on just one occasion during that week.'

Coupland nodded. 'I can see I'm going to need to keep my eye on you,' he said, picking up the typed list. He signalled for Ashcroft, who was at his desk checking through emails, to come over. 'Can you cross check the owners of these cars against the passengers that came forward to give DNA samples?' he asked. 'Anyone who hasn't come forward yet, I want to know about it.'

'Will do,' Ashcroft said, taking the sheet of paper from him. Krispy's face fell.

'Teamwork makes the dream work,' Coupland reminded him, then remembered something he wanted checking about Sharon Mathers. 'Actually, you couldn't give the bus company a ring could you?' he said, giving the DC his winning smile.

An hour later Krispy returned to his desk with the

bus company tapes. 'What's boy wonder doing?' Ashcroft asked as he passed Coupland's desk. It was the end of the college day; Ashcroft was heading back to see where Vinny went after he finished his shift. His lunchtime check had revealed nothing, Vinny's car hadn't moved from its original spot and Ashcroft had spied him eating chips from a polystyrene container on one of the college benches.

'So far we've checked out passengers travelling on the evening Sharon was murdered, I want to see who the regular travellers are, see if any patterns emerge.'

'What? Someone might have been doing a reccy to see which were the quietest stops?'

'Something like that.'

'So he's an opportune killer, waiting for that unguarded moment? In which case if Vinny parks up at home then heads out for a tram tonight we should be worried.'

Coupland laughed but it was hollow, something niggled at the back of his brain. 'Look, I need to go and see Mallender, can you ring me the moment Scrote Features deviates from his route home, even if he stops for a newspaper.'

'Will do, Sarge,' Ashcroft said amicably.

DCI Mallender's office door was closed. Coupland knew he was still in the building as his car was in its parking space by the main entrance. Probably ensconced on the floor above, having his testicles felt by Curtis, but he knocked anyway before trying the handle. The door opened to reveal the DCI sitting behind his desk, biting down onto a quarter pounder by the look of it, a large cup of something fizzy beside it. He normally looked after himself, ate healthily, only drank decaf, an occasional cigarette when he thought no one was watching. He'd been a drinker once, Coupland had heard the rumours, but didn't touch the stuff now, kept his distance with after work drinks, though wasn't averse to leaving money behind the bar which endeared him to many. 'Christ, can I not get five minutes to eat in peace?' he muttered, glaring at Coupland's silhouette in the doorway.

'I only need two minutes,' Coupland said, undeterred. In his line he was used to trying to talk to people who didn't want to engage. He stepped into the room, closing the door behind him. The waft of grilled cheese and ketchup made Coupland's stomach rumble and he remembered he'd thrown away his bacon roll several hours earlier in a fit of pique. He wondered if it could be microwaved back into edible form. 'Our man so far has picked victims on a bus route and a train route,' he said eagerly, plonking himself down in the chair opposite Mallender without being invited to do so. 'We need to get someone on the trams, sharpish, see if we clock anyone checking out the quiet stops.'

Mallender put down his half-eaten burger, wiped his mouth with a thin paper serviette. He studied Coupland. 'Are you serious? Are you actually suggesting we move our beat officers from the streets and have them spend the evening riding the trams in some vain hope our killer will be filling out a tick sheet on 'most likely destinations to do someone in'? Are you out of your mind?' He peered closely at Coupland as though checking to see if his pupils were dilated. 'You were banging on earlier about this college handyman, now you're veering off in another direction again.' Mallender sighed. 'I'm as frustrated as you, in fact more so, since I'm the one dragged upstairs for a dressing down at the end of each day. I simply can't allocate more resources – Curtis has made his position clear on this.' Coupland remained quiet while the boss grappled with his conscience. 'The only option is divert the personnel we have, but quite simply, without some sort of plan – which night, which trams, what exactly we're looking for – I can't sanction this.' He didn't cave in after all.

Swallowing disappointment, Coupland pushed himself up from his chair. 'See, I told you it would only take two minutes,' he said brightly, 'and I was right.' *Though it's the only thing I've been right about since this investigation began,* he thought sourly.

The row of terraced houses had seen better days, there was no denying it, but with the housing crisis such as it was homes that would previously have been condemned were deemed liveable; better to have a roof over your head than be homeless, some would say, even though those saying that were unlikely to face such a stark choice themselves. Amid the peeling paint and loose brickwork a couple of properties had had a makeover, new windows and doors fitted, fronts rendered, sky dish attached to a dodgy chimney. Coupland double parked his car alongside Ashcroft's, lowered his driver's window, indicated for the DC to lower his passenger window so they could talk without getting out of their vehicles. They were parked across the road from Vinny's flat, obscured by a council work van.

Ashcroft greeted him with a salute. Coupland inclined his head in the direction of the main road. 'Been here all evening,' Ashcroft stated, 'parked up at tea time with a carrier bag full of shopping, haven't eyeballed him since.'

Coupland nodded. 'Go on, I've got it covered from here.'

Ashcroft raised his brows, ''Scuse me?' He squinted at Coupland in much the same way that Mallender had.

'You heard.' Coupland held his ground. 'Skedaddle, chances are he'll be in for the night anyway. I'm the one with my boxers in a twist over him, stands to reason I take over the night shift.'

'But DCI Mallender specifically said…'

'I know what the boss said, but I'm here now and ready and willing to pull my weight, where's the harm in that?'

A pause. 'I dunno…' Ashcroft looked from Coupland to Vinny's home and back again but Coupland could tell he'd won him round.

'Look, how about I call you if he moves from here, that way you can pick up where you left off so to speak, except there'll be two of us on his tail. Can't say fairer than that… The boss'll see the logic in that too,' he added.

Ashcroft grimaced; Coupland was one of the old guard, preferred following his instincts even if that meant he was skating on thin ice. 'It's a deal, but you call me straight away, I can make it back here in ten minutes if I have to. I'm your wing man, you hear me?'

Coupland flashed his most convincing smile. He might have skirted round the edges of regulations over the years but he wasn't about to put a blot on someone else's copybook. He pulled into the space Ashcroft vacated, lifted the lid off a Costa Coffee he'd picked up on the way over. He took a sip, already eyeing the bag of shortbread biscuits he'd bought with it to keep his sugar levels up. He ripped it open; it was good to have something sugary with a coffee, especially since he'd left his sweeteners in his desk drawer. He hunkered down in his seat, pulled up his jacket collar and opened a Metro newspaper at the sports page, a dejected England squad climbing onto the team bus after another disastrous outing. Coupland tutted, glancing at Vinny's front door before checking his car was still visible just in front of the works van. He turned on the radio, a singer he'd never heard of before sang *I wasn't expecting that*. He swore at the song's ending, picked up another biscuit.

His phone rang, the caller ID telling him it was Lynn. '*Are you not bothering to come home tonight?*' she asked lightly, but he knew she worried about him, especially since Todd's murder a couple of months before. The young DC hadn't been in the team long, was a rookie in every sense of the word but his loss was palpable, more so because Coupland felt in some way responsible.

'I told you I was working late,' he reminded her, eyeing the empty bag of biscuits beside him, the crumbs scattered cross his lap.

'*There's late and then there's what the hell is he really doing late, which one of those is this?*' she demanded.

Coupland hesitated, his missus was like a human MRI scanner, she could see right through him in a heartbeat. 'I'm on surveillance.' He hoped she'd take the hint and leave him to his work.

'*So why not just say? Why the big mystery, Kevin?*' She waited, the way she always did when she felt he wasn't telling her the whole truth. He could already feel himself squirm.

'Because you'll only go off on one,' he confessed, keeping his eyes trained on Vince's front door.

The penny must've dropped because the groan seemed to come from the pit of her stomach. '*Oh, for God's sake*

Kevin, tell me you're not following Vinny? Coupland hung his head even though Lynn couldn't see him. '*You're actually stalking him. You know that's an offence now…*'

'Before you start,' he cut in, 'I've got a reason to be suspicious about him.'

Lynn exhaled a long, slow breath. '*Seriously?*' She sounded sceptical. '*About what?*'

'These murders…'

It took a moment for her to understand what he was saying, '*No!*' she gasped, and then, '*Does Amy know?*' Coupland said nothing. Lynn's tone had changed from frustration to concern in a heartbeat. She didn't ask what had made him suspicious; she trusted his detecting skills, at least. '*Don't you think you should tell her if you are that worried?*' There was an edge to her voice which implied he was putting Amy at risk by saying nothing.

This was serious rock and hard place territory. He felt the familiar rush of blood pulsing through his veins when he thought of Vince and his daughter, but so far his fear was all gut feeling with nothing concrete to substantiate it. 'I don't have any actual evidence at the moment,' he admitted, 'he was caught on CCTV getting a light for his cigarette from one of our victims on the night she was murdered.'

'*Oh, God,*' Lynn whispered and immediately Coupland could have kicked himself, he hated stoking worry at her door. 'That doesn't mean much in itself,' he added hurriedly, 'which is why I'm keeping an eye on him, see if there's a solid reason for us to pull him in. At the moment the boss thinks it's a grudge match.' Lynn said nothing. Coupland heard her breathing get heavier and doors closing as though she was moving from one part of the house to another.

'Where's Amy now?' he asked.

'*She's here, revising for an exam tomorrow; she's not seeing him tonight.*' Coupland thanked God for small mercies. '*Be careful Kevin,*' Lynn said quietly, '*Amy's going to be devastated no matter which way this goes, even if you're wrong. And if he catches you at it, she's going to find that hard to forgive.*'

'Then I need to make sure he doesn't find out,' Coupland muttered.

Just then Vince's front door opened and he stepped out into the darkness. He was dressed in black, jogging bottoms and a slim fitting hoodie, black gloves and trainers. Dressed to kill? Coupland crouched down in his seat, ended his call with a brief 'I'll phone you later.' Surely he wasn't going to make this so easy? Coupland watched as Vince spoke into his phone, talking animatedly, his eyes darting up and down the street before letting himself into his car then pulling away. Coupland glanced down at his own phone still warm in his hand. He had reassured Ashcroft that he'd not go chasing after Vince on his own but they both knew he hadn't meant it. Reluctant to lose visual contact Coupland threw his phone onto the seat beside him before pulling out into the traffic behind Vince's car.

CHAPTER 10

The drive across Salford saw pedestrians make their way home through windy streets, pulling jackets and scarves tight against the cold night. This was what Coupland protected. Ordinary people, their lives shaped by normality. A body builder in a tight tracksuit waited while his Doberman squatted on the pavement outside a Tesco Metro. He didn't bother clearing its mess up. 'Makes it all worthwhile,' Coupland muttered into his chest.

Vince pulled into an Aldi car park. The store was about to close and only one other vehicle was parked there – a white Ford transit – so Coupland kept his distance, parking on the main road but keeping the engine running as he adjusted his rear view mirror to keep tabs on what was happening. Vince got out of his own car, glancing around to make sure no one was watching before climbing into the van's front passenger seat. Almost immediately the van drove off, turning left at the car park's exit, pulling into the flow of traffic approaching the city. Whatever he was up to, it wouldn't be kosher. Why else was he dressed up like a Ninja? Coupland pulled out into the traffic behind them, keeping his distance. The road was quiet for that time of night, enough to keep tabs on the van while hanging back, letting others pull in front, accelerating only when approaching traffic lights. They were driving towards Salford College. Coupland followed as the van turned into the main entrance. Security lighting lit up the approach. Evening visitors to the campus were signposted to a brightly lit block straight ahead but Coupland ignored this, kept on Vince's tail albeit from a distance. The van veered left to a part of the college cloaked in darkness. Coupland hesitated. A sign ahead stated Catering College Deliveries Only. Moving down the gears Coupland nudged his car along. The van pulled up abruptly beside a loading bay causing him to swear and turn off his headlights before executing a three-point turn. He headed back towards reception, choosing a better lit area of the campus, parking his car beside a building marked Adult Learning Centre. A large rectangular block had lights on in every window and a dozen or so vehicles were parked close to the entrance. Coupland climbed out of his car and doubled back down the side of the building towards the catering faculty.

He hung back behind a hydrangea bush, in a small landscaped patch close to the administration block he'd found himself in several days earlier when he'd had the bright idea of approaching the college principal. The landscaped area was on a slight incline and from this position he had a clear view of the loading bay. The van had been reversed into position so that its doors were nearest to the entrance; its doors were open and two men were carrying boxes of varying sizes which they placed into the back of the van. Stockier built than Vince, both men were also dressed in black with hoods pulled low. Vince was standing beside the college doors looking shifty.

'Well, well well…' Coupland shivered involuntarily, resisting the urge to light up in case they spotted him across the tarmac. One of the men stopped what he was doing and said something to Vince but he shook his head and backed away, ignoring the man's shouts as he ran towards the car park exit. Coupland ducked down so he wouldn't be seen. The man shouting after him called him a wanker then barked at his mate to get a fucking move on. His mate pulled a crow bar out of the back of the van and proceeded to batter the loading bay entry in an attempt to make it look like a burglary rather than an inside job. Torn between apprehending the robbers and going after Vince, Coupland jogged back to his car. An ear-splitting alarm shrieked into life but that didn't offer any reassurance. By the time the call was responded to the men would be long gone, probably with what they'd come for, but at least there would be CCTV footage to try and identify them later. Coupland guessed Vince was heading to the Aldi car park to pick up his own car so he decided to get there ahead of him and wait.

He was puffing away on his electronic cigarette by the time Vince arrived. He'd already smoked through two Malboroughs in a row; the scrote wasn't as fit as Coupland had first thought. He'd parked beside Vince's car, only putting his lights on as he bent double, clasping his knees while he got his breath back. 'Fancy seeing you here.' Coupland grinned, lowering his car window. Vince's head shot up at the sound of Coupland's voice, confusion giving way to alarm when he clocked his beaming face. For once he was on the back foot, his eyes giving away the fact his little brain was trying to think up a lie. 'And before you start concocting some story about running out of milk I've just seen you,' Coupland warned him.

'Seen me what?' Vince sneered, already regaining his composure.

Coupland stepped out of his car. Even though he had the upper hand he didn't like the perceived advantage of this toe rag staring him down. He moved towards him. 'Assisting in a robbery at the college to start with,' he shot back.

Vince's face fell. 'No, you've got it wrong, I didn't actually break in.'

'No,' Coupland was enjoying himself, 'but you brought the keys, and you'll have tipped your mates off as to the best day to nick supplies. I guess it's all the frozen food and meat packs they've taken?' Food that could be offloaded easily. 'Everyone knows it'll take ten minutes for a police car to respond, long enough for three strapping blokes to empty a store cupboard,'

'No, it wasn't like that,' Vince persisted. 'I said all along I couldn't get involved in the break in.' He jerked his thumb back in the direction he'd come. 'They asked me to give 'em a hand loading the van but I said no way…'

'So you scarpered, big deal. This gets back to your probation officer, you'll be back inside before morning.'

Vince's hands fluttered beside him. 'They're mates, they won't dob me in.'

'Ya think?' Coupland growled. 'CCTV'll show three men were involved, they'll soon cave in if it saves their own skin.'

'If it was working, yeah,' Vince started to smirk. 'Only it went on the blink yesterday. Funny that, what with the timing and everything.'

Coupland bared his teeth as he slammed Vince back against his car. 'I saw you there, I can place you at the scene,'

'And be the nasty bastard that got me sent down again?

Amy'd love that.'

'She'd get over it.' Coupland leaned in close, his fists curling round the collar of Vince's hoodie.

'Not if she knew I was doing it for her.'

'What?' Coupland stepped back, he didn't want to breathe in the moron's breath any longer. How Amy could stomach him he couldn't understand.

'I care for Amy,' Vince said, all traces of humour gone. 'But it isn't easy staying out of trouble when you've been inside. I never wanted to be a bad guy.'

Coupland snorted. 'You forget I was the one carted you off that lad, it would have been a murder charge if I'd been five minutes later.'

'And if you'd have been five minutes earlier you'd have seen how he went for me. He and his mates had it in for me the moment I walked in that bar.' Vince shook his head. 'His type are the worst kind of hard case, the ones who give no warning. I was tanked up, yes, but I was minding my own business. Next thing he's accusing me of spilling his drink, eyeing up his bird, anything to give him a reason to have a pop. Fast forward and I'm in the back of a police van covered in some nutter's blood.'

The pub was notorious for trouble. It wasn't the kind of place you went in for a quick drink. You went in because you thought you were a player. It was true Vince had no previous prior to the assault, he certainly hadn't come under Coupland's radar before, and if he wasn't going out with Amy he wouldn't be bothering with him now; petty theft at the college would be dealt with by uniforms.

'Look,' Vince continued, 'I'm trying to keep my nose clean, honestly. I met one of those guys inside, and you know what it's like, they come searching for you when they get out, safety in numbers and all that. He heard I was working at the college and he's been pestering me to tip 'em off about the best time to do over the kitchen ever since.' There was always a market for stolen meat, if they touted it round the local pubs over the weekend it'd be snapped up by closing time, the landlords given a cut for turning a blind eye. Coupland forced himself not to lose sight of why he was really there.

'What were you doing on Tuesday night?'

Vince blinked. 'What?' His eyes screwed up in confusion.

Careful. He couldn't be questioned without a caution, and you could trust an ex con to know his rights. Coupland was treading on very thin ice if he went any further down this road. 'Is the question too difficult?' he persisted, staring Vince out.

'I went into town,' he shrugged, 'walked around the centre. If you've not been inside it's hard for you to understand but I can't get enough of being out in the thick of it, crowds, music. I went round a few pubs, got a bag of chips, went home.'

'Did you go past the Dog and Duck pub?' Coupland couldn't stop himself.

Vince shrugged. 'Probably, I don't know. What is this?'

'Did you speak to anyone?'

'Whao, are you trying to fit me up with something?'

Coupland could have kicked himself. 'It's not like that...' he said, too quickly for his liking.

Vince's gaunt face spread into a grin. 'Do your superiors know you're here? Better still, does Amy?' The cocksure swagger returned once more. He had Coupland over a barrel and he knew it. But instead of milking the moment he shook his head. 'Look, I get that I'm not what you had in mind for your daughter but I care about her, you know. If you stopped trying to think up ways to try and lock me up again you'd realise we're on the same side. Think about that.' He took Coupland's silence as permission to move. Coupland, still kicking himself over his stupidity, knew better than to say any more. He'd played into Vince's hands and they both knew it. Coupland's face was impassive as he watched him climb into his car, his fist clenching onto an imaginary nerve in Vince's neck.

Coupland returned home with a sinking feeling. He tried not to brood over Scrote Feature's parting shot. If his feelings for Amy were genuine then the chances of their relationship fizzling out like Ashcroft predicted looked less likely by the second. All he could hope for was that Amy came to her senses instead but she was smitten. Of all the boys – or men, Coupland grudgingly accepted – she had to parade under his nose at home, why did it have to be this one? Vince was trying to drive a wedge between them, he could feel it, and Coupland had just gone and made it a whole lot wider.

He'd no sooner stepped into the hallway and closed the front door behind him than Amy launched herself down the stairs, shouting at the top of her voice as though she'd been lying in wait for him to return. 'I CAN'T BELIEVE YOU FOLLOWED HIM!' she screamed, standing in the middle of the narrow hallway. Feet planted wide with hands on hips she resembled a stroppy toddler and though fearful of her mood he found it hard not to smile.

'Hello to you, too,' he saluted, stifling the urge to ruffle her hair. Her scowl warned him to keep his distance. He hoped Lynn was close at hand, she could defuse a row in seconds – as long as she was on his side. He cocked his head towards the kitchen but Amy wouldn't budge.

'Do you know how embarrassing what you've just done is? It's bad enough that my dad's a cop...' she added, staring at him like he'd crawled out from under her shoe.

Coupland raised his hands in mock surrender. 'I know, I know, you've told me often enough,' he said amiably, trying to joke her out of her temper. It used to work, when she was ten years old.

'...but now you're shaming me by persecuting my boyfriend.'

Coupland pulled a face at the word. The thought that Vince was in a relationship with his daughter jarred with him on some primitive level. Amy wasn't his property, he knew that, but it still felt like something of his was being plundered. 'Can I at least get into my own home before you start giving me a hard time?' he pleaded, glancing into the sitting room looking for the cavalry. There was no sign of Lynn. 'He was a possible suspect in a murder enquiry,' Coupland explained, 'he needed to be eliminated.'

If only that were possible.

'So you think he's a killer now?' Amy demanded, her face a picture of disbelief.

Coupland placed a hand on her shoulder but she jerked it away. He let his arm fall to his side. 'Look, I saw him on CCTV footage talking to our victim, what the hell am I supposed to do?' he hissed. 'Stand back and let him kill you too?'

'But he hasn't killed anyone though, has he?' she said triumphantly. 'Look, are you talking about the two women on the news?' Her voice was calmer now, though the tone still reproachful. Since when had the tables turned? he wondered, as he stood before his child being reprimanded.

He nodded in answer, a sigh hissing out of him like a slow puncture. 'He asked the first victim for a light for his cigarette.' His tone was weary, already he was regretting tonight's action.

'So that makes someone a killer in your book now, does it?' Her voice rose slightly.

'No,' he said through gritted teeth; he had already blown PACE protocol by questioning Vince without a caution. He didn't want to give Amy much more information in case she passed it on; he didn't want another bollocking from DCI Mallender, especially while Curtis was so set against him.

'Anyway, wasn't the second woman murdered on Thursday evening?' she asked.

Coupland nodded once more.

'You do know I was with him then… remember when I stormed out? – It was the day you took it upon yourself to go over to my college.'

How could he forget?

'I stayed over,' she added spitefully.

Coupland winced, stepping around her to go into the kitchen. He needed reinforcements, and fast.

'She's gone up,' Amy informed him.

Coupland's heart missed a beat. 'Is she all right?' He glanced at his watch; he wasn't that late. Depending on shifts Lynn'd often wait up until he got back. His colon twitched at the thought she was unwell again. 'Have you been giving your mum a hard time?' His accusation made Amy draw back, startled, his fear of upsetting her eclipsed by anger Lynn was getting caught up in the crossfire.

'No!' But she didn't meet his eye.

Coupland had had enough. 'Move!' he bellowed. It was the voice he used in the city centre at closing time when it was kicking off. The one he saved for scum bags off their faces, not his precious daughter. Amy's eyes widened before she turned on her heel. Throwing him a filthy look she ran upstairs, slamming her bedroom door behind her. Coupland, focussed on Lynn, took the stairs two at a time, his chest thumping as he went into the bedroom they shared.

His wife was sat up in bed reading, a cup of camomile tea on the bedside table beside her. The scent of lavender permeated the air. As she unplugged a pair of ear phones from her ears, the sound of pan pipes could be heard over the hiss. 'Welcome to Beirut,' she said, tapping a bookmark onto her kindle before placing it on the empty half of the bed.

'Christ, no flies on His Nibs then. He must have rung her the moment I drove away,' Coupland muttered, removing his jacket and tossing it onto the pile of clothes on the chair by his side of the bed. Lynn was after getting an ottoman but he didn't see the point. 'Not like you'd ever see it,' he muttered, whenever she brought it up. He was a creature of habit. Too long in the tooth to start changing.

'He saw you then,' Lynn prompted.

Coupland lowered his head. 'I waited for him…'

'Oh, Kevin!' she groaned, thumping her hand against the top of the quilt in frustration. 'Stop trying to score points!'

'I'm not!' he said quickly, sitting on the edge of the

bed as he turned to face her. 'I thought he was up to something when he left his flat and I was right. I caught him helping a couple of mates nick food supplies from the college.'

Lynn sighed, 'So he's not a killer, then?'

'Is it not bad enough that he's on the rob?'

Lynn shrugged. 'Yes, but you made it sound so much worse earlier.'

Coupland ran his hands through his hair. He supposed it was relative, that it depended on your moral compass, or what you thought of someone else's moral compass, at any given time. His daughter's boyfriend had a history of violence and had now branched out into burglary, but at least he wasn't a killer.

Oh joy.

He unbuttoned his shirt and put on an old t-shirt he used as a pyjama top. He took off his trousers, laying them neatly across the top of the clothes pile.

'Do you want me to heat up your dinner?' Lynn asked, already pushing back the bedclothes. 'It's your favourite – humble pie,' she grinned.

Coupland scowled as he stepped into his pyjama bottoms. Just then Amy's stereo blasted into life, American rappers obsessed with folk who do unmentionable things to their mothers.

He pulled a face. 'Don't bother,' he pouted, his appetite lost.

CHAPTER 11

Fresh sobs burst from the woman's throat as he stifled a yawn. No fight in this one, just fear. A vein in his head throbbed guiltily. It wasn't her fault things had turned out the way they had, but then it wasn't his either. They were victims of circumstance, that's what they were. The woman wasn't a pretty crier; slugs of snot trailed over her mouth which she wiped away periodically with a sleeve. She tried to say something but she was crying so hard it was impossible to understand.

'Say it again,' he said patiently, like he imagined she'd be with a pupil learning to read. Her words tumbled over themselves between hiccupping sobs. He still couldn't understand her. 'You're going to have to speak nice and slow.' He smiled, but it was the kind of smile that made her hold her breath. There was something profoundly wrong with it.

Insincere.

The woman exhaled, slowly, quietly, and begged through her snot covered mouth: 'Please don't kill me.'

Tuesday morning

Coupland knew his day was about to get a whole lot worse long before it actually did. Amy had got up early so she could make a point of blanking him in the kitchen. She flounced around in an oversized t-shirt, slamming her coffee mug onto the counter while she waited for the kettle to boil, using the last of the milk to spite him. Lynn, back on days, hadn't bothered to get up yet, even though her breathing told him she was wide awake. 'If you stay on that fence much longer you'll get splinters in your bum,' he whispered as bent to kiss her, though he didn't blame her waiting until the coast was clear before venturing downstairs.

'He's a passing phase, Kev,' she sighed, 'don't rise to the bait and he'll be gone soon enough.'

'That's what they said about Hitler,' Coupland grumbled. 'Look how that turned out.' At least Lynn was speaking to him, unlike Amy, who preferred shouting.

'HOW COULD YOU, DAD?' she called after him when she failed to get the response she was expecting.

Coupland turned, his heart flipping over as it always did at the sight of her. 'How could I what, love?' he sighed. 'Worry about you? Care for you? Want what's bloody best for you?' He held her gaze.

'How could you betray my trust?' she said quietly. 'You promised you'd leave him alone.'

'I don't think I actually promised that,' he reasoned lamely. 'And by leave alone, I meant not try to strangle him.' The words died in his throat because instead of raising a smile she just scowled.

'I ended up going over to see him last night,' she said defiantly, 'you know, to check everything was still alright between us.' She watched Coupland's face for a reaction. 'I'd have stayed over if I wasn't supposed to be revising and all my books are here. Anyway, we're still good, though no thanks to you. We talked about moving in together as it happens, I can study for my exams just as well at his place as I can here, better even, given the current climate… so I'm going to move some of my things over this afternoon.'

Coupland felt as though someone was squeezing his heart. He opened his mouth to speak but shut it again. He didn't want to talk anymore because he was frightened of what he would say. He turned away.

'Whatever.' He muttered into the ever growing space between them.

The call came before he'd even unlocked his car, his mobile piercing the silence. Robinson: *We've got another body, Sarge.*

Coupland's shoulders sagged as he took down the address, pausing to repeat it in case he'd misheard, his notepad balancing on the roof of the car, his body itching for a lungful of smoke. 'Is the DCI there?' he asked, his voice clipped as he went onto autopilot.

'He's on his way.'

'DC Ashcroft?'

'He'd just arrived as the call came through.'

'Tell him I'll meet him there. Oh, and Robinson.'

'Yes Sarge?'

'We need as many cars there as possible, put a ring of steel round the place till we get the measure of it.'

'Will do.'

A pause. 'Does the Super know?'

'Yes, Sarge. He left pretty sharpish after the call came in so I guess he's on his way over there now.'

Just what Coupland didn't need.

*

The body of Kathleen Williams, reception teacher at Bude Hill Primary school, had been found in the school playground by John Kennington, school caretaker for ten years, due to retire at the end of term. He thought at first

she'd suffered a cardiac arrest, had rung for an ambulance before giving her chest compressions until the paramedics arrived. A classroom assistant had had a stroke the previous year and the local education authority had sent all school staff – teaching as well as ancillary – for emergency first aid training. 'So his prints are all over the bloody body,' Benson muttered when Coupland arrived.
'Cause of death?' Coupland hoped like hell the pathologist would give him a straight answer rather than a spiky comment.
'She's been strangled,' he said irritably. 'As to whether that was the primary factor I won't know until I open her up, Sergeant.'

Coupland walked towards the victim with some trepidation. She'd been moved from her original position by the over-zealous caretaker; Ashcroft was with the man now at the far end of the playground trying to ascertain the position she'd been found in. He watched as the man lay down on the floor playing dead while Ashcroft summoned the photographer over to take his picture. It wasn't normal protocol but normal had left the building and crazy had stormed right in. The paramedics who'd been summoned to deal with the original emergency had stood down after taking one look at the victim, waiting until the police arrived once they'd called it in. They'd had to respond to another shout before Coupland arrived but had left their contact details with one of several uniformed officers deployed to the school. More officers turned up from every direction; many had children in the school, wanted to make sure pupils arriving early didn't see more than they bargained for. The school secretary had been allowed into the building so that she could contact parents and the local taxi firms who had contracts to transport children with special needs; the education authority would contact the bus companies. There would be no school today. The local radio station had been contacted to broadcast a message just before the school run was due to start that Bude Hill was closed *'due to unforeseen circumstances,'* and that pupils were to remain at home until further notice. The parents would love that.

The crime scene manager was a bald-headed DS from South Manchester that Coupland had met once before but hadn't taken to though he couldn't recall why. Quinlan, if he remembered rightly. The man was thin like a whippet with narrow eyes. Coupland headed over in his direction. 'Someone moved the boundary overnight?' he quipped. 'I'm afraid I'm going to have to ask to see your passport.'

Quinlan turned to Coupland but didn't return his smile. 'Handful of us have been seconded to the investigation by those who must be obeyed,' he responded, 'may be more of us by the end of the day if your Chief Super can't convince the ACC you lot know what you're doing.'

Coupland let the remark go. 'Anything I need to know?' he asked as he changed into the CSI suit Quinlan handed to him.

The other man shrugged. 'All will be cascaded during morning briefing, I've no doubt. I've already updated your SIO.'

Coupland bristled at the snub but kept his response in check. So, Curtis had been summoned by the Assistant Chief Constable. He would be under pressure to give assurances that his murder squad would catch the killer before he struck again, assurances he was in no position to give. If his arse was in a sling he'd need a sacrificial lamb should things go belly up, and no prizes for guessing who'd be at the top of that particular list. Coupland looked around for a familiar face. A white forensic tent was being erected over the body. Two SOCOs walked over, rustling in their bodysuits, their features impossible to distinguish beneath plastic hoods. Metal fencing, the type used to prevent the public from gaining access to construction sites, had been erected around the perimeter of the school, crime scene tape secured to it like a ribbon around a present. A press helicopter had already flown overhead and as word spread press association syndicates would begin camping outside the school gates cooking up all sorts of scaremongering stories to keep the public glued to their television sets. Curtis would be forced to give a press conference, promising transparency at every step while reassuring the public they were safe. *There was a killer at large, but have a nice day now*. Coupland understood why Curtis would want to visit the crime scene prior to making the trip to police headquarters. He'd want sound bites he could take into his meeting. Coupland sighed; just his luck to be saddled with an arsey crime scene manager with ideas above his station. Even Turnbull would have been preferable to this.

'Personal belongings?' Coupland asked.

Quinlan raised an eyebrow. 'All bagged and signed for.'

Coupland held out his hand. 'Let me look at the damned inventory then.'

Quinlan handed Coupland his clipboard. A large handbag had been found beside the victim. In Quinlan's spidery handwriting he had logged the following contents: purse, car keys, make-up bag, mobile phone, iPad, make-up wipes, perfume and underwear.

'Sarge.'

Both men turned in the direction of the voice. The South Manchester CSI team had finished erecting the tent around Kathleen Williams' body; the victim could be viewed once more. Coupland nodded, handing the clipboard back to Quinlan before making his way over to the tent. Benson was already inside, kneeling beside the victim as he scraped beneath her nails. 'Is she wearing underwear?' Coupland asked.

Benson nodded. 'There's no sign of any sexual activity, if that's what you're thinking.'

'I'm not sure what I'm thinking, to be honest,' Coupland muttered, moving closer to study her face. 'Make-up's a bit heavy for a primary school teacher, don't you think?'

Benson, who was single, hadn't got children of his own. He shrugged. 'How would I know?' He squinted up at Coupland. 'Though I seem to remember my old teacher had whiskers.'

Coupland recalled his own reception teacher, a fierce woman named Mrs Faulkner who always spoke in the third person. Amy's teacher had been small and round, not an edge to her. The kids all cried when they moved up to the next class. 'She just seems a bit dressed up to be spending the day surrounded by sticky little fingers,' he shrugged.

'Well, that's where this gets interesting,' Benson said smugly. 'She was found what, an hour ago?'

Coupland nodded.

'At best, I'd have expected rigor mortis to have given her the beginnings of the death stare, that slight grimace you often see on a corpse when the Adenosine Triphosphate drains from their facial muscles.'

'Yeah, I was thinking the exact same thing.' Coupland's voice dripped with sarcasm. 'In English, please, if you don't mind.'

Benson swallowed his impatience. 'Look at her, man! She's rigid from head to foot; she's been dead for some time.'

'What are you saying?'

Benson regarded him as he might a particularly dense student. 'That if your man over there really did find her in the middle of the playground she wasn't killed on her way into school. She was killed on her way out.'

So, she'd been here overnight. Coupland digested this information. 'And given the fact she'd put a lot of effort into her appearance – and the make-up wipes and spare knickers in her bag – the poor cow probably thought she was on a promise.'

The pathologist's demeanour changed as someone behind Coupland caught his eye. 'Looks like you've got a royal visit on your hands,' he murmured and Coupland didn't need to turn round to know Curtis had arrived.

'A word please, DS Coupland.' Mallender called him over. Coupland clenched his jaw and tried to lift his shoulders as he made his way back to the primary crime scene cordon where Superintendent Curtis waited beside the DCI. The Super must've been reluctant to get in Benson's way; either that or he baulked at donning CSI clothing over his pristine dress uniform in case it creased. He made eye contact with Coupland, the first time in days since he'd done so.

'I've called a press conference.' His tone was neutral, as though Coupland didn't irritate him one little bit, his eyes locking onto the detective's as he drew near. 'What the hell do you suppose I can tell them?'

CHAPTER 12

Incident room, Tuesday morning

All hell had broken loose. The Major Incident Team from south Manchester had arrived en-masse, bringing with them detectives, crime scene investigators and major incident room staff responsible for operating HOLMES2 (the Home Office Large Major Enquiry System). Hi-Tec crime staff had set up camp in the CID room and were now examining Sharon Mathers' and Maria Wellbeck's laptops, together with Kathleen Williams' iPad and all three victims' mobile phones. Force policy meant that seven and 28-day reviews were to be carried out into the investigation of a serious crime if a case was unresolved. The clock was ticking; no wonder top brass were pulling out all the stops.

A new incident board had been erected for Kathleen Williams. A formal picture of her that normally hung in the school corridor had been stuck onto the centre of the board. Coupland was right, her day time make up was minimal, her long hair secured in place with metal hair combs. Beneath it someone had placed the photograph of her body taken when the murder squad arrived, and beside that the photograph of the caretaker mimicking the position he'd found her in. In both pictures the victim was lying on her back; the main difference between the photos was he'd straightened her head to commence CPR. It was likely his fingerprints would overlay those of the killer but the poor man had only been doing what he'd been trained to, preserving life, not dealing with one that had been wiped out.

The incident room was close to overcrowded. Standing room only and even then you'd need a body mass index below 20 if you didn't want to get intimate with the person standing in front of you. Health and Safety would have a field day if they saw this. Coupland squared his shoulders as he pushed his way to the front of the room to stand beside Mallender and DS Quinlan. He didn't need to move to the front but he was marking out his territory, in the same way a dog might piss on a patch of grass. A pre-emptive strike, should Quinlan try punching above his weight. Quinlan was wearing a black suit, narrow lapels and thin tie, his long hair giving him the appearance of the frontman in a 1980s tribute band; either that or a creepy undertaker. His cronies, standing close to him, saw him clock Coupland as he moved towards the front of the room. They looked on with interest.

'We heard you were struggling, Coupland,' Quinlan smiled, his fingers straightening his greasy tie, 'came as fast as we could to lend a hand.'

Coupland ignored the jibe. 'This is a joint investigation not a sparring match,' he pointed out as he positioned himself between Quinlan and the DCI, easing the other DS off to the side. 'We haven't got time for handbags at dawn; all offers of help are gratefully received.'

'And so they should be, don't want you putting any more of your squad in danger.' The reference to DC Todd Oldman's murder made Mallender and several officers take a sharp intake of breath. The temperature in the room dropped several degrees.

Coupland regarded Quinlan with steely eyes. 'What was it Muhammed Ali once said about Sonny Liston? Ah, I remember now: *"You're so ugly the sweat runs backwards just to stay off your face."* Can't for the life of me think what's reminded me of that.' True to form Coupland's team sniggered, some of Quinlan's too although they tried their best to hide it as they looked to their leader for a response.

DCI Mallender stepped forward, as much as he could given the layout of the room. 'For Christ's sake, the clock's ticking, can we please attend to the matter in hand?' A manilla envelope was clamped under his arm. 'The DNA results are through for the commuters at the train station,' his voice lifted as he spoke, 'and we've got a match.' He opened the envelope and was about to read out a name he'd highlighted in fluorescent yellow when Coupland butted in.

'Edward Kershaw, Sir,' he said, bursting the DCI's bubble, 'that's the guy night shift brought in off his face a few days ago, Turnbull's been over to see him to get a statement.'

'Going by the look on your face I take it he's not our man?'

Coupland's expression was pinched. Lynn said it made him look sour faced but there was nothing he could do to change it now. Too set in his ways. 'He's got a cast iron alibi for the first murder,' Coupland informed him. 'Best case scenario we thought he might have seen someone or something on Thursday evening but he was too far gone.' Coupland mimed the universal hand signal for having a drink.

Mallender tossed the DNA results onto the desk

behind him. 'So we're back to square one,' he sighed.

He turned back to DS Coupland and DS Quinlan. 'I want the two of you to work together to allocate today's actions. Can you both please ensure you report back with any significant leads, Christ knows we need some good news to give to Curtis for his bloody press conference.'

Quinlan's team were given the bulk of the actions. They'd been drafted in to ease the burden on the murder squad at Salford, a squad already stretched with two high profile murders in the space of one week. A third would have hindered progress already made, and in turn impacted morale. No one wants to think they're doing a shoddy job, not when it was obvious a killer was at large. At this stage Coupland was reluctant to reassign tasks; instead where someone had been given a specific line of enquiry they were buddied up with their south Manchester equivalent whose role was to extend that action to include Kathleen Williams. It meant both teams had to integrate, but they were grownups. Well, Coupland wasn't so sure about Quinlan but the rest of his team looked like any cop in the face of a serial killer – hungry to stop the bastard in his tracks.

Quinlan's officers stuffed their hands in their pockets as they filed out of the room, catching the eye of their sergeant as they left. 'Play nice,' he called out, as the door shut behind them. Coupland volunteered to go and speak to Kathleen's husband, along with Ashcroft. Quinlan was for the moment to stay back at base and co-ordinate responses as they came in.

Driving down the East Lancs Road Coupland flicked on the radio. More bad news about some terrorist atrocity; major job losses following the closure of a steel plant. Coupland cared, but his head was full of other stuff, three dead women and their grieving families. He switched to the local radio; Ed Sheeran belted out a love song. 'Preferred it when he sang about Crack,' he grumbled, turning down the volume.

'That's what I'm learning to love about you, Sarge, you're all heart,' Ashcroft tutted into his chest.

'You want me to turn it back up?'

'No, you're fine.'

Coupland resisted the urge to light up. Instead he felt around in his jacket pocket, found a couple of loose mints that had seen better days. He offered one to Ashcroft, who took one look. 'You're kidding, right? I mean, do they even make these anymore?' Coupland ignored him, threw both into his mouth crunching as loud as he could.

'Who delivered the death message?'

'One of Quinlan's men. Not quite a rosy garden there, it seems. They were going through a separation but sharing a house as neither could afford to move out.'

Coupland shook his head. 'Be careful what you wish for, eh? The number of times he must have wished for the place to himself, no squabbling.'

'Husband is distraught by all accounts. Hoped by staying under the same roof they'd get back together again. Thought he was playing the long game.'

'I take it he had no idea she was on a promise then?'

Ashcroft blew out his cheeks. 'I guess we're about to find out.'

The front room curtains on the Victorian semi-detached were drawn. Two cars were parked on the tarmacked driveway, one haphazardly as though someone had arrived in a hurry and couldn't be arsed straightening it up. Raised voices could be heard coming from the hallway as the detectives waited for someone to answer the door. A female police officer he didn't recognise let them in barely glancing at their warrant cards, her face set in a grimace as she did so. 'The son's just arrived,' she whispered, looking behind her to check she couldn't be overheard. 'No love lost there as it goes, playing merry hell, saying it's his dad's fault they broke up.'

Coupland remembered accusing his own father of the same thing. There was truth in it; his dad had treated his mother like a skivvy, expecting her to tiptoe around his drunken moods. Though Coupland didn't blame her for going, he could never fathom why she hadn't taken him with her.

'HAPPY NOW YOU BASTARD? GOT WHAT YOU WANTED?'

Coupland followed the shouting into the living room. A youth not much older than Amy squared up to a middle-aged man. The youth had a slender build, his wiry frame resembling that of a long-distance runner. Dark hair clung to his scalp; his face was unshaven, reminding Coupland of a gunslinger in a spaghetti western. The man squaring up against him was a heavier, greyer version of the youth, with lines around his mouth and eyes, which were now bloodshot.

'Can we take it down a notch?' Coupland urged, forcing his way between them like an overzealous referee in a boxing match.

'You heard him,' Ashcroft added, hovering behind the boy in case he swung a punch in his old man's direction. Coupland stood his ground, waiting for the spark of anger to defuse. The man stepped back, compliant, as though relieved someone else had taken control. He sank into a sofa behind him, staring up at Coupland, waiting to be told what to do next. The youth, now he had no-one to rail against, threw himself onto the sofa opposite, burying his head in his hands. 'They were very close,' the man explained. 'This was bound to hit him hard.' The words came easily, suggesting a lifetime of making excuses.

While everyone drew breath Coupland looked about the living room; it was a good size, two settees forming an L-shape around a wooden coffee table, a modern gas fire mounted halfway up the opposite wall. The books piled atop the coffee table suggested an interest in art and DIY. The TV remote control was positioned arm's reach from where Kathleen's husband sat. Coupland's gaze fell onto the indentation in the seat cushion at the other end of the sofa. He pictured them sitting like book ends, each careful not to encroach on the other's territory. Living under the same roof when things were going well was challenging; to do it after a relationship had ended must be nigh on impossible.

Coupland plonked himself beside the youth, close enough to make a grab for him if tensions flared again. The FLO lingered in the doorway, stepping forward to make introductions now there was a ceasefire. Kathleen's husband was called Derek and their son, Raphael. 'But everyone calls me Raph,' he added quickly. Coupland nodded, his glance returning to the art book as though it was somehow responsible for the boy's out of sync name. Ashcroft must've clocked the dent in the sofa too, as he followed the FLO into the kitchen, returning with a wooden chair which he placed beside the coffee table.

'Who would do this?' Derek asked. He hadn't taken

his eyes off Coupland, as though he would have answers for them both that would explain the way the day had panned out.

Coupland shook his head. 'We don't know that yet,' he said. 'That's why we're here, to find out more about Kathleen so we can build up a picture that'll help our investigation.'

'I bet it was a pupil,' Raph cut in, 'you hear about it on TV, some child of Satan takes a knife into school because they got a detention the day before.'

'It's a primary school,' Derek said, his eyes remaining on Coupland, 'no one'd do that in a primary school.' His face took on a pained look.

'You're doing it again!' Raph challenged. 'Smiling apologetically as if to say "the kid's talking bollocks, ignore him…" you did it before with that woman cop.'

Derek turned to his son. 'Well, you are talking bollocks! It won't be a pupil, Raph. Besides, she wasn't stabbed, she was strangled.'

Raph closed his eyes; when he spoke next it sounded as though something was wedged in his throat. 'It could be someone she used to teach, someone now at the high school, or older.'

Ashcroft pulled out his notepad and pen. 'Raph, can you think of any names we should be looking at? Anyone in particular that you feel could be responsible?' He wrote the names Raph suggested into his notepad but Coupland knew they wouldn't do anything with this, not unless forensics came back suggesting this murder wasn't connected to the others, which was unlikely. Ashcroft was appeasing him, making him feel involved in some way. That was the hardest thing for the victim's relatives, the feeling of helplessness, and it sometimes spilled out into aggression.

'What about you, Derek?' Ashcroft prompted, turning to him. 'Can you think of anyone who would want to harm your wife?'

Derek shook his head. His brows creased as though he was trying to recall something. 'I saw you,' he said in a low voice, turning back to Coupland, 'in that press conference on the TV, you didn't say anything but you were there, weren't you?' He turned back to Ashcroft. 'You were there too.' Both detectives nodded. 'The guy in the uniform, Chief Superintendent somebody or other, he's the one in charge?' Coupland nodded once more. 'He didn't seem happy when your colleague said the murder of those two women may be linked. Is that what's happening? There's a killer out there picking off women randomly?'

'You mean this has happened BEFORE?' Raph stormed. 'And these jokers could've stopped it?' He was on his feet again, up on his toes like a boxer dancing round the ring.

'We don't know anything for sure yet,' Coupland said, getting to his feet, pulling himself to his full height.

'Raph, sit down,' Derek pleaded, dragging his hands through thinning hair, 'let them do their job.'

'Their job was keeping Mum safe and look how that turned out! Have you even put out a public warning yet? Why haven't you told people to be on the lookout?'

'There was no obvious link at first, and by the time we established the possibility the murders were connected it was…' Coupland let his words trail off, unwilling to rub salt into their wounds.

'It was already too late!' Raph spat, turning on Ashcroft

who had remained seated. 'Why did you ask me for those names?' he demanded. 'Were you just taking the piss?'

'No…' Ashcroft stuttered, looking to Coupland for help, 'we're still trying to identify potential suspects—'

Raph wafted Ashcroft's words away. 'Yeah but it won't be a bloody school kid, will it? You know what? I'm done here.' He stormed out of the room; seconds later the front door slammed, followed by the sound of a car engine stalling.

'Has he got far to go?' Coupland watched as Raph crunched through his gears to put his car into reverse before accelerating off the driveway.

'His flat's ten minutes away,' Derek answered. 'He'll be back when he's calmed down.' The way he said it hinted at countless sparring, as though bitter exchanges were the normal mode of communication between the two of them.

Ashcroft cleared his throat. 'Does he blame you for your marriage break up?'

Derek laughed, but there was no humour in it. 'He blames me for a lot more than that,' he pursed his lips, 'but yeah, you could add that to the list of things I've done to let him down over the years, right up there with being his dad.'

Coupland nodded in sympathy. 'Can I ask why you and Kathleen split up?'

Derek looked away. 'It's no secret, I suppose. Ask anyone around here and they'll tell you soon enough. I used to work for the local council. Lost my job in their last round of cost cutting exercises. I started drinking. Only problem was I didn't know when to stop. Kathleen stood by me through some pretty grim times, Raph was so fed up of seeing her upset he used to beg her to leave, take him with her. She refused, but I could feel things had started to change between us. By the time I'd cleaned up my act there was no going back. She said she was tired, needed a fresh start. By then Raph had got his own place, I guess the thought of having to deal with me on her own if I lapsed horrified her. We put the house up for sale six months ago but there's been very little interest from buyers. Neither of us can afford to move out until it's sold so we agreed to stay here for as long as it took. That suited me fine; we were civil enough to each other. I always thought… hoped… that she'd wake up one morning and change her mind, say she was willing to give us another go. Twenty-five years is a long time…'

'Did she tell you she was going out after work?'

A pause. 'We weren't each other's keeper any more. She didn't need to tell me what she was doing.'

Coupland nodded, as though conceding the man's point. 'It would be helpful if you could answer the question though, just so we're clear?'

'She didn't tell me, no,' Derek snapped, 'told me often enough her life was her own.'

'So, she was seeing someone else then?'

Derek shook his head. 'No, I'd have known,' he lifted his chin defiantly, 'that's what made me think there was still a chance for us. I mean, it's not as if she started going out on dates. If anything, she spent more and more time at home, albeit in the spare room… I mean her bedroom.'

Coupland glanced briefly at Ashcroft. 'Do you mind if I take a look?'

Derek rolled his shoulders. 'If you must,' he muttered. Ashcroft began to ask him about the couple's life together before the split; Derek relaxed as he spoke of them as one solid unit, the tension in his face easing as he recalled happier times. Coupland left the room.

There were three bedrooms upstairs, a small, boxy room with posters on the wall of groups long since disbanded; Coupland struggled to remember their names. The single bed had been stripped and on it a set of weights had been left. The curtains were still drawn in the master bedroom, the double bed unmade. It had been early when Derek got the knock on the door, probably got him out of his bed. The room wasn't unduly messy. A pile of clothes lay on what Coupland took to be Kathleen's half of the bed, or rather used to be. He moved towards the window to open the curtains, looked out at the unsuspecting city beyond. The wives, mothers and daughters going about their business, unaware of the peril facing them. Coupland's shoulders sagged as he turned to survey the room. There were indentations in the carpet where a piece of furniture had been removed. The en-suite bathroom was empty save for a toothbrush and toothpaste dispenser, a shaving kit beside it. A damp towel lay across the floor. The toilet seat was left up revealing several skid marks inside the toilet bowl.

The spare room was smaller than the master bedroom, but that hadn't stopped Kathleen from squeezing in a dressing table beside her bed, a chest of drawers on the other side of it. A clothes rail ran the length of the opposite wall, crammed with garments hanging from wire hangers. A laptop sat open on the dressing table stool. The room was tidy, despite the lack of space. Coupland guessed that if he checked in the family bathroom at the end of the hall it would be spotless, her toiletries displayed in that way women had, as though visitors actually gave a toss what deodorant you used. Coupland pulled a pair of nitrile gloves from his pocket and slipped them on, turned the laptop towards him as he tapped one of the keys. The password prompt came onto the screen. He typed 'Raphael' into the box, smiling as the laptop whirred its approval. The desktop photo was a picture of Kathleen with her son, a holiday snap by the look of it, both tanned and smiling for the camera; the boy was a couple of years younger, less angry looking. Derek had probably taken the photo. Saved airbrushing him out later, Coupland supposed. He clicked onto the internet explorer icon, pressed the history tab. A list of frequently used sites appeared down the right hand side of the screen. He skimmed down the clothing and beauty links, a holiday site that specialised in singles and a couple of dating websites. Coupland closed the lid on the laptop, placing it under his arm as he removed his gloves before leaving the room, pausing briefly to touch something on the wall beside the bedroom door.

The front room was silent as Coupland walked back into it. Derek was showing Ashcroft something on his phone. Ashcroft, nodding politely, looked relieved to see him standing in the doorway. 'Holiday snaps.' The DC widened his eyes.

Coupland stepped into Derek's line of vision. 'Can you tell me what happened yesterday?'

The widower reared his head in Coupland's direction. 'You mean apart from my wife being murdered?'

'I mean the part where you saw fit to punch a hole in your spare room wall.'

'How do you know it was me?' he challenged.

Coupland's gaze fell to the swollen knuckles on his right hand.

'I thought he'd got that during the run in with his son,' Ashcroft muttered, wrong footed.

'I suspect that's what he hoped you'd think, our timing couldn't have been better this morning, arriving just as you two were practically laying into each other…' Coupland perched on the arm of the settee. 'Now tell me what happened.'

A sour look passed across Derek's face but it was fleeting. 'She'd been all perky the night before. Seemed to be enjoying my company, hadn't snapped at me or pulled me up for something I had or hadn't done.' Coupland could see how that would seem like a good thing. He nodded for Derek to continue. 'Even so, she still went to her room early as usual. I followed her upstairs, hung around outside the bedroom door to see if she was on the phone to someone but she wasn't, though I could hear her tapping onto her laptop. The next morning I slipped into her room while she was making herself some breakfast – she doesn't like me hovering about her, prefers if we eat at separate times…' and this was a man who thought they were on the verge of a reconciliation, Coupland thought, not unkindly, '…and had a snoop at her emails. There she was,' his face clouded once more, 'emailing some guy about meeting up that night. She came back to her room and went mad because she'd caught me prying "in her personal business" as she called it – but can you blame me? She practically suggested I'd driven her to it with my irritating ways and I'm afraid I saw red and…'

'Put your fist through the wall,' Coupland finished for him.

'I regretted it straight away,' Derek added. 'She left then, shouting "Don't bother waiting up." It was the last thing she said to me.'

'What did you do after she left?'

Derek's eyes fell onto the laptop nestled under Coupland's arm. 'I tried to see if I could find out who it was that had scuppered my chances of getting back into her good books.'

'And?'

'Funnily enough it wasn't someone she'd met on a dating site, it was a parent from school.'

Coupland regarded him sharply. 'What makes you say that?'

A shrug. 'I dunno, I got the impression their paths crossed through her job, going by the messages they exchanged. He could be a teacher I suppose, but then they wouldn't need to email each other if he was at the same school, would they? It's not like she went out much, so I can't see how else they'd have been introduced... Anyway, however they met it looked as though they were finally going on a date.' Coupland furrowed his brow. 'She was wearing her good jacket,' Derek explained, 'and I noticed her slip her makeup bag into her briefcase.'

Good job he hadn't seen the knickers in her handbag then, Christ knows what state her room would have been in. Coupland caught Ashcroft's eye; the look the DC gave him told him he'd been thinking the same thing. 'So why did you tell me you didn't know what she was doing after she'd finished work?'

'Who'd want to admit their wife was going off to meet another man? I didn't want to admit it to myself, never mind you lot.'

Coupland studied him pointedly. 'When did you decide to repair the wall, Derek?'

Derek looked away, shoved his hands deep into his pockets to stop him wrestling with his conscience. A sigh. 'I decided straight away to fix it, if Raph had caught sight of it he'd have gone berserk, tried to get her to move out properly.'

Coupland's mouth formed a thin line. 'I'll put it another way, Derek, shall I? When exactly did you repair the wall upstairs?'

'You know when!' Derek spat, glaring at Coupland as the detective turned his hands over to show white marks on his fingertips. 'You mean the wet paint on my hands?'

Coupland said, 'I want to hear you say it, Derek, and I want you to explain why.'

Derek's voice sounded choked, as though he'd swallowed razor blades or had a bad bout of tonsillitis. 'After the two cops had left this morning... before *she* came,' he indicated the FLO standing outside the kitchen's back door, puffing on a cigarette while checking messages on her phone, 'I went upstairs. I wanted to be close to Kathleen, to be surrounded by her things. Only the first thing I clapped eyes on was the damage I'd caused the day before and realised how it would look. I thought it was better to repair it before someone got the wrong idea.'

'And what idea would that be?'

'That maybe I'd hurt her, or at least... that I wasn't the doting husband I made out to be.'

Coupland sighed. Kathleen was going out on a date. Whether she'd met this fella online or through the school where she worked it didn't really matter. The soon to be ex-husband had confessed to throwing his weight around in a fit of jealousy on the day she was killed. 'We're going to have to take you in.' Coupland shouted for the FLO to get rid of her fag and join them in the living room. 'Get onto control,' he ordered sharply, making a point of looking at her collar number. Blotches of red spread along her cheeks as she reached for her radio. Coupland turned back to Derek as the widower gripped onto the sofa's headrest to steady himself. He felt some sympathy for the man. 'It's standard procedure,' he explained, 'the sooner we get you eliminated as a suspect the better, but in the light of what you've just told me…'

The custody suite at Salford Precinct was half empty. Derek was processed at the desk and led to a cell where he sat motionless on the dark grey mattress. Coupland watched him for a moment on the CCTV monitor which jumped after a few minutes to different occupants in the neighbouring cells. He turned away from the screen towards the custody sergeant. 'I'll get one of Quinlan's team to question him. He isn't a person of interest but we need to go through the motions, make sure we don't miss anything in case some bloody lawyer later down the line claims this was a case of domestic abuse.'

The custody sergeant nodded. He'd not long come on shift; a good night's sleep and a decent breakfast behind him had made him biddable, certainly more so than the other day. He took a swig from a coffee mug and made a note on the custody record.

While Ashcroft went in search of DS Quinlan to update him Coupland slipped outside for a puff on his vape stick. He'd read somewhere the idea was to keep to his smoking routine so he didn't feel the change from cigarettes so acutely. He wasn't convinced. His lungs waited for the hit of nicotine that was refusing to come.

Ashcroft ambled towards him, licking his finger and thumb. 'Someone's brought cakes in,' he explained. 'Don't worry,' he added, clocking the look on Coupland's face, 'I've put one in your desk drawer.'

Coupland nodded in gratitude. 'We'll make a good detective of you yet,' he grinned.

'What did you make of the pair of them?' Ashcroft inclined his head in the direction of the custody block.

'What? The arctic freeze between father and son? It happens.' Coupland rolled his shoulders. 'Most likely they've both got a point, just too pig headed to realise.'

'I wouldn't dream of disrespecting my old man.' Ashcroft shook his head as he said this, the way someone would who'd only known a happy childhood. Coupland had spoken out of turn just the once, grabbed hold of the fist raining down on him, told his old man if he raised his hand to him again he would kill him. For both their sakes he'd moved out that night. Lynn had paved the way towards a ceasefire, a barest acknowledgement that each other existed. Not every family got it right all the time, he'd seen enough over the years to know that. But Christ, he shuddered at the thought that an unsuitable boyfriend could come between him and Amy.

Coupland barely recognised anyone in the incident room. Quinlan's team had bagged the desks that had been brought through, some were busy on phones following up actions they'd been allocated earlier, others were typing up reports and cross-referencing data from HOLMES. Quinlan's voice grated in the hallway long before he appeared, carrying two coffees, his tongue poking out through his lips as he tried not to spill them.

'You shouldn't have.' Coupland helped himself to one as Quinlan placed them on a table in front of the incident board.

'I didn't,' he shrugged, mouthing an apology to a DC already seated there.

'Don't mind me,' the detective said, getting to his feet, 'time I was back out there anyway.'

Coupland pushed the coffee towards the man guiltily, only to feel worse when he waved it away. 'How's it going?' he asked, by way of compensation.

The DC pulled a face that implied frustration. 'There doesn't appear to be anything linking these women. We've checked out jobs, social circles, hobbies, even schools.' The man was wiry, with a lined face that'd give Mick Jagger a run for his money. There were dark circles under his eyes but the night shift did that, and a weariness about his mouth that made it turn down at the corners. Nicotine stained fingers suggested a smoking habit Coupland could only aspire to. He looked a grafter though, one of those men who didn't make a big deal of it, could be trusted to get on with the job in hand.

'Maybe it's not about the women,' offered Coupland, 'maybe they are simply in the wrong place at the wrong time.'

Quinlan blew across the top of his coffee, 'But there's usually a trigger,' he said, 'the way they look, the way they speak, the job they do, or simply the access he's been given to them – how does he meet them? He could be a cab driver, client, shop assistant…'

'I can look into that, boss,' the DC piped up. 'I've drawn a blank on just about everything else I've looked at.'

Quinlan nodded, patting the DC on the back as he

headed towards the door.

'Seems a decent guy,' Coupland observed.

'Whitehead? Salt of the earth, fifteen hours straight but he won't knock off until he finds a lead. He's like a hungry dog searching for a scrap.'

'Thought he'd have bypassed you by now then, what with you being a lazy bastard.'

Quinlan's laugh was genuine; he was known for not liking to get his hands dirty, was more than happy keeping a professional distance. 'Since when was it about ability?' he smiled. 'C'mon, you should know better than that. Whitehead's thoroughness has got up noses in the past, not enough to ostracise him, but I daresay the powers that be think it's better to keep him out of harm's way.' You can't get anyone's backs up if you don't have any clout.

'Who've you sent to question Derek Williams?'

'DC named Baxter, ten years plus on the clock, he knows what he's doing.' He saw the look on Coupland's face. 'No one on my team'll let you down, it's in all our interests to get this bastard off the streets.'

Coupland nodded, though it pained him to think Quinlan was talking sense for once.

Sometimes during an investigation it was possible for a case to develop mission creep; his role was to keep the team focused on the critical lines of enquiry. This investigation needed him to take off his blinkers and view the case from a number of different dimensions, gather evidence from an ever-increasing range of sources until something clicked. He just wished that click would come sooner rather than later.

Ashcroft spoke next. 'What about potential links

through their partners? You know, sports clubs, gym memberships, bars. Maybe they frequent the same casino, have run up a few debts at the local bookies…'

'So someone decides to wipe out their partners because they're owed a few bob?' Quinlan pulled a face. 'That's not how you go about getting a debt repaid.'

'I know, but someone has done just that, and even if the motive turns out not to be money, that doesn't mean any other reason is more deserved.'

Ashcroft had a point. 'We push on in every direction,' Coupland reminded them. 'At the moment we don't have the luxury of being choosy.' He turned to Quinlan. 'Just make sure you're sending out guys like Whitehead and Baxter, we haven't got the manpower to keep going back if someone less experienced misses something.'

Quinlan's eye flickered at the slight but he was professional enough to know that now wasn't the time to take offence at ill-chosen words; he took out his note pad and wrote down actions he would allocate as each detective returned.

Coupland's desk phone rang and he signalled for a passing DC to answer it. 'Chief Superintendent Curtis wants to see you,' the DC called over.

The Super's meeting at HQ hadn't lasted long then. Coupland clenched his teeth, along with other body parts, as he made his way to Curtis's office. The door had been left open; Coupland grazed it briefly with his knuckles as he entered the room. Mallender had been summoned too by the look of it; he was already seated. Both he and Curtis were staring at a flat screen TV watching news coverage of the aerial view of Bude Hill Primary School playground where Kathleen Williams' body had been found. The camera focussed on the tent erected in the middle of the playground; the red ticker tape along the bottom of the screen reported the breaking news that a third woman's body had been found in Salford in the space of a week, before the image on screen moved to footage of the press appeal put out only four days earlier for information relating to the murders of Sharon Mathers and Maria Wellbeck. The main image was of Curtis although Coupland could be seen clear as day in the background. If there was one thing he hated more than looking at photographs of himself it was looking at his moving image on screen, and this footage did nothing to change that view. It was the standing still that got to him. He might not make it onto the Jamaican sprint team any time soon but he was fit for his build, always ready on the balls of his feet to tear after someone if he had to, or move out of the way sharpish when needed. Everything about his demeanour yelled *Fight or Flight*. Although he'd been nothing more than part of the back drop in the appeal, his expression was easy enough to read. The pursing of his lips when the Super was asked a question, the widening of his eyes when he answered it. Coupland would never rise above the rank of sergeant, a badge of honour he wore with pride. Sometimes he found it hard to hide his disdain for those who flaunted their ambition. He'd lost count of the number of times he'd been told to keep his poker face on when in the presence of the press. His gaze flickered away from the screen and back to the senior officers seated before him. He placed his hands behind his back, waited for a bollocking that didn't come.

'Seems we have managed to pacify Sharon Mathers' brother, Sergeant,' Curtis began. 'He's been in touch with me today to say he will not be making any official complaint relating to the manner in which the investigation had been handled originally. As far as he is concerned the matter was dealt with satisfactorily on his arrival.'

Coupland gave the merest incline of his head. He hoped Curtis wasn't looking for gratitude; at a push he could toe the line when needed but absolutely refused to blow smoke up the Super's backside. He kept his expression neutral.

'I hear you've brought in Kathleen Williams' husband for questioning.'

'That's correct, Sir.' Coupland wasn't going to offer anything up unnecessarily; if Curtis wanted information he was going to have to work for it. Better men than him had tripped themselves up in an eagerness to please. Curtis sighed, flicking an irritable glance at Mallender. The DCI widened his eyes at Coupland as if conveying he really should play ball.

'I take it you're just being cautious?' Mallender coaxed, eyeing Coupland steadily.

'There was evidence of a domestic, Sir, one that required her husband to repair a bedroom wall an hour after getting the death message. When we arrived he was going head to head with the couple's son, and he made it clear to us he'd been hoping for a reconciliation.'

'The couple were estranged?' Curtis narrowed his eyes as he asked this, as though Coupland was somehow the reason for their marital break-up.

'Looks like she was meeting someone she'd been chatting to online, Sir, hubby was none too happy about it.'

Scowling, Curtis looked at Mallender. 'Be hard to make the public sympathise with that domestic set up,' he chimed. 'Any press appeal needs to focus on her colleagues and the school community. Hardworking school teacher and all that.'

Coupland didn't know what surprised him most, Curtis's ability to view everything from the perspective of a sound bite, or the fact that he was still surprised by something the Super said or did. 'Anything else sir?'

Curtis's gaze bore into him as he turned to leave. 'How are the South Manchester team settling in?'

Coupland's mouth turned up at the corners. 'We're like the Brady Bunch, Sir,' he replied, eyes dancing.

'Is that so?' Mallender observed, keeping his smile in check. 'Just so long as Mom and Pop play nice in front of the children.'

Back in the incident room another white board had been wheeled in. Someone had written the heading 'Connections,' at the top of the board, but so far the space beneath it was blank. Coupland moved over to the techies' desk where Kathleen's laptop was being put through its paces by a young DC with a virulent crop of acne around his mouth and jaw. No wonder he preferred working in the backroom. Coupland's smile when he approached him was sympathetic. 'How're you getting on?' He made a special effort to focus on the young man's hairline.

'The victim had bookmarked a couple of dating sites Sir, and had just paid her first subscription to Match.com. But although she was meeting someone on the night she was murdered it wasn't anyone from those sites.'

'So who was it?'

'She'd been corresponding via her school email account with some guy who'd pranged her car at the school gates. Next thing they're messaging each other like bezzie mates, then two nights ago he asks her out for a drink.'

'Can you trace his details from his email account?'

'That's what I'm working on now.'

'Where did they arrange to meet? If this guy is innocent he'll have been waiting for her to show up, are there any messages from him later asking where she'd got to?'

The spotty guy shook his head. 'He'd offered to pick her up from school, her car had gone into the garage for repairs and she didn't want him turning up at the family home.'

'So either he didn't turn up – or he's our killer,' Coupland surmised. 'Good work...' he added, nodding at the DC, '…sorry, I didn't catch your name,'

'Ross, sir,' the young detective answered, his spots turning a deeper shade of red as he acknowledged the compliment. 'DC Ross Bateman.' Bateman's eagerness to please reminded Coupland of his younger self, not long out of uniform and eager to make his mark. Back in the day when he thought a life sentence meant just that. That the killers he put away would never harm another soul. He'd been in the job long enough now to see murderers get parole, return to towns where their victims' families still grieved, their lives consumed by loss, even as they tried hard not to be defined by it. It was impossible not to work on the cases he had and not be tainted by the sorrow people caused. It was a rite of passage in his line of work, he supposed, to learn to expect the worst. A form of survival. He studied Bateman and wondered when it would happen, when the spark in his eye would be replaced by caution, when his shoulders would stoop with fatigue, when he treated everyone he met with suspicion. Coupland smiled ruefully. 'Go and grab yourself a coffee, stretch your legs a bit. it's okay to take a break, you know.'

'Will do, Sarge,' Bateman replied, but they both knew he wouldn't.

'Sarge?' A stocky detective not much younger than Coupland was making his way across the incident room. 'DS Quinlan's asked me to let you know I've finished interviewing Derek Williams.' DC Baxter, if he recalled it right.

'How did he seem to you?'

'Numb,' came the reply, 'and embarrassed at getting caught covering his tracks, but he's not the first fella to put his fist through a wall.'

'No history of domestics then?'

'While he's been here their FLO's had a chance to speak to the son alone, went over to his place. The lad maintains his dad's a knob, but there was never any suggestion of violence while he was growing up.'

Coupland studied the floor as he listened, as though he'd taken up counting carpet tiles for fun. Baxter cleared his throat. 'Do you want to speak to him, Sarge?'

Coupland shook his head. 'Let him go.'

'Want me to arrange for uniforms to give him a lift back?'

Coupland considered this. 'Nah, he can ring his son, it's about time they started learning how to get along together, today's as good a day as any to start.'

Talking of mending rifts, Coupland decided to take a detour on his way home. He'd been tempted to ring ahead but the policeman in him won out, deciding there was a lot to be said for the element of surprise. He parked outside a Nisa store, bought a packet of mints and the Evening News. He hadn't intended to buy a paper, but the headline had jumped out at him: *Top Cop Confesses Killer at Large*. He'd listened to the statement Curtis had read out to the press assembled on the station steps, his tone neutral as he laid out the facts. He'd refused to answer any questions, nor would he be drawn on resourcing issues in the wake of recent budget cuts. All in all as far as statements went it achieved what it intended: an announcement saying nigh on precious little. No wonder the press went into overdrive with their headlines, Coupland mused, though to be fair this one wasn't that far removed from the truth.

Leaving his car outside the shop he walked along the street until he found the house he was looking for. The postage stamp front garden had been left to ruin. Weeds jostled with each other for space. The front doorstep was chipped and dirty. He rang the buzzer, watching a familiar figure approach behind the frosted glass. The safety chain slid in place before the door opened just a crack. 'Come on, Amy, don't be like that,' he coaxed. 'I've come to say I'm sorry.' A sigh. The door was pushed to while she slid the chain back. Coupland glanced up and down the street. Crisp packets blew across the road in the wind. More dog owners that didn't clean up after their pets. The net curtains at the ground floor window were nicotine yellow. The front door opened wide. 'I can't believe you're dating a smoker!' he sniped, unable to stop himself. 'All the years of grief you've given me and you go and hitch up—'

'—Here we go,' Amy shot back, 'you've not been here two minutes and you're having a go at me.' Her words stopped him in his tracks. Since when had she become so irritated by him, mistaking his concern for criticism?

'Come on Ames,' he attempted, 'we're better than this.'

'We were, Dad, but if you can't accept my boyfriend I can't see how we can ever go back to how it was.'

Something inside Coupland twisted. 'Christ, does he really mean that much to you?'

Amy's eyes widened. 'Hello? Take a look at this place.' She opened the front door wide so he could see the peeling wallpaper and manky carpet. 'Do you think I'd give up my home comforts just to make a point?'

Coupland stepped inside. He'd been in worse places, he reminded himself, but then he was a cop on a murder squad, his terms of reference were knocking shops and crack dens. He tried to imagine how a normal parent would feel on stepping inside but he couldn't make the leap. He'd never known normal. The place was tidy enough, he noticed, moving into the front room. The settee, though sagging in the middle, was covered in a throw Coupland vaguely recognised. The coffee table had been given a wipe and coasters partially covered the cup rings just visible beneath them. The carpet was a cheap nylon affair, the type that'd go up in seconds if a cigarette was dropped on it. The rug beneath the coffee table looked new. 'I see your mother's been here then,' he observed. He didn't blame Lynn, she hated friction, would do everything she could to smooth things between them.

Amy smiled for the first time. 'She helped me clean it up, along with Vinny's mum. He works long hours at college, he's tired when he gets in, and then there's his open learning course.' Coupland furrowed his brow. 'He's doing an access course online, he wants to get some qual-

201

ifications behind him so he can earn a decent living. He doesn't get paid much at the moment. Mum brought over a few things to make it more homely.'

Coupland wouldn't have gone that far to describe the place but he knew what she meant. 'Of course, you could just come back home,' he said.

'I like being with Vinny all the time,' she said shyly, 'would he be able to come too?'

Coupland tried not to let the horror show on his face. 'I can't see how that's going to work, Amy,' he said cautiously. 'I mean, we don't exactly get on, it'd be a disaster waiting to happen if you ask me.'

Amy's face registered her disappointment. 'Why does it have to be about you?' she snapped. 'Couldn't it be one nice thing you could do for me?'

'Come on, love, that's not fair, I nicked him for Christ's sake, you can't blame me for not wanting him under my roof.'

'Well if that's how you want it you'd better leave.'

Coupland turned sharply in the direction of Vince's voice, kicking himself for not checking where he was when he'd arrived. He'd assumed he wasn't in; that kind of mistake could be fatal in his line of work, but then this wasn't work, he reminded himself, this was his life.

'You don't come into my home and disrespect me,' Vince sneered, 'so do us all a favour and piss off.'

Coupland resisted the urge to punch him by shoving his fists deep into his pockets. Vince may not win any popularity contests any time soon but he could no longer accuse him of being a killer – he'd been under surveillance at the time of the latest murder. The fact was the guy was just a jerk, pure and simple. Coupland turned back to his daughter, 'Amy—' he spread his arms out wide, though if he thought she'd run into them he was mistaken.

'—He's right, Dad.' She stood her ground, unable to meet his eye. 'It's better if you go.'

'Come on, please don't be like this…'

Amy lifted her gaze to meet his. 'JUST LEAVE ME ALONE!' she yelled. Coupland's legs felt as though they'd got lead weights on the end of them. He moved slowly, giving Amy time to change her mind and call out to him to stop, to say she was sorry, that she didn't mean it after all. He paused as he opened the front door, cocked his head to pick up the slightest sound.

None came.

CHAPTER 13

Coupland's reception at home was no warmer but not because Lynn was in a huff with him – she was out. His wife had accepted Amy's moving out as a compromise she was willing to live with as long as their relationship with her improved. Coupland decided to keep his impromptu visit quiet. For now. He moved about the downstairs rooms like a lonely ghost. Lynn's absence felt like a missing limb. There were times during her cancer treatment when she'd been confined to the house, nausea and tiredness making it impossible for her to get out. During her recovery she'd returned to work, though she'd cut down on her shifts, and Coupland supposed he'd just got used to her being around more when he got in. Now she was well she was making up for lost time, as the text that pinged into his phone testified:

Gone for a drink with the girls after work. Shouldn't be late back.

Shouldn't be late. He wanted to laugh out loud. A serial killer was going about the place and his wife sends him a glib text saying she shouldn't be late. Dropping his car keys onto the hall table he tutted as he speed-dialled her number. Voicemail. 'Lynn it's me… oh, bollocks…' he rang off, wishing he'd not bothered. He didn't want to make a drama out of it; she'd only have a go at him later. He re-dialled her number. This time when the voicemail came on he was ready for it: "S'only me, love, let me know where you are and I'll come and pick you up when you're ready.' He'd tried to make it sound like it was no big deal, but he knew he wouldn't settle until she called him back. He put his phone in his jacket pocket as he moved about the empty rooms, unaccustomed to the silence. There was a time once when he longed for a bit of peace and quiet to hear himself think but those days were long gone. Lynn's diagnosis made him savour the noise, the constant chatter of women unable to do anything without a running commentary. 'You never join in, Dad,' Amy would say and he'd tell a rude joke or make daft impressions of the people he worked with and Amy would laugh while Lynn scolded him. 'What sort of a role model is that?' she'd say. His face fell when he thought of Vince. Was he to blame? Was his unsuitable humour the reason why Amy had aimed so low? After five minutes he checked his phone in case he hadn't heard it ring.

No missed calls.

Sighing, he reached for his car keys.

The first pub he went to was a regular for off-duty nursing staff and medics. Situated across the road from Hope Hospital's main entrance it was convenient and cheap. The landlord had had a heart attack three years before and this was his way of giving something back. The décor was tired and the music lame but it provided a chance to wind down with minimum fuss and was a place to go to celebrate someone's birthday when no one could be arsed making a proper effort. The landlord was in his regular position on the punter's side of the bar reading the Salford Reporter when Coupland walked in.

The barmaid, a young woman he hadn't seen before smiled as he walked up to the bar. 'What can I get you?'

she asked.

'On the house,' the landlord called over as he greeted Coupland.

'Make it an orange juice,' Coupland said quickly, his eyes scanning the bar for Lynn but the place wasn't that full and he could see she wasn't there.

'You here on business then?' the landlord asked, folding his paper, his interest piqued by a visit from CID.

Coupland shook his head. 'Said I'd pick the wife up, must have got our wires crossed about where she was going.'

'Likely as not gone to The Grey Mare if they're wanting food,' he said amiably, 'we offer a limited menu here and it's the chef's love of fry ups that put me over the road in the first place.'

'How is the old ticker?'

The landlord pulled a face. 'Mustn't grumble. I've cut back on my smokes and if red wine counts I'm getting my five a day.'

Coupland nodded, he'd long since questioned the benefits of healthy eating, though that was an opinion he kept away from his better half.

'I see you've got your hands full at the moment,' the landlord said, pushing the folded newspaper in Coupland's direction. Coupland unfolded the paper before scanning the headline: 'Local Murders are Connected.' *Police confirm that they are treating the murders of Sharon Mathers, Maria Wellbeck and Kathleen Williams as connected in some way given the timing and proximity of death…* He skim-read the remaining article but he got the gist; the police didn't know what they were doing, couldn't find their backsides with two hands and a mirror. It was the truth, but seeing it in black and white didn't make it any more palatable. 'No one puts much faith in the press anymore,' the landlord commented, 'vultures, the lot of 'em, only out for the headline, don't care what their scare mongering does to ordinary folk. Don't know why I bother buying it to be honest, apart from the crossword.'

Coupland knocked back his orange juice; raising his hand in farewell as he left the pub, happy to let someone think he had a strategy in place when really he had bugger all.

The décor in The Grey Mare wasn't any better but there was a designated seating area where punters could eat once they'd paid for their meal up front at the bar. A chalk board by the till listed the day's specials. Coupland didn't bother going up to the bar; instead he walked around the periphery looking for anyone he recognised. It wasn't unusual for most people who saw him coming to break eye contact quickly enough, but he was used to that.

'Detective Sergeant Coupland as I live and breathe!' He turned in the direction of the familiar voice, though he had to study the face a while longer to put a name to it.

'Christ, you still pulling pints Breeda, I thought they'd have put you out to pasture a long time ago.'

'They wouldn't dare!' she chuckled, her hand automatically reaching for the pump. 'I'm driving,' Coupland told her.

'Half then,' Breeda insisted and he knew better than to argue. 'Seriously, I can't think when I last saw you, I was certain I'd heard you'd retired.' Breeda inclined her head in the direction of the bar and the back room beyond it. 'Our Johnny runs it now, took over as landlord from me a few years back but I stayed on doing the books and helping out when he can't get cover. He doesn't like me out front mind, says I frighten punters off, remind 'em of their mothers – or their grandmothers,' she grinned, 'thought I'd get that in before you put in your two pennorth.'

'You could run rings around the best of 'em I'm sure,' Coupland said gallantly, sipping his half pint while looking around the bar.

'Lost someone?'

'I thought Lynn might be here, there was a few of 'em went out after work.'

'I've only come out front to collect glasses while Johnny takes a break, maybe she's been and gone. Glad to hear you two are still going strong, not so many manage it these days.'

'I know, but then I always knew I was punching above my weight.' The secret of a successful marriage was keeping your head down; go along with everything the missus said, shame it took him twenty years to work it out.

Breeda nodded her head vigorously. 'Very true,' she concurred. Just then two men about Amy's age walked behind the bar, conjuring the words brick and shithouse to mind. The men were identical, shaven heads upon barrel shaped bodies. Both men were dressed in black: jeans, boots, zip-up jackets. Each in turn greeted the old woman with a kiss. 'You remember the twins, Sergeant?' Breeda asked as both men helped themselves to a soft drink before returning to their nan's side.

'I remember them well enough,' Coupland said, 'only they were knee high last time I saw them.'

Breeda beamed. 'Take after their dad, and his dad

before him, God rest his soul.'

'She's got you working on the doors then?' Coupland observed.

The men eyed him cautiously, their curiosity about the stranger talking to their nan getting the better of them. 'We work the bar, normally,' one of them answered, his voice was an octave or two higher than Coupland had expected and he tried not to let his surprise show.

'Only there's a match tonight,' his sibling continued, his vocals the same falsetto pitch as his brother, probably explained the body builder look they were working so well, 'Dad likes us to be out front, says we frighten off potential trouble.'

Coupland nodded, he could see how that would work, just so long as they didn't speak. He'd been so wrapped up in the case he'd forgotten City were playing tonight. 'You get much trouble here, then?'

'Not now,' said Breeda, 'not like in the early days when I ran the place with Jim. We'd not long taken over when we discovered this was the stomping ground of an old football firm, they'd meet here to plot their trips down south for the away matches, always with a ruck in mind,' she sucked in a breath, 'all came to a head when one of 'em was murdered. We all thought there'd be a full scale war after that but the police caught the fella responsible pretty sharpish, took away the need for revenge attacks. Your lot needed half a dozen vans to cart everyone away for DNA testing. After that we realised we had to change things round here, appeal to a different clientele otherwise we'd get dragged under. We offered weekday discounts to local professionals and it worked. We get a whole new crowd in these days, the lads here going on the door is just our way of putting down a marker, reminding everyone where we stand, that if you're looking for trouble you need to look somewhere else.'

Coupland nodded. 'Talking of looking, I'd better go find the missus,' he said, placing his empty glass on the bar, even though in theory Lynn didn't know he was looking for her.

By the time he'd located his car and headed further into the direction of town the streets were filling with revellers out for the night: the heels were higher, skirts shorter and as far as he could see not a single coat in sight. After-work drinkers were heading home, briefcases and rucksacks marking them out, that and a heavy footstep knowing they'd be doing it all again tomorrow.

Work. Drink. Sleep. Repeat.

Just then his mobile pinged, signalling a text. It was from Lynn:

Don't bother coming to pick me up, just heading for a cab now.

He hadn't realised how worried he'd been until he received her text and the tension began to ebb from his shoulders. The taxi rank was on the other side of the square but for once the one-way system worked in his favour. She was standing with three other women, deep in conversation while keeping their eyes peeled for a returning cab. Lynn's face was flushed, her arms moving animatedly as she spoke. He should have known she would be fine. Lynn didn't take unnecessary risks, apart from marrying him of course. He pulled up alongside her at the kerb. 'Taxi for Nurse Coupland?' he grinned, clocking the surprise on her face.

'Lucky you were passing,' she said, staring at him in

that way she had. He checked his rear view mirror to break eye contact but he could see a smile playing on her lips. 'Get in girls,' Lynn instructed, ignoring one pal's plea that she lived in the opposite direction. 'Nonsense, Kevin doesn't mind giving you all a lift home,' she said firmly, making it impossible for him to refuse without looking like a selfish shit.

'Course I don't,' he said lamely as the women climbed in, engulfing him in perfume and alcohol fumes. 'Where did you get to?'

'We fancied a pizza from that Italian that's just opened, after a couple of glasses of red we couldn't be bothered moving onto anywhere else. So what's your excuse?'

Coupland shrugged, reaching automatically for his pack of cigarettes then remembering just in time his vaper was in his pocket. A couple of puffs would buy him time to think up a suitable answer.

'It's okay,' Lynn said quietly as his brow furrowed in concentration, 'I get it, I guess I'm lucky to have my very own knight in shining armour, aren't I?'

'Christ, how much have you had to drink?' he shot back, while hoping her rose-coloured mood would last at least until bedtime.

'Lynn said you're on the team looking for that killer,' a woman with bloodshot eyes piped up from the back seat, Elaine or Ellen, Coupland couldn't remember which, but now it was his turn to stare at Lynn. At least she had the grace to blush.

'I can't really talk about it…' he said, indicating to pull out into the traffic. 'Come on, Kev, you can do better than that,' the woman chided him, 'this is us, remember?' She was seated beside a woman with long black hair and heavy eye make-up who stared into his rear view mirror until he made eye contact. Connie, if he remembered rightly, worked in the special care baby unit almost as long as Lynn, lost a lot of weight last year causing her face to go all jowly; the heavy liner around the eyes was meant to provide a distraction. She'd looked contented when she was hefty, now she resembled an embittered witch. How the babies in SCBU got to sleep at night with her staring down at them was beyond him. Lynn had a lot of respect for her though, said you could open her veins and the initials NHS would run right through them. It had to be that way, he supposed. In many ways nursing had a lot in common with policing – there were much easier ways to earn a bloody living.

'Seriously,' he began, turning the car around the moment he was able to and taking the turn off to Eccles so he could drop off those living closest to the hospital first, '…we're pursuing several lines of enquiry at the moment. It would be—'

'—Is that really the best you can do?' Witch Features said spitefully. 'Trot out the same old drivel that you do for the papers? I used to think cops said that kind of stuff to lull the bad guys into thinking they hadn't got a clue when they had a master plan up their sleeve… but you really haven't, have you?'

Coupland's grip tightened around the steering wheel. The temperature in the car seemed to drop several degrees while he contemplated his answer. One of the women giggled nervously. Lynn stared ahead in the passenger seat; he could feel her willing him not to get arsey. 'The problem with giving out too much information is the press can get ahead of themselves, turning throw away comments into headlines; look at the way that teacher from Bristol was treated, hung drawn and quartered according to the news syndicates and the public were all too willing to believe what they read about him. When you're running an investigation you have to keep sight of the facts, you don't make a move until you've gathered compelling evidence.'

'Like I said, you've got nothing to go on, then...' the witch concluded.

Coupland's shoulders sank.

*

It was still dark when Coupland's phone startled him awake. He fought and lost a battle with his bedside lamp, sending it crashing to the floor. 'What time is it?' he barked into the mouthpiece, turning to check whether by some miracle Lynn was still asleep. A glare before turning to face the other way told him she wasn't.

'I'm sorry to be ringing you so late, Sarge,' Ashcroft said dutifully, although he didn't sound sorry at all. In fact, there was an excitement there that made Coupland's pulse start to race.

'What is it?' He pushed himself into an upright sitting position whilst squinting at his wristwatch which he kept at the side of his bed. It had been a gift from Lynn for his fortieth, had dots rather than numbers going around the dial. Given the bedroom was cloaked in darkness and the only light came from the street lights seeping through the curtains, he had to squint to work out the time. 5 am. 'Tell me you've had some kip.'

Ashcroft paused. *'Couldn't sleep,'* he said, *'something Sharon Mathers' partner said kept bugging me, had a theory I wanted to try out for myself.'*

'Care to elaborate?'

'Probably better you see for yourself.'

A pause. 'Give me half an hour.'

Incident room, daft o'clock, Wednesday morning

By the time Coupland returned to the station he found Ashcroft in the incident room drawing a spider gram on the whiteboard that had been headed up 'Connections'. On it, he'd written the names of the murdered women: Sharon Mathers centred at the top of the board, Maria Wellbeck to the bottom right hand corner and Kathleen Williams to the bottom left hand corner. He'd written their partners' names beside them in brackets. A series of lines jutted out diagonally across the board. The diagram had been drawn using a black marker and the names written around its perimeter were in black too. At the moment the centre resembled the artwork of a three-year-old, with jagged lines leading to one name then stopping abruptly while another name had a new line coming from it going into another one before coming to a halt. Ashcroft's shirt was crumpled as though he'd slept in it. Two days' stubble covered his chin and bags under his eyes were beginning to rival Coupland's. His face became animated as he saw the DS approach.

'I've been working on the statements taken by Quinlan's team from Kathleen Williams' friends, family and colleagues up at the school.'

'And you found something?'

'Not at first, no. We'd been trying to find links between the women – which so far hadn't resulted in anything positive. The addition of Kathleen in to the mix only made it harder; where we may previously have identified something that two of the women may have had in common, trying to find any similar trend with the third victim was proving impossible. Yesterday we widened the trawl to include the women's leisure interests and social circle to see if there were any new links emerging.'

'We already know there isn't anything connecting the victims or their husbands,' Coupland said irritably. 'I don't need a diagram to tell me what we've already worked out.'

'Yeah, but what about this?' Ashcroft wrote a name on the board that seemed vaguely familiar. Nathaniel Mathers. Coupland studied it for a moment, tried it out in his mind a couple of times but his memory wasn't playing ball. Ashcroft had written it above Sharon Mathers, the first victim. He then wrote Harry Sandford above Maria Wellbeck, the second victim, and Coupland's pulse quickened. By the time Ashcroft had added the third name, Lewis Carruthers, above Kathleen Williams' name, Coupland was standing as close to the board as a child in front of a toy shop window before Christmas. He watched in silence, his mind racing.

Ashcroft picked up a red marker pen. 'Can you tell what it is yet?' he teased.

'Steady, the last bloke who said that was sent down for a very long time,' Coupland cautioned, but he didn't need to watch Ashcroft draw a line from one name to another to know they would all join up. 'Jesus Christ,' he muttered as it clicked.

'You put 'em all away, Sarge?' one of the night shift DCs asked, who'd been watching the exchange with interest.

Coupland spluttered, the DC had missed the point

completely. Ignoring the question he turned to Ashcroft. 'Who are they in relation to the women?' he asked but already he knew in the case of Sharon Mathers, her brother had told him when they were standing on the station steps.

'Their fathers,' Ashcroft said hurriedly. 'It was something Sharon's partner said when I interviewed him that got me thinking, about her upbringing being so strict because she was a copper's daughter. All I needed to do was check with the others and, well, there's your pattern.'

'Good work,' Coupland muttered, his head already full of the implications of this information. A thought occurred to him. 'Curtis will self-destruct when he hears this,' he said aloud. He turned to the night shift DC who'd asked if he'd put them away.

'They're all cops,' he said simply, 'and I suspect for a time they were based here.'

CHAPTER 14

'Shit.' Several detectives around the room reached for their phones at the same time to warn loved ones and other colleagues, causing a knot to form in Coupland's stomach. 'Our killer isn't targeting the families of serving officers,' he said quickly, adding, 'These men are retired now.'

'One's dead,' Ashcroft corrected him, 'natural causes.'

'Either way, this is probably related to something that happened in the past, not the present.' He tried to sound reassuring, but his colon was twitching nonetheless.

'Someone with one helluva grudge,' one of Quinlan's DCs muttered.

'Someone they put away who's just been released, more like,' said another.

Ashcroft nodded eagerly. 'We can pull out the records for cases that all three of them worked on together, it might be laborious but it's the best lead we've had.'

'I'll give you a hand,' the detective who'd spoken up earlier offered. He had a South Manchester ID card hanging around his neck from a lanyard. He was a big fella with thinning hair. His rolled up shirt sleeves marking him out as someone unafraid of getting stuck in.

'Me too,' said a woman with hair scraped back in a ponytail, freckles so dark they looked drawn on. Coupland nodded. These were Quinlan's officers but beneath the rivalry they were all on the same side, and when facing a threat to their own it became tribal. When Ashcroft headed over to the records office there were six detectives in his wake. Satisfied, Coupland pulled out his phone, tapping it against his chin for a moment before hitting speed dial. It wasn't yet 6am, but Mallender would want to hear this development immediately.

The DCI's familiar MG pulled into the car park heading for the reserved bay close by the station's entrance. Either he had already been up and dressed when he got the call or he shaved on the drive over, but either way he arrived at the station as immaculate as ever, freshly pressed shirt, clean suit, hair with just enough product on it to not look like he was trying too hard.

Coupland waited for him in the car park; he'd needed a smoke to put his thoughts in order. He cast his memory back to when the retired policemen had been serving officers. They were a good twenty years older than Coupland, probably preparing to hang up their boots while he was just a probationer. Prison was the perfect place to hold a grudge and let it fester; many a con carried that anger with them during their sentence but upon release found their contacts – and their strength – long gone. At best the threats made from the dock as they were being led away amounted to nothing, yet on this occasion someone had the will – and the ability – to see it through.

Crushing the remains of his third cigarette underfoot Coupland approached Mallender. He'd already briefed him on the phone, and the DCI informed him that Superintendent Curtis had been updated and was expecting a full report on his desk by the time he arrived in just under an hour. It was to be expected, for once Curtis escalated this information up the food chain he would be summoned to HQ to brief the ACC before most organisations would have had time to switch their coffee machines on.

There was no time for normal pleasantries. Mallender got straight to the point. 'How far back are we looking?'

'I know one of the men retired around the mid-nineties.'

'So we could be talking about someone who was put away as far back as 1970?' Mallender regarded Coupland keenly.

'In theory, yes, sir, but if that was the case they'd have been released the same time as the men retired, so why not do something then?'

Mallender nodded in agreement. 'That was my thought. Besides, it suggests our killer was a young man back then, otherwise he'd be operating a mobility scooter now and presumably be no threat to anyone – apart from other road users.'

Coupland blew out his cheeks. 'Yeah, and it also means he got a hefty sentence, which I'm guessing was for murder. I joined the force in '90, but I wasn't let loose on anything major till I had a few years under my belt.'

A look came over Mallender's face that Coupland couldn't fathom.

'Sir?' he prompted.

A sigh. 'If you must know I'm wondering why you hadn't picked up the police link earlier, just as well your wing man's thorough.'

Coupland ignored the rebuke; Mallender was right. He'd been aware that Sharon Mathers' father had been a beat cop – Damian Mathers had told him so on the day of the press appeal – but he hadn't made the connection to the other victims' fathers the way that Ashcroft had. Too busy letting Amy's boyfriend distract him from doing his job properly, though as an excuse that was pretty lame and he knew it. He followed Mallender inside; staring at the back of the DCI's head as they walked by the CID room. With floor to ceiling glass it was commonly referred to as the goldfish bowl. Most of the inhabitants were used to being gawped at, though some of Quinlan's team had taken offence and begun staring down passers-by. The lack of progress was making everyone edgy. Right now the office was deserted. Coupland explained that a small team had been dispatched to the records office sifting through case files from 1970–1995 looking for investigations where all three officers had been involved.

'Christ, what's that going to cost in overtime?'

'It's not my job to keep a smile on the Chief Super's face – that's yours,' Coupland threw back. 'Besides, most of the records will be computerised, the challenge will be whether we can rely on the cross referencing facility. In my experience it's better to sift through it by hand, all it takes is for one of them to have been sloppy with his paperwork one day and it'll be like he never existed. Assuming statements and court files have been stored away correctly we should be able to trace back to the serving officers who worked each case.'

'Fool proof then,' Mallender's mouth was a grim line, 'not like anything ever gets misfiled or deleted in error these days, eh?'

'Granted,' said Coupland, 'but we've got to start from somewhere…'

Mallender nodded, blowing out his cheeks. 'Curtis is going to need names and dates… I know I'm asking the impossible...'

Coupland looked at his watch. It was 6.30am. 'Give me an hour,' he suggested, 'we may not have a suspect by then, but I hope to Christ we'll have some background on the retired officers.'

Ashcroft's grin split his face in two when he popped his head around the goldfish bowl door some thirty minutes later. 'I'm starting to worry about you,' Coupland said, 'you're getting more like Pollyanna the longer you've been here. I don't have that effect on people as a rule, normally by now they've got the Police Federation rep's number on speed dial.'

Nobody enjoyed digging around in old record files, but Ashcroft appeared to be relishing the task. He approached Coupland's desk, waving a piece of paper under the senior man's nose. 'Human Resources don't open until nine, so I can't be sure when all three men joined and left the force exactly, and I'm even less certain whether they started here or they transferred here at a later date, never mind whether they transferred elsewhere later.'

'Leave HR to me,' Coupland informed him.

Ashcroft nodded. 'I was hoping you would say that,' he smiled. 'I just wanted to give you a heads up that the men were certainly here in the 90s, and at one point were involved in a team targeting the football violence that was rife at the time. At the moment we can place two of them on the same case but not all three.'

Coupland nodded; it wasn't much but it was a start, and that's all they needed. Just then Krispy Kreme walked into the room, wiping his hands down the side of his trousers. Coupland guessed he was returning from the toilet. He waited while the DC settled himself at his desk before walking over to him with a large smile. Krispy looked up at him alarmed, his eyes darting to his desk drawer where Coupland suspected he now stashed his sugar fix. 'I need you to look up football hooliganism in and around Salford during the 90s. Who the major players were, what stories the press were peddling back then.' Coupland remembered something he'd heard Breeda say when he called into her pub looking for Lynn. 'See what comes up relating to The Grey Mare.' The DC nodded eagerly, scribbled some notes onto a pad and set to work immediately.

Human Resources didn't exactly put out the flags when Coupland called but they didn't give him as hard a time as he expected. He hadn't bothered waiting until 9am to phone them, he knew the HR manager of old, she was married to a beat cop, travelled in with him on earlies to save on petrol – if she answered the phone she'd not send him packing. 'DS Coupland?' she repeated, as though her ears were deceiving her. 'What's wrong?' Her tone changing to suspicious, no one called HR voluntarily. An incident the previous year involving Coupland and a civilian call handler had got messy. HR had needed to step in to stop it blowing up in his face. Still he cringed at the memory. The HR manager wasn't known for bearing grudges, she treated Coupland the same as anyone else – apart from a few wise cracks.

'Is this about the email I sent you at the start of the year about annual leave?'

He laughed politely. She was someone he'd have to tread around with care but she was married to a cop so she couldn't be all bad. Her tone was friendly enough, though he did suspect at one point she was recording the call to play back to any disbelieving colleagues. When she realised the serious nature of his enquiry she ceased with the teasing, her voice taking on a serious tone. 'OK, so you want to know when these men joined the force and when they retired, and specifically the dates they were based at Salford?' Coupland grunted a yes. 'Give me thirty minutes, an hour at most; I'll put the information into an email. Whether you open it or not is up to you,' she added.

Forty minutes later she was as good as her word. Her email confirmed:

Nathaniel Mathers joined the force in '74, Henry Sandford, (known as Harry) joined the same year as Lewis Carruthers, in '78. All men were stationed at Pendleton but did stints at Little Hulton, Swinton, and Salford Precinct when required. Mathers retired in 1999, followed by Lewis Carruthers in 2003. Henry Sandford had taken early retirement in 1995 due to ill-health.

Coupland reached for his mobile, dialled Ashcroft's number. The DC picked up straight away. 'You said one of the men had passed away, was it Henry Sandford?'

'No, Lewis Carruthers, why do you ask?'

'Sandford took early retirement on the grounds of ill-health, made sense that it was him, that's all. How did Carruthers die?'

'Open verdict,'

'And what does that mean exactly?'

Ashcroft faltered. *'Your guess is as good as mine,'* he admitted.

'You told me originally it was natural causes.'

'Hang on a minute.'

Coupland heard the sound of paper shuffling alongside a slow outward breath. Pollyanna was in the process of leaving the building. Ashcroft came back on the line. *'I knew I'd made a note of it somewhere, he died of exposure on top of a hill somewhere in the Peak District.'* His power of detail was beginning to rival Turnbull.

'Okay.' Coupland filed the information away in his head. 'I'm going to forward you the email I've just got from HR.' He typed Ashcroft's email address into the mail recipient line as he spoke – together with Mallender's, for onward transmission to Curtis.

'How come you managed to get hold of them so early?'

'Sometimes having a reputation for all the wrong reasons has its advantages,' Coupland said grimly. 'The email's got the dates all three men were serving officers, can you pass it onto the rest of the team you've got working on this then meet me in the car park? I think we need to pay Lewis Carruthers' widow a visit.'

*

Elba Carruthers lived on an executive development in Clifton, a cul-de-sac of mock Tudor homes looking onto a three-storey apartment block. Coupland pulled up in the car park beside the block and consulted his notes. 'Flat number 6,' he said, stepping out of his car. 'She's remarried,' he said across the car bonnet to Ashcroft as he bleeped the car locked. 'Goes by the name of Dunleavy now.' Coupland had telephoned ahead so when he pressed the buzzer the door clicked open without an enquiry to see who was there. The flat was on the first floor, accessed by a communal stairwell, clean and recently decorated if the smell of paint was anything to go by.

The door to Elba's flat was already open; a man with a thick mop of white hair stood in the doorway waiting for the detectives as they walked across the landing. 'Elba asked me to get the coffee on; I expect you'll be glad of a cup?'

Coupland nodded, 'I take it you're her husband?'

'Yes! Sorry! Where are my manners? I'm afraid ever since we got the news… My name is Gerald, I was a friend of Elba and her husband before his death, I'd not long been widowed myself, knew what she was going through. I know to some we probably seemed a little hasty with our nuptials, but we're none of us getting any younger, are we?'

Coupland inclined his head in agreement. 'How is she?' he asked, as he drew close.

'She's beside herself,' the man replied, 'this is the worst possible news. She and Kathleen were so close. She was upset when Kathleen's marriage broke up, worried about how it was going to affect her grandson but this is off the scale… nothing prepared her for this.' He led them into a small hallway. A door leading off from it was partially open. 'Please, go through,' he said. 'Elba's waiting…'

The woman seated on the corner unit stared at Coupland as he approached her. She looked older than he expected, white hair peppered with grey and deep lines on her forehead which added ten years to her face. Her eyes were red rimmed and her face was blotchy. She was squeezing the life out of a crumpled tissue in her hand. It was only when they were standing in front of her that she seemed to notice that Coupland wasn't alone, that Ashcroft was lurking somewhat uncomfortably behind him.

'Thank you for agreeing to see us.'

A thread of snot threatened to drip onto her upper lip, she dabbed at it with the well-worn tissue. 'Please, take a seat,' Gerald instructed, moving into the open plan kitchen to pour boiling water into a cafetiere before carrying it through to the lounge area where he placed it upon a coffee table, cups and saucers already set out. He poured coffee into three cups.

Elba's cup already had liquid in it, tea or coffee it was impossible to make out. 'Why do people always insist on making drinks when someone dies?' she sighed. 'I had to put up with this when I lost Lewis, like it was supposed to help in some way when it doesn't help at all. Not one little bit.' She glared at Gerald as she said this, but he concentrated on offering the detectives milk and sugar, as though his wife hadn't spoken.

She turned her attention to Coupland. 'Why would anyone want to hurt Kath?' she asked. 'She was a schoolteacher, for goodness' sake.' People often said this, as though there were occupations that deserved murder as a possible outcome, but Coupland didn't agree. Apart from traffic wardens perhaps; he could make an exception for them, and anyone from HMRC for that matter, or politicians…

'Every resource we have has been allocated to this investigation, I promise you. I know there's a lot to take in but please be reassured that we'd like nothing more than to bring the person responsible to justice. But for now, we'd like to talk to you about your husband…' Coupland cast a glance at Ashcroft, signalling permission to step in if he was too heavy footed. 'Your late husband…' he corrected himself, '…what with him being in the job…'

'Married to the job more like,' Elba remarked, not unpleasantly. 'Are you married?' She directed the question at both detectives but only Coupland responded.

'Yes,' he replied, 'a work in progress at the best of times…' he let his words trail off while he thought how to get the conversation back on track. Sometimes honesty really was the best policy. 'Look, I'm really sorry about intruding on your grief like this, but I don't think this can wait.'

Elba regarded him sharply, 'Why? Lewis has been dead nigh on a year. Do you think there's a connection?' She looked at Gerald as though prompting him to step in.

'How can my wife help you, Sergeant? You can see she's distressed.'

Coupland sighed, moving so that he stood in front of Gerald thereby blocking him from Elba's line of vision. 'How did your husband die?'

Elba's head reared back sharply. 'You couldn't have got this information from someone else?'

Gerald's brows knotted together as he moved to sit beside his wife. Ashcroft chose that moment to speak. 'We discovered this morning that two other women, murdered the same week as Kathleen, are daughters of officers who served in the force the same time as your late husband. You can appreciate that tracking down the coroner who recorded an open verdict at his inquest could take some time, and if we approach your GP they won't speak to us without your permission.'

'So here we are,' Coupland picked up, 'and we don't have all day.'

Gerald took his wife's hand, gave it a squeeze. Elba sighed. 'Lewis loved hillwalking. It's what he did in his spare time, man and boy, climbing God forsaken peaks just because they were there. Selfish I always thought, that on his days off he'd prefer to head out to the middle of nowhere.'

'You didn't share his passion, then?'

'Not at all!' Elba wrinkled her nose in disgust. 'At best I'd go and stay in the nearest B&B while he went off on his adventure… but it was lonely, to tell the truth, hanging around all day waiting for him to come back. And when Kath came along I had a ready-made excuse to stop going. He loved his solitude so much; sometimes I wondered why he bothered marrying. Oh, that's unfair in a way, he was good company when he made the effort, but something changed in him and over the years he became withdrawn.'

'Any idea what?'

Elba studied her hands. 'Well… I can't be certain. It wasn't something he confided in me you understand, but I know he blamed himself for a colleague getting injured when they were on foot patrol.'

'When did this happen?'

Elba looked off into the middle distance. 'Well, now you're asking, I can't be certain… early nineties, maybe?'

'Do you know what happened?'

She shook her head. 'Not exactly. I mean, I know that they were policing outside Old Trafford and that the crowd turned on them. I'm afraid what I'm about to say doesn't put Lewis in a good light, but, well, it seems he ran off, leaving his colleague to the mob. Harry – that was his colleague – suffered appalling leg injuries.'

'Can you remember his surname?'

A shrug. 'Sandwell?' Close enough. 'He was confined

to desk duties when he finally returned to the job after leaving hospital, pensioned off not long after that. Lewis told me about the incident and Harry's injury, but he never confessed to me about running away and leaving him on his own. If he thought I knew the cause he'd have been deeply ashamed.'

'So how do you know all this?'

Elba lowered her head, 'I heard him on the phone once, to Harry.' She looked across at Gerald whose expression said it was the first time he'd heard this story. 'I was embarrassed, even a little ashamed, I didn't want to discredit his memory by mentioning it after he'd gone.'

'Very wise,' Gerald replied, patting her hand.

'So, you heard him on the phone to his pal...' Coupland prompted her.

'No, they weren't pals,' Elba corrected him, 'they didn't mix out of work, Lewis had barely spoken of Harry before his injury, and afterwards, well, Lewis barely spoke full stop.'

'Why did he phone him, then?'

Elba shook her head, 'I can't be certain... I didn't catch the first part of the call.' She looked down at her lap, at Gerald's hand stroking hers. She placed her free hand on top of his. 'I'm ashamed to say I listened in on the phone's extension.' She looked up at Coupland shyly. 'He'd stopped sharing his life with me, Sergeant, I thought there may have been another woman.'

'But instead it was Harry.'

'Yes, and he was saying the most hateful things. That Lewis was a coward, that because of him he'd been cheated out of a career and the least he could do was to keep to his side of the bargain.'

'What did he mean by that?'

'I don't know, Harry put the phone down on him and from then on Lewis seemed to shut down even more. It wasn't his way to share his problems with me and I couldn't own up to eavesdropping. But something was gnawing away at him; I'd always assumed it was the fear of Harry discrediting him to me at some point. Truth was, I was so relieved he hadn't gone off me that if he'd told me he'd left Harry to his own devices that day I wouldn't have berated him. Besides, Harry didn't sound like a very nice man… which is why I took Lewis's death so hard afterwards… I blamed myself, you see, that my silence had left him carrying the burden of a secret that no longer existed.'

'What do you mean?'

'After that phone call he became more withdrawn, he couldn't wait to get away from here.' She laughed bitterly. 'I know a lot of retired cops head for the sun but not my Lewis, in fact the colder and bleaker the destination the better as far as he was concerned. Then one day he headed out and just didn't come back.' She shuddered, as though something cold had settled on her shoulders.

Coupland leaned forward, dipping his head as he spoke. 'Can you tell us what happened?'

Elba turned to look at Gerald who nodded in encouragement. 'It just wasn't like him… He was very organised, you see, as thorough as a boy scout, you know, prepared for anything. Over the years he'd amassed all the right climbing equipment and professional clothing, and he always remembered a back pack full of provisions in case he got stranded somewhere. Only on this particular day when he went out he didn't return to the B&B at the time he told them he'd be back. They didn't waste any time raising the alarm but it took several hours for the mountain rescue team to find him and by then he was dead. Hypothermia.'

Who wouldn't freeze to death if they got lost on a mountain top? Coupland supposed. Instead he asked, 'Where did this happen?'

'Kinder Scout, he went there three or four times a year.' Elba tutted as she looked over at the lounge window and the grey sky beyond.

'What is it?' Coupland asked, more sharply than he liked.

'He was an experienced climber, DS Coupland, on a mountain range he was familiar with, yet he'd gone out without protective clothing, no equipment and no means of raising alarm. There was an inquest several months later, the coroner recorded an open verdict but the truth of it was clear to see for anyone who bothered looking.'

'And that was?'

'He set out that morning never intending to come back.'

*

Once they'd returned to his car Coupland checked his phone; he'd turned it off while he was with Elba Dunleavy out of respect. He had two missed calls, both from Amy. He tapped the screen to call her back but her phone rang out.

'Suicide then,' Ashcroft observed as he fastened his seatbelt.

'Sounds like it,' Coupland agreed. 'Just need to find out what he was running from.'

'You don't buy that shame theory, that he was embarrassed about leaving another officer to fend for himself?'

Coupland pulled a face. 'I'm not sure. I suppose Sandford could have been blackmailing him, pay up or I tell your wife, but blackmailing someone on a police pension isn't exactly going to fund an extravagant lifestyle.'

'Says the man who just came back from Vegas,' Ashcroft joked.

'Hmm, with the credit card bills to prove it,' Coupland grumbled, 'and what would blackmail have to do with a convicted killer murdering their daughters?' The facts kept pointing to something Coupland couldn't quite put his finger on.

'Shall we go and speak to Harry Sandford?'

Coupland hesitated, 'I think I'd rather speak to Nathaniel Mathers first, see if he can paint a picture of what the relationship between these two men was like.' He pulled a face. 'Don't much like the idea of breaking that particular bit of news to his son, though.' He blew out his cheeks as he reached for his phone. 'Here goes.'

CHAPTER 15

Incident room, Wednesday afternoon

The afternoon briefing showed that progress was being made. The officers tasked with searching for cases where PCs Mathers, Sandford and Williams had worked together pulled out a series of raids and stop and searches in and around pubs with a reputation for being frequented by known local football firms during the eighties and nineties. 'You know the kind of thing,' one of Quinlan's DCs advised, 'making sure home and away fans didn't mix on the approach into Old Trafford. Visiting fans would be escorted from the station to the game, or met off coaches where they'd be searched, especially if the coach was dropping them off at particular pubs that had an affiliation to one team or another.'

Coupland remembered the stories from older, battle-worn cops, the weapons found inside gang members' coat linings: carving knives, machetes, ice hammers, carried by men who held responsible jobs in the week but turned feral come match day.

'Good work,' Coupland said. Quinlan nodded his appreciation. Coupland turned to Krispy Kreme. 'Does any of that feature in the digging you've done online?'

The DC nodded. 'There was a murder in '92 at a derby game, the leader of a City firm, Eddie Garside, stabbed during an altercation inside a multi-storey car park.' He hesitated, looked over at the detectives seated close by.

The teams were still gravitating towards their own packs, Coupland noticed, but the gap in the aisle between them was narrowing.

One of Quinlan's DCs, a woman with close-cropped hair and large glasses, waited for Krispy Kreme to finish before speaking. 'We've cross referenced the date of that murder and all three officers were on patrol that day. In fact not only were they in the area, two of them were present when the suspect was picked up. Nathaniel Mathers was the arresting officer.'

'Was he indeed?' Coupland muttered. 'Funnily enough I've arranged to pay him a visit first thing tomorrow.'

Mallender's head shot back in alarm. 'With his son present, of course,' Coupland assured him, 'though not in a professional capacity.' He half turned to Ashcroft. 'I hope.' Turning back to Krispy, he asked, 'What was the convicted man's name?'

'Lee Dawson.'

Coupland instructed Turnbull to check with the probation service the date of Dawson's release. 'And check what kind of supervision he's getting,' he added.

'You reckon he's our man?' Turnbull asked but Coupland didn't want to be drawn.

'He's the best lead we've had so far,' was all he'd say. He turned to Ross Bateman, avoided staring at the cluster of angry red spots across the young DC's jawline by speaking to his chest. 'How are you getting on tracking down the mystery man emailing Kathleen Williams?'

Bateman looked downcast. 'Still trying to find an IP address for him, Sarge.'

'Great.' Coupland's shoulders sagged.

'I've done a bit of digging, though. Their online

conversation began after he pranged her car at the school gates so I checked out the story with the school caretaker. He remembers someone clipping the side of her vehicle as she was leaving one evening. He was clearing out the lost property box in the school office when he saw her get out of her car to inspect the damage. The other driver was already out of his vehicle, handing her a slip of paper which the caretaker assumed were his details so he didn't bother going out to see if she needed any help.'

'Can he give us a description?'

Bateman shook his head. 'Didn't have his glasses on.'

'Jesus, not even a colour?'

'Do you mean the vehicle, or the man who pranged her car, Sarge?'

A nervous titter went around the room. Those who knew Coupland were cautious; he'd been known to kick off over a lot less. He counted to ten. 'Either,' he said on an outward breath.

'The male was white, Sarge,' Bateman stuttered, as though answering a trick question. He glanced down at his notebook. 'The caretaker wasn't sure about the vehicle, other than he had only clipped Kathleen's passenger door with his bumper so it was unlikely to have suffered any damage.'

'Especially if he timed the prang just right.'

Bateman nodded, 'We checked with the garage where her car's gone in for repair – turns out they were going to call her as the insurance details written on the note were fake.'

'Surprise, surprise. What've you done with the note?'

'I've sent it off to see if we can get any prints but the world and his wife had handled it at the garage so I wouldn't hold your breath.'

Coupland rubbed the back of his neck as he surveyed the room. Robinson raised his hand. 'Sarge? We found the murder weapon used on Sharon Mathers.' About time. 'Uniforms recovered a large stone with traces of blood on it from the wall of a resident's garden backing onto the recreation park. It was sent away for analysis this morning, but we're confident it's the weapon used. It had been placed inside a damaged part of the wall but it didn't match the other stones used and the homeowner doesn't remember putting it there.'

It was something, Coupland supposed. So long as the killer had a police record. 'Get the results fast tracked.'

Robinson dropped his gaze. 'Will do, Sarge, only…'

'What is it?'

'Everything's being fast tracked at the moment…' which meant for all intents and purposes the lab was choked; there were only so many urgent tests it could carry out without impacting normal service delivery. Coupland nodded, trying hard not to let his frustration show. The team weren't to blame for lack of resources.

One of Quinlan's men loomed in the doorway. DC Whitehead. He looked as though he hadn't slept for days. 'Sarge?' he ventured, stepping forward. 'I've been questioning some of the local mums close to where Maria lived.'

'Neighbours? Won't that have been covered in the house to house?'

The DC shook his head. 'They go to a mother and baby group, there's a sign advertising it in the family's medical centre.' Lateral thinking. Coupland smiled appreciatively. 'It's held in the local church hall when the weather's bad, on good days they go over to a park nearby. Maria was a regular.' Quinlan's chest expanded at the prospect of reflected glory. 'They said there had been a van parked by the entrance to the church hall a couple of times, didn't think any more about it until it started showing up by the park.'

'Did they get a look at the driver?'

Whitehead was already shaking his head. 'Said he wore a beany hat, looked like a builder but they never saw him get out of the van.'

'Did they report it?'

'They didn't think too much about it until I turned up asking if they'd seen anything suspicious.'

'Have we got a description on the van?'

'Other than it was white – and dirty – no,'

Coupland turned to Quinlan. 'Got to be our man.'

'Agreed. Once he knew her pattern all he had to do was sit and wait. She probably passed his van while talking to the other mums about the night out she had planned, completely oblivious he was eavesdropping. Again, all he had to do was turn up at the train station on the right night – and if he knew where she lived it'd be pretty obvious which station she'd use – then bide his time.' Coupland tried to temper the mounting excitement in the room. 'So we're looking for White Van Man,' he commented. 'Piece of cake.'

Coupland reported on his visit earlier in the day to Elba Dunleavy and her recollection of her late husband's suicide on Kinder Scout. 'His widow's convinced that something was preying on his mind,' he added. 'Whilst a serving officer, Lewis Carruthers left PC Harry Sandford at the mercy of a gang of thugs during a derby match, suffering a severe injury to his leg as a result. It's why he took early retirement.'

'So he felt guilty at letting a fellow officer down?' Robinson asked.

'Maybe.' Coupland's mind was elsewhere. 'Can you get onto HR, check the date of Sandford's injury, mention my name if they sound like they're going to drag their feet.' He was thinking back to Elba Dunleavy's concern that something had been preying on her late husband's mind. What if it hadn't been about guilt over Sandford's injury, what if it was over something much worse? These officers were connected in some way; they just had to work what it was. Coupland's meeting with Nathaniel Mathers couldn't come soon enough.

*

Thursday morning

Nathaniel Mathers lived in a modest house in Swinton. A 1930s semi on a main road, the property was set back, obscured from passers-by by a bank of mature trees along the pavement edge. The front lawn was well tended, Hydrangeas beneath a bay window and an olive tree in a pot beside the heavy wooden front door. Coupland was about to ring the doorbell when the door swung open, Damian Mathers greeting him with a cursory nod. The lawyer was wearing jeans, good ones going by look of them, and a pinstripe shirt which was open at the neck.

'Who's this?' He glared at Ashcroft, before turning back to Coupland with a sad smile. 'I expected more from you.'

Coupland felt himself bristle. 'I told you I was bringing my partner,' he said firmly. 'What am I supposed to do, not bring him to avoid you thinking he's been helicoptered in especially. Christ, the world's gone mad.' He shook his head as he said this. 'Not to mention we don't have the budget.'

Mathers sighed, held up his hands in mock surrender. 'Look, I'm sorry, blame it on lack of sleep, my sister's murder has knocked all of us for six.'

Coupland blew out a long breath, nodded his head in understanding. 'It's been tough on all the families, Damian, but I think we're making progress.'

'Please, come through, then, my father's keen to know how he can help.'

Nathaniel Mathers was an elegant man. Tall, slim built, with fine chiselled features. He got to his feet when Coupland walked into the small front room behind his son; if he was surprised at seeing Ashcroft he didn't show it. He stepped forward to shake both detectives' hands while his son made introductions, before pointing to a patterned settee. 'Please take a seat,' he invited them, moving to stand behind his wife who was seated in a high-backed chair. She was a small woman, who barely glanced in their direction, preferring instead to gaze at a framed photograph of Sharon placed on a coffee table in the centre of the room, a single lit candle beside it. A box of tissues had been placed on her knee; a pile of used tissues had fallen into the crevice of her seat cushion.

Nathaniel made to clear away the debris, talking over his shoulder as he did so. 'It's all changed since I was a serving officer.' He tossed the tissues into a plastic carrier bag he pulled from a drawer in the sideboard behind him, tying the handles together in a knot before heading into the kitchen. Moments later the kettle could be heard being filled and cupboard doors opening and slamming shut. Nathaniel Mathers was a man who didn't like to sit still; his garden vouched for that.

'Dad I'll do that,' Damian said firmly, following his father into the kitchen, gently cajoling him back into the sitting room. Though his steps were heavy, his shoulders sagging, he carried himself with an air of dignity. He spoke softly as he lowered himself into an armchair opposite his wife.

'Damian is right, I should let him help more, but it's when I sit down, or stop and think for even a moment that it hits me our daughter has gone.' His chin began to wobble as he spoke, he stared at the detectives before clearing his throat several times. Coupland had never felt more like he was intruding. Mathers wanted to grieve, but not in front of visitors.

'We think the person who killed Sharon is someone you put away before you retired.'

Mathers didn't react. 'I arrested many men, Detective Sergeant,' he responded, 'some for serious crimes, but they will be old men now.' His tone was measured. Even. A good man to have in a crisis.

'We've identified a person of interest, we're just checking with the prison service for his release date. If we're right he would have been a young man when he was jailed for murder.'

'Who?'

'Lee Dawson, sent down for the murder of Eddie Garside in '92.'

Nathaniel remained silent.

'What we need to find out is what you, Lewis Carruthers and Harry Sandford could have done to make this man bear a grudge against you throughout his life sentence.'

Nathaniel cocked his head, 'Hang on… are you saying the other women on the news… women you think have been murdered by this man… are their daughters?'

Coupland nodded.

Mathers dropped his head into his hands; his bald head was shiny in parts, the sunlight coming in through the bay window reflected off it. 'I had no idea…' His shoulders dipped, his breathing came in a succession of slow sighs.

'Did you keep in touch with either PC Carruthers or PC Sandford after they retired?'

Nathaniel lifted his head, squinting at Coupland as though surprised he was still there. 'Not really, we weren't exactly buddies, I got invited to a couple of drinking sessions when other folk retired – they'd often be at those, we'd rake over old ground for an hour or two, but we didn't keep in touch beyond that.'

'Did you know Lewis Carruthers is dead?'

A nod. 'I sent a condolence card to his wife. I'd met her a couple of times over the years, while we were still serving, seemed like the right thing to do…'

'Your son mentioned that you witnessed some prisoners being mistreated whilst in custody. I wondered if this could have happened in this case.'

'He had no right to speak out of turn.' His raised voice carried into the kitchen.

When Damian came out carrying a tray of coffee he avoided his father's eye. 'It was an off the cuff remark, Dad.'

'So off the cuff they're round here asking me about it!' Nathaniel said harshly, and in an instant they reverted to how it must have been between them, an imposing father presiding over unruly boys and a headstrong girl. Boys that did as they were told or there'd be consequences. Pocket money withheld or a clip around the back of an ear at worst. His own father had preferred fists and a belt, until Coupland grew taller than him and learned how to resist. Against the law today of course, if he was a kid now he'd probably be in care. The thought brought him no comfort; he'd arrested enough care leavers over the years to know that wasn't always a better option.

'Sarge?' Ashcroft prompted him.

Coupland cleared his throat. 'Either his conviction was unsafe or he was mistreated in custody.' His tone was sharper than he'd intended. 'Which is it to be?'

'Now look here—' Damian Mathers exploded; he'd placed the tray on the coffee table, leaving him free to move towards Coupland.

'I can fight my own battles,' his father objected, holding onto his son's arm. 'Why don't you leave us, I'm not ready for the knackers yard quite yet.'

'I'm going nowhere, Dad,' Damian shot back, obliterating all traces of the child he'd once been, 'and this time I'm here as your lawyer.'

Coupland sighed. 'If you feel that's necessary,' he said evenly, 'maybe we should continue this down at the station.'

'Maybe we should start over again,' Ashcroft attempted, 'we all want to catch Sharon's killer, right? So we need to find out more about Lee Dawson. Our colleagues are out looking for him as we speak but he's been clever, there's no DNA, nothing as yet to incriminate him, we're going to have to build a strong case – and finding a motive is a start.'

Coupland caught Ashcroft's eye. The DC had bailed him out of a cock up of his own making and he nodded his appreciation. 'You've already told us that Carruthers and Sandford weren't your friends,' he added.

'I didn't say that exactly…' Nathaniel objected.

'But it's what you meant.'

Nathaniel didn't contradict him.

'So why are you trying to protect them?'

'I'm not!' Nathaniel snapped. 'Sandford was an idiot, prone to showing off if the mood took him. Every once in a while he'd bring someone in who he'd roughed up on the way to the cells, no one ever complained, the men were usually guilty of something, burglary, drunk and disorderly, domestic abuse, they'd take the beating as part of their punishment and go on their way. Carruthers wasn't like that, he wasn't cut from the same cloth as Sandford but in many ways he was just as bad. He was in cloud cuckoo land, you see, turned a blind eye to Sandford acting up because he wanted a quiet life. But on the night Lee Dawson was brought in I know nothing happened to him.'

'How can you be so sure?'

Nathaniel gave Coupland a look to say his answer was obvious. 'Because Sandford was admitted to hospital that afternoon, underwent surgery the same night as I remember it. To be honest I was relieved he wasn't there.'

'Why do you say that?'

A sigh. 'It had been a long day and I was glad to get home. I was sick of having to babysit Sandford to make sure things didn't get out of hand and he'd really taken against Dawson. If he hadn't been incapacitated I'd have had to stay on after my shift.'

243

'Why would you do that?'

Another sigh. 'There was no love lost between him and Lee Dawson. I was there when he first encountered him. It was the day of the Manchester Derby. We were carrying out searches on a group of Red Army supporters. The powers that be had pulled out all the stops, police dogs and handlers, riot vans, mounted police, you name it, they weren't taking any chances. You could hear the chanting half a mile away. Taunts, threats and counter threats The brief was to put a ring of steel around Old Trafford but even with beat cops drafted in from other areas the best we could do was focus on keeping the opposing football firms apart. We had a group of supporters lined up against the exterior wall of a pub and began to search them. Lee Dawson was impatient at waiting his turn in the line and started singing. He was a Jack the Lad, pure and simple. The other supporters joined in the song and laughed when he started messing about while Harry patted him down. Harry didn't like that; he pushed him against the wall and yelled at him to shut it. Dawson just grinned, tried to carry on singing but Harry dragged him to the ground. Dawson was tall but slender with it, no match for Harry, he was heavy in those days; he pinned him down on the tarmac, told him if he stepped out of line or opened his fucking mouth again it would be shut for him properly.' Nathaniel eyed Coupland. 'Those were his words, Sergeant, not mine.'

Coupland didn't doubt it.

'A tag team of officers escorted them to the football ground, but as Dawson passed Harry he started miming…' Nathaniel mimicked the universal wanker sign, 'Harry was all set to go for him but I held him back, told him not to be so damned stupid. I've seen a lot worse in my time, Sergeant, not worth escalating things for the sake of it.'

Nathaniel's wife began to sob, pulling out several sheets of tissue to dab her eyes and nose. 'Wait a minute,' Nathaniel pushed himself up from his chair, taking his wife's hand as he helped her to her feet before leading her from the room. 'Her GP gave her a sleeping tablet before you got here, with any luck she'll be knocked out for the rest of the day. It'll give me a chance to start making arrangements… I don't suppose you know when Sharon's body will be released to us?'

Coupland shook his head. 'Soon as we can…' was all he promised. After a couple of minutes they heard an upper room door close followed by footsteps on the stairs. Nathaniel entered the room with a large box file under his arm. He regarded both detectives as he placed the file on the coffee table, pushing the untouched coffee to one side. 'Some cases you never forget,' he said, 'and some cases won't let you forget because so much is written about them.' He opened the file, pulled out a yellowed newspaper clipping and passed it to Coupland. He passed Ashcroft another, further articles he placed onto the coffee table around the file. His son leaned over Ashcroft's shoulder to get a better look.

Most articles had used the same images – an enlarged photo of an angelic looking schoolboy had been placed beside a picture of a scowling youth being led into court from a police van. Nathaniel pointed to the angelic schoolboy. 'Eddie Garside twenty years before his murder. A more appealing picture than the thug he turned into. Convictions for GBH and ABH, all football related. These days he'd be banned from matches but back then there was no way of really enforcing that. Instead surveillance teams were set up to monitor what they were doing. The gangs were well organised, you know, like mini corporations, with a lynch pin heading up each faction. Eddie was the leader of a local firm; he'd inflicted countless injuries over the five years of his reign.'

'No loss to society then.'

'He was still a victim of a terrible crime,' Nathaniel replied. 'His family were entitled to justice.'

'And this is Lee Dawson.' Ashcroft pointed to the photograph of a youth being led away in cuffs.

Nathaniel nodded. 'No previous record, wasn't known to any of us before that day, bit of a jack the lad by all accounts,'

'Says here,' Ashcroft picked up another yellowed cutting and began to read aloud a statement made by Dawson's boss, owner of a local joinery firm: '"This has come as such a shock to those that know Lee. He doesn't get into fights, he doesn't go to games for trouble, he just loves his football." A teacher from his old school, who preferred not to be named, said: "He could be cheeky at times."'

'No law against that, last time I looked,' Coupland said

Ashcroft read some more: '"The hostility between rival fans was palpable that day," said a police spokesman, "with opposing firms antagonising each other, culminating in a stand-off inside a multi-storey car park. It is believed the men broke away from the crowds to settle their score privately."'

Nathaniel caught Coupland raise his eyebrows at Ashcroft. 'Does that bit strike you as strange, Sergeant?'

Coupland grunted a yes. 'A gang is about protection and reflected glory, why would they 'break away' from the others?' The men fell silent as they pondered this. 'Did Dawson know his victim?'

Nathaniel shook his head. 'They supported rival teams, didn't frequent the same pubs. He'll have known his reputation. I guess it was just a case of bravado gone wrong.'

'Was he drunk?'

Nathaniel nodded. 'No more so than anyone else, we did our best to stop drink being taken into the ground but all that meant was they made sure they were tanked up when they arrived.'

Coupland remembered as a probationer making up the police line that shepherded supporters from Manchester Piccadilly onto shuttle buses going back and forth to Old Trafford or Maine Road. The drinking was done on the way up on the intercity trains, the home team supporters frequenting back street pubs.

'Was it you that found the body?'

Nathaniel didn't bother looking up but the shake of his head was clear. 'No, I was responding to a call for assistance. An officer was down.'

'Harry Sandford?'

'Yes. I'd stayed put doing stop and searches, Harry had been sent to escort supporters out of the stadium but things had started to turn ugly, though by the time we arrived he'd gone.'

'Who was "we"?'

'Sorry?'

'You said things had turned ugly by the time "we" arrived. Can you remember who was there?'

'Not after all this time!' Nathaniel said irritably.

Damian Mathers fixed Coupland with a stare. 'In case you haven't noticed, my father is doing all he can to help you despite the distress he's in.'

'I know that,' Coupland said carefully, 'bear with me, Nathaniel, I just need to know who was with you. Did Lewis Carruthers respond to the call?'

'What?' Nathaniel looked up at Coupland, his brow knotting as he squinted his eyes. 'No, he was already in the vicinity; he was one of the officers that got caught up in the squall when it started kicking off. I didn't see him until much later.'

'After the body had been found.'

'Yes, obviously, sorry didn't I make it clear? It was Lewis who found the body. Well, him and Harry really. Lewis radioed it in and as I was closest I was the first officer to respond. It's funny, Harry hadn't liked the look of Dawson from the moment he clapped eyes on him, turned out he was right not to. Certainly his instincts on that day were better than mine. He told me he'd seen tensions escalating between Dawson and Eddie Garside when they were leaving the ground. He followed them into the multi-storey car park which given the injury to his leg was a brave thing to do. Got a commendation for it if I recall. Lewis had run into the car park to check Sandford was OK. By the time he got there Dawson was nowhere to be seen but he found Garside lying on the ground.'

'And he didn't see anyone leaving?'

'You'd have to check his statement at the time but I guess not.'

Nathaniel picked up another newspaper clipping and held it up for the detectives to see. The headline read:

Scarf Convicts Football Derby Slayer, and referred to 'the crucial evidence that convicted Dawson was his Burberry scarf which had been found beside the victim covered in his blood.'

'It had his DNA on it and everything,' Nathaniel informed them, 'he never denied it was his, to be fair, though he'd have struggled with that given we had CCTV footage of him wearing the scarf earlier that day.' The newspaper had printed a grainy picture of an army of men wearing Lacoste tracksuit tops over polo necks and baggy jeans. One man's face had been circled. He wore a Pringle jumper over a Fred Perry shirt. Adidas Three Stripe trainers. A Burberry scarf was wrapped around his neck several times. Nathaniel placed the clippings in the centre of the coffee table. 'Lee Dawson and the scarf that gave him away.'

He shook his head as though ridding himself of some terrible thought. 'Could he really have killed Sharon?' He held Coupland's gaze. 'Could he really be targeting us after all this time?'

Coupland chose his words carefully. 'We think it's likely; remember, he's been cooped up all these years, he's not had the chance to go after anyone before.'

'But why not come after me? If he was angry with me why come after my daughter?'

'Because this would hurt you more.'

'But then why kill Lewis's daughter? He's dead, how can killing her hurt him now?' He had a point.

Coupland shrugged. 'Maybe he didn't know Lewis was dead. Remember revenge isn't rational, you're trying to apply a logic that isn't there.'

Nathaniel's demeanour was changing before Coupland's eyes. 'If I'm to blame for this, for losing Sharon, how can I ever forgive myself?' He turned to Damian. 'How will your mother ever forgive me?' His dark skin took on a grey tinge, beads of sweat formed on his brow. His body was going into shock.

'You need to leave now,' Damian Mathers said firmly. 'My father needs to rest.'

Coupland got to his feet, signalling for Ashcroft to do the same. He pocketed the news clipping he was holding.

A long sigh escaped from Nathaniel. 'Why would he do this to us?'

Coupland shook his head in reply as he followed Ashcroft into to the hall. They were about to let themselves out when his mobile pinged, signalling a text. He grabbed his phone. It was Robinson: **Harry Sandford sustained a leg fracture on 14 March 1992 after a derby match. Returned to desk duties but was retired out not long after.** This confirmed Elba and Nathaniel's recollection of events. But still… Coupland pulled out the newspaper clipping he'd pocketed and re-read it. He stopped in his tracks. 'Wait a minute…' he muttered, turning around and marching into the sitting room where Damian was kneeling in front of his father, a hand resting on the older man's shoulder. Nathaniel seemed to have aged in the short time they'd left the room. Coupland waved the yellowed paper in front of him.

'Where was the scarf found?'

Nathaniel lifted his head, 'Underneath Garside's body. I moved him when I tried to do CPR.'

Coupland stared at him in alarm, 'I thought it had already been radioed in that he was dead.'

'It had, Lewis had done it himself, but Harry thought he saw a movement, he asked me to check the body for signs of life.'

'So you moved him to do CPR?'

A pause. 'Yes.

'And that's when you found the scarf?'

'Yes.'

*

They were driving back along the East Lancs Road, Coupland was unusually quiet; something in the scenario Nathaniel had described didn't make sense. 'The article said the scarf had been found beside the body, yet Nathaniel only found it when he moved Garside which suggests it was underneath him.'

'So?'

'Only one version can be right and my money's on Nathaniel.'

'Does it matter? If Dawson didn't have a criminal past and it was a spur of the moment spat that got out of hand it is conceivable he wouldn't have been thinking how to cover his tracks, he probably just scarpered and didn't realise he'd lost his scarf in the scuffle.'

Coupland considered this. 'The scarf was bound to be covered in blood if it had been lying beneath someone who'd been stabbed,' he said aloud. 'Doesn't mean it was the owner of the scarf committed the crime, though.'

He blew out his cheeks as he switched on the radio. Another scandal involving a member of the cabinet, the refugee crisis reaching breaking point. He cared, but right now his head was throbbing. He turned to Ashcroft. 'You listening to this?'

'Not really.'

He switched to the local radio station, turned up the volume when he recognised the track. 'You're not a fan, are you?' Ashcroft was unable to keep the surprise from his voice.

'I'm not a complete dinosaur,' Coupland grumbled, hoping to Christ he didn't ask him to name the band, like Amy often did, then snigger when he got it wrong. He wracked his brain, Hosiery or Hooters, or maybe something in between. The local news followed, headlining with an update on the murder enquiry.

"*Police have today confirmed that they are making significant progress in the hunt for the killer of Sharon Mathers, Maria Wellbeck and Kathleen Williams.*" Coupland looked over at Ashcroft, raising his eyebrows. "*A spokesperson for Greater Manchester Police confirms that public response to the recent television appeal has resulted in several significant lines of enquiry opening up which investigating officers are following up.*" A familiar voice loomed out from the dashboard: "*Greater Manchester Police would like to thank the people of Salford for their continued support during this investigation,*" Curtis. Coupland tipped his head and saluted the radio. "*Furthermore, we would urge residents to remain vigilant until this evil perpetrator has been apprehended.*"

He turned to Ashcroft. 'Do you think they actually believe that stuff when they read it out? I mean, they must know it's drivel written by some pen pusher paid to put a positive spin on everything.'

'Can't have the public losing faith in us,' Ashcroft reminded him.

'Suppose.'

The truth was most of the calls made following the

appeal had fallen into two categories: members of the public settling old scores by naming someone they'd recently fallen out with, or psychics and tarot card readers claiming they had messages from the victims they wanted to pass on. Very few of the calls made to the incident room warranted following up. It was more a PR exercise, made the public feel they were doing something to help. Appeals were more successful following reconstructions, which may well be the next step if the lead regarding Lee Dawson went cold. Coupland glared at a woman talking into a mobile phone as she overtook him. He made a note of her registration to pass onto traffic. He turned to Ashcroft. 'Can you chase up the enquiry regarding Dawson's release date? I thought we'd have heard something by now.' Ashcroft nodded, pulling out his mobile while turning the sound down on the radio. He hit speed dial, grunted into the mouthpiece when his call was answered.

'Who is it?' Coupland asked.

Ashcroft covered his phone with his hand. 'Turnbull,' he mouthed.

Coupland nodded, satisfied. Turnbull was one of those people who shouted into his phone no matter where they were, he'd be able to hear his reply loud and clear from where he was sitting: Dawson had been released from prison in February last year. The parole officer supervising his release was on annual leave, Turnbull had left a message with a colleague who was covering his caseload, was waiting to hear back.

'Can you get him to chase it up?' Coupland growled. It appeared Turnbull's wasn't the only voice that amplified down the phone line as his short reply made them both smirk.

Ashcroft ended the call. 'He'll call us the moment he gets an address.'

Harry Sandford's home was a bungalow on a new estate on the outskirts of Ellendale. Five hundred homes and counting. The local school now needed to be extended; an extra locum sought for the medical practice. Long term residents had seen the town blown out of all proportion. 'No community spirit. They're right about that,' Sandford said as he opened the door to Coupland, 'only moved here because we need to be on one level now, what with my leg.'

Coupland had telephoned ahead; with the property being new it wasn't yet on Google Maps, his GPS had tried to send him the wrong way round a mini round-about. He made the introductions, apologising at turning up at such a difficult time.

'Not like it'll get any easier.' Sandford's voice caught. 'You both know that, you'll have seen it enough times I daresay.'

'Even so…' Coupland acknowledged, letting his words trail off.

'Sheila's helping my son-in-law with the babies,' Sandford informed them, 'but I take it from your call it's me you want to speak to?' He led them into a bedroom that was being used as a study; a desk and computer had been placed beneath a large window looking onto the street and the houses opposite. 'It makes me look busy when really all I'm doing is spying on the neighbours.' He laughed but there was a hollowness to it. 'I suppose that's all going to change now,' he said quietly. 'I mean, Pete can't cope, Sheila's already said she wants them all to move in here, not like we haven't got the room. It's not what I imagined being a grandparent would be like though, but then none of us saw this…'

Coupland remembered the anguished look in Sheila's eyes as she held the twin babies close; she was at the sharp end, could see where this was heading, where it'd likely end up. Harry might lose his study but hers was the life that'd change the most.

Sandford looked Coupland up and down. 'You'd likely be wet behind the ears as I was at the point of hanging up my boots… and you'd still be a twinkle in your old man's underpants I reckon,' he added to Ashcroft.

'I'm older than I look,' the DC told him, 'good genes.'

Sandford's head nodded as though it had a life of its own. 'You black fellas never look your age,' he agreed, 'no offence like.'

'None taken,' Ashcroft responded.

Coupland cleared his throat. 'There are a couple of things I wanted to check with you, face to face like, if I may?'

'Fire away.' Sandford perched a buttock on the edge of his desk, motioning for the detectives to sit on the bed settee opposite. 'We're all on the same side here.'

Coupland didn't respond.

'You never fancied inspector though?' Sandford prodded.

Coupland shrugged. 'Happy where I am.'

'Best way,' Sandford agreed. 'Now, what did you want to know?'

'About the murder of a football supporter, Eddie Garside, happened in March '92.'

Sandford looked off into the distance as he blew out

his cheeks. 'Now you've got me… hang on though… Manchester Derby just after Easter, yeah, though for supporter read hooligan.' He sucked in a breath, curling his lip in disgust. 'Nasty, back then it was like patrolling the Shankill Road.'

'I only saw the tail end of it.' Coupland shook his head as he spoke. 'Heard a lot of the stories though.'

'It was like a war zone on match days, believe you me. Bastards didn't come for the game, just the trouble around it. There were a lot of criminal firms back then, gave themselves daft names, had lapel badges made, scarves, tattoos, the leaders thought they were heading up a fuckin' battalion. Came to a head when the trouble spilled overseas. The gangs were travelling to away games in Europe, giving decent Brits a bad name. Politicians had to put a stop to it but it was a long drawn out process, wasn't pretty. Most forces were running surveillance by that time; even so it was the likes of us that bore the brunt of it.'

Coupland considered this. 'Yet the lad who you put away for the murder, Lee Dawson, he had no previous, wasn't even known to the local police, never mind Interpol – didn't you think that was odd?' He held Sandford's gaze for a beat or two.

'What is this?' The retired cop narrowed his eyes. 'Do I need a solicitor present?'

The atmosphere in the room changed. 'Do you think you need one, Harry? I'm only trying to get the facts right in my head.'

'You've read the report, seen the statements taken at the time?'

'Sketchy to say the least,' Coupland replied. 'Don't

get me wrong,' he added, holding up a hand against the protest he was certain would come, 'I'm the world's worst when it comes to paperwork, and I know it was harder back then to cross check criminal history but even so, the guy you lifted for the murder had no previous whatsoever, unless you count not returning his library books on time.'

'You're over egging the pudding a bit there, son,' Sandford sniped, 'he was a mouthy little gob shite, all told,'

'A lot of 'em are at that age,' Coupland retorted, 'doesn't make 'em killers.' He ignored the glance Ashcroft sent in his direction. He was aware that's how he'd responded to Amy's boyfriend, automatically thinking the worst of him, but that was different, the moron was going out with his daughter.

'What does it matter anyway?' Sandford shrugged. 'Water under the bridge now.'

'Except we think he killed Maria.'

Sandford's face froze. 'There must be some mistake.'

Ashcroft shook his head, 'No mistake,' he answered, 'turns out he was released last year.' A look passed over Sandford's face but he said nothing.

'Are you aware of anyone following you or your family over the last few months?'

Sandford was already shaking his head. 'No… If I had I would have reported it, wouldn't I?'

'Any idea why he'd want to come after you?'

He pulled a face. 'None whatsoever, other than holding a grudge because he was caught.'

'We're waiting on an address so we can bring him in for questioning.'

Sandford nodded, moving from the edge of his desk

to his faux leather office chair. 'Bastard,' he said to no one in particular, 'but why come after my daughter?'

'Maybe he wanted to hurt you where it mattered most. He's killed Lewis Carruthers' and Nathaniel Mathers' daughters too. Those names mean anything to you?'

Sandford's eyebrows shot into his hairline. 'You're joking? We were all serving officers about the same time…'

'It was the women's husbands who did a press appeal on TV the other night.'

'I saw that, I had no idea.'

'Seems you were all involved in Lee Dawson's arrest.'

A pause. 'I suppose.'

'I understand you were the first to find Eddie Garside's body?'

Sandford shrugged, shifty now. 'It was a long time ago. I seem to recall Lewis wasn't far behind,' then, under his breath, 'typical Lewis.'

'You know he's dead, don't you?'

Sandford nodded. 'Heard it was a climbing accident.'

Coupland looked at him sharply. 'Only if you consider an experienced climber walking out into the middle of nowhere without any kit an accident.'

'Happen he had a lot on his mind.'

'Mebbe.' Coupland waited a beat. 'You were pals though?'

Sandford pulled a face. 'Hardly.'

'What do you mean?'

A shrug. 'Doesn't matter now.'

Coupland fixed him with a stare. 'Try me.'

Sandford frowned. 'Bit of a wimp, that's all, not much of a team player.'

'Were you, back then?'

'I like to think so. Put it this way, *I* wouldn't have left someone to get a good kicking. It's how I got this.' He lifted his left leg and gripped his damaged knee. 'Lucky for me I managed to get away.'

Coupland didn't respond, he was miles away, mulling something over. 'As I understand it Lee Dawson's conviction rested on his scarf being discovered at the scene of the crime, covered in Garside's blood.'

'You've done your homework.' Sandford's tone was sharp. 'Not sure what you need me for…'

Coupland regarded him. 'To fill in the gaps, of which there seem to be many.'

Sandford made a sound like a slow puncture. 'It was a long time ago, I can't see how anything I say will help you.' Not so convivial now, even a touch shirty. A look of anticipation flitted across his face as Coupland reached inside his jacket and pulled out a small notebook, the corner folded down to mark a particular page.

'Fourteenth of March, Nineteen ninety two,' Coupland said, his finger running down what was in reality a blank page. Ashcroft sat back with his arms folded, studying him with interest. 'The Manchester Derby. You and PC Lewis Carruthers stumble across a body on the ground floor of a multi-storey car park.' He looked across at Sandford, who nodded, his face flooded with relief now they were on safe ground. Coupland flicked on a few pages, glancing at invisible notes. He locked his gaze onto Sandford.

'So who got there first?'

'Well, me technically.' Sandford shifted position in his chair, as though a buttock had gone numb. 'I'd just taken a beating; I dragged myself over there to get away from the marauding gang.'

'And you found the victim lying on the ground?'

A nod of the head.

'Was he dead at this point?'

'He didn't look too bloody clever, if that's what you're meaning.'

'So why didn't you call it in?'

Sandford changed position once more. 'By the time I realised it was a fatality, Lewis – PC Carruthers had arrived. He said he'd do it.'

Coupland held his gaze steady. 'He got there quickly, didn't he?'

Sandford looked at him unsure, then nodded.

'But still after you got there?'

A slower nod. Sandford swallowed, leaning forward to catch a glimpse of the notebook. Coupland tilted the book away from him. 'But I thought he'd run off and left you?'

'He had.'

'So how could he have arrived so fast on your heels?'

'He was already there.'

Coupland screwed up his face. 'So he found Garside?'

'No.' Sandford folded his arms across his body, hunching his shoulders. 'I found him,' irritable now.

'Was PC Williams already there or not?' Coupland barked.

'He'd been hiding out in there! After he scarpered and left me to a beating he legged it into the car park, only I didn't know that until he crept up behind me when I was checking Garside over.'

'To see if the victim was still alive,' Ashcroft added

for him.

'What? Yes.' He shifted a little more in his seat.

'So why did you ask PC Mathers to check the body for signs of life when he arrived?' A pause. 'Come to think of it, it's funny how you didn't find Dawson's scarf while you were checking the victim yourself.'

Sandford blinked.

'Look, I thought this was all about me helping you track down the bastard who killed my daughter. That's what you told me on the phone. It's the only reason I agreed to you coming over.'

'It helps me understand why this might be happening,' Coupland shot back. 'If Dawson is targeting the people who he thinks were responsible for his conviction I want to know what happened on the day of Garside's murder, otherwise how the hell do we work out who he's going to target next…'

A sigh. 'OK, I get the picture. He felt he was wrongly convicted, but if he thinks Lewis did him harm hadn't he paid for what he'd done with his suicide?'

'Sometimes it's a question of coming clean…'

'And if there's nothing to own up to?'

Coupland stared him out. 'Lewis made a call to you shortly before his death. Can you tell me the nature of that call?'

'How do you know that?'

It was Coupland's turn to sigh. 'Just answer the question.'

'I would if I could remember, but to be honest I don't recall Lewis contacting me. Now if you don't mind…'

Ashcroft got to his feet, waited for Coupland to get to his. 'Sarge...?' he prompted.

'We're done,' Coupland said, tucking his notebook back into his jacket as he stood up, 'for the moment.'

Coupland's mobile rang as he climbed into his car. It was DC Turnbull: '*Dawson's probation officer got back to me Sarge, or rather the one covering her caseload.*' He cleared his throat. '*It's not good news.*' Coupland could feel the contents of his stomach plummet. He glanced over at Ashcroft who nodded that he could hear. Even so Coupland put the phone onto loudspeaker.

'Go on.'

'*Lee Dawson is dead, Sarge. Pancreatic cancer. Died last year six weeks after diagnosis.*' Coupland felt something inside him pulsate. Ashcroft gazed back at him wide-eyed. 'Are you sure?'

'*Positive, I got his address from the probation officer and went round there myself. He'd been placed in a hostel in Little Hulton, I've just finished speaking to the duty manager who arranged for him to go into a hospice when he couldn't look after himself.*'

'Christ.' Coupland rubbed the heel of his palms into his eyes. He felt tired, as though someone had sucked the air right out of him. 'I was sure we had him,' he said eventually, 'everything about it fit.' He ended Turnbull's call and pulled out his pack of cigarettes. He offered one to Ashcroft, but the DC was already waving the pack away, 'I forgot your body is a temple…' Coupland said absentmindedly as he lit his cigarette, lowering the car's front windows to compensate. He slumped back into his seat, inhaled the nicotine as far as it would go. 'Shit,' he muttered eventually.

Ashcroft turned to him, 'Bit of a coincidence don't you think…' he said slowly, 'that one of the cops responsible for his arrest that day took his own life the same year he died.'

Coupland exhaled reluctantly. He could no more fathom the reason for that than he could the solution to world peace. 'It might explain the reason for Carruthers' call to Sandford. His widow only heard part of it, but what if he'd been informing Sandford of Dawson's death?' Coupland's brain cells were on go-slow, but they turned nonetheless. 'But how would he have found out in the first place?' He grazed his hand over his chin, puffed out his cheeks. 'If that was the thing that he felt guilty about – knowing an innocent person had gone to jail, maybe he kept track of him over the years, wouldn't be difficult with the contacts he'll have made during his career. Maybe he hoped for an early release, a reunion with his family and a happy ever after.' The reality was seldom like that. On leaving prison the chances of ex-offenders moving into employment were slim; with family members reluctant to take on the responsibility of keeping tabs on them, life in a hostel beckoned. It was no wonder they returned to old haunts, likely that was the only welcome they would find.

'Even if Carruthers didn't have a contact inside he could find information like that from press archives or the internet.'

'When did Carruthers kill himself?'

Ashcroft tapped the screen on his phone and scrolled down. '31 March 2015.' He said. Coupland hit the redial button on his mobile, Turnbull picked up first time:

'*Sarge?*'

'When did Lee Dawson die?'

A pause as papers were shuffled around his desk. '*1 March 2015.*'

Coupland nodded to Ashcroft. 'Turnbull, get Krispy

to do a search on Dawson's death, see whether it was reported at the time.'

'*DC Timmins?*' Turnbull clarified, but the fact he'd correctly identified who Coupland was referring to meant already the nickname had stuck. '*I'll get him on to it right away,*' he said before ending the call.

Coupland started piecing the timeline together. 'I think poor little Harry in there has been telling us porkies…'

'Shall we go ba—?' Ashcroft stopped mid-sentence. Coupland was already out of the car, jacket flapping in the wind as he stomped up Sandford's driveway. He caught up with him as he banged on the front door.

'What the hell do you call this?' Sandford spluttered, using his body to block Coupland's entry. 'I'm not having you barge in here like I'm some common criminal. What do you want?'

'I want the truth!' Coupland spat. 'And this time I won't be going round the houses to get it. You'll either answer my questions or I'll bring you in for obstruction.'

Sandford reared his head back as he stared at both men on his doorstep. 'On what basis?'

'That you already knew Lee Dawson was dead yet failed to tell me that when I questioned you. Now why would you do that?' Coupland leaned in close so that his face was only inches from the retired cop.

'I didn't know he was dead!' Sandford protested, though his heart wasn't in it.

Coupland's nose was practically touching Sandford's now. 'You either cooperate with me or I go round to your son in law's place and tell him and your wife that Maria's death rests firmly on your shoulders.'

'Sarge,' Ashcroft warned, resting a hand on Coupland's arm, 'we don't know that for sure,' he said in his ear. Coupland spun round, locking eyes with the DC but his threat had already worked its magic.

'You'd better come in,' Sandford said quietly.

The front door had no sooner closed behind them than Sandford raised his arms in mitigation. 'I didn't like the little scrote, okay? Sometimes it happens like that, you don't take to someone or they rub you up the wrong way and let's not forget these are football hooligans we're talking about, not boy scouts on a day trip.'

'It was that attitude that caused Hillsborough,' Coupland said evenly, 'police treating fans like they were less than human.'

'Don't give me that politically correct bullshit!' Sandford sneered. 'Don't tell me certain folk don't get on your nerves.'

'Oh, I hate certain folk alright,' Coupland mimicked him, 'I hate killers and rapists and men that rob little old ladies, but right up there on the top of my twat list is people who waste police time. You get that?' Sandford nodded. He was a large built man, could hold his own under normal circumstances, but Coupland was twenty years younger and raging. 'So tell me what happened,' he ordered, clenching and unclenching his fists, 'the condensed version.'

Sandford hung his head. 'I first clapped eyes on Dawson before the match when I was carrying out a stop and search. He was a mouthy little sod—' he saw the look on Coupland's face and raised his hands once more, '— Fine! Fine! But there's no escaping he rubbed me up the wrong way. When he finally buggered off to the game I saw his scarf lying on the floor where I'd pushed him to the ground. I shoved it inside my jacket. God knows I had no idea what I was going to do with it. Probably would have just thrown it away but things sort of progressed.'

Coupland eyed him steadily. 'In what way?'

'After the match me and Lewis got separated from the rest of the officers escorting supporters from the ground. The crowd turned on us and Lewis wimped out, leaving me to take a pasting.' He pointed to his knee once more, just as he had during the detectives' earlier visit to his home. 'I needed a new plastic socket, pins and everything.'

'Like I give a toss,' Coupland growled.

Undeterred, Sandford continued. 'I managed to get away, limped into a multi-storey car park close to the stadium to hide. On my way in I collided with a supporter. I recognised him from previous run-ins; he was a member of one of the most feared local football gangs. He stopped and stared at me as though daring me to question him… he was carrying a knife and there was blood on it, and I didn't need to be Einstein to know what he'd do to me if I didn't play my cards right, so I told him to get out of there.'

'Who was it?'

A sigh. 'I didn't know his name, honestly. We were beat cops, weren't kept in the loop when it came to the Who's Who of Salford gangs. It didn't stop us recognising their faces, though.'

'Yet you let him go, even though you suspected he'd stabbed someone?'

Sandford didn't even blink. 'I was hardly in a position of strength, was I? I certainly didn't want to be his next victim. I let him go on his way and he let me go on mine.'

'And then you found the body?'

'Yes,' Sandford replied, only quieter now, 'and that's when it dawned on me. That I could teach that little fucker Dawson a lesson he wouldn't forget. I pulled his scarf out of my jacket and placed it beneath the body.' His eyes slid in Coupland's direction, 'Next thing I know Lewis appears from behind a parked car, tells me he'd witnessed the stabbing and had called it in. He wanted to know what I was doing with the scarf. When I told him he went ballistic, but as I reminded him, he was in no position to take the moral high ground, what with leaving me to take that beating. We were arguing the toss when Nathaniel arrived and everything just fell into place, I asked him to check for signs of life telling him I thought I could feel a pulse, next minute he spots the scarf while checking Garside over and seeing as the victim was already wearing a team scarf realised this could lead us to the killer. I left him to piece the rest of it together and hey presto, someone pulls out CCTV from the main routes into and out of all the pub car parks where we'd searched supporters that morning and lo and behold Dawson is in several shots wearing his Burberry scarf, clear as day. Further footage of him going into the stadium shows him minus the scarf. A search went out for him; Nathaniel tracked him down that evening and arrested him. My only regret was that I got carted off to the hospital; I didn't get to see the look on the little tosser's face… Lewis kept his silence over the years, well for the most part, every once in a while he'd try sounding me out to come clean but what was the point? Then after all this time I get a call from him last year, he'd read that Dawson had died shortly after his release. He said we'd ruined a young man's life and that we owed it to his memory to come clean to his family about what we'd done. "No point now is there?" I told him. I guess Lewis just couldn't live with it.'

'I guess he couldn't,' Coupland said.

Sandford regarded him irritably. 'What's the point of raking over this when you know Dawson is dead? He can't be the killer.'

'No,' Coupland said evenly, 'but he's the reason this is happening.'

Just then his mobile rang, its tone shrill amid the tension in the room. Coupland barked his name into the mouthpiece causing Krispy Kreme to stutter. '*Sarge? You wanted me to check for old articles relating to Eddie Garside's murder in '92? The Evening News ran a main feature following his death, headline:* Gang Leader Knifed in Unprovoked Attack. *The reporter claimed that Garside's own knife was still concealed in the lining of his jacket,*' Coupland noted that internal leaks were as prevalent then as they were today, '*that he was caught unawares because he never went anywhere without his foot soldiers to protect him.*'

'So his killer could have been someone he knew and trusted.'

'*As you know the local papers headlined with Dawson's back story, how his friends and work mates said he was a decent guy. Well the Echo goes on to show a picture of his 'distraught girlfriend' as the caption describes it, walking down the crown court steps following the guilty verdict.*' He paused. '*She was pregnant, Sarge.*'

'I'm on my way in,' Coupland barked, pushing Sandford out of the way to get to the door.

CHAPTER 16

Incident room, Thursday afternoon

The incident room phones were on meltdown by the time Coupland returned to the station. Krispy and DC Whitehead had been tasked with tracking down Lee Dawson's girlfriend and child. 'The girlfriend's name is Patsy Doyle,' Krispy informed Coupland when he approached his desk, 'she was interviewed by the Evening News after the trial, who had her down as living in Walkden. She gave birth to a boy at Hope Hospital on 3 September 92. I'm checking with the housing department and private landlords registered in the area to see if I can find her.'

'Good work.'

Coupland turned his attention to DC Whitehead, seated beside Krispy. 'I'm checking with the local schools to see if a boy with either of their surnames attended,' he informed him.

'Try nurseries and childminders too,' Coupland added. Whitehead nodded.

As he approached the open door to Mallender's office the DCI was already on his feet. 'I was just on my way to see you, I heard about Dawson.' He moved round to the front of his desk to perch on a corner whilst Coupland took a seat. 'So who the hell's got an axe to grind on his behalf, and while we're on the subject, what's their motive?' His eyebrows knotted together as he considered the possibilities.

'Well, I suppose I'd better fill you in on that,' Coupland responded, getting up to push the office door to.

The atmosphere in the incident room was charged. They were on the brink of tracking down a significant person of interest. Coupland didn't want to call him a killer yet, didn't want to repeat the mistakes that had started this tragedy in the first place. When they tracked Dawson's son down they would bring him in, and Coupland and Mallender would interview him. Ashcroft was sipping from a takeaway cup that he'd brought back from the canteen. He leaned over Krispy's shoulder to read something on the junior detective's desktop. A matching take-out coffee cup sat on Coupland's desk. He gave Ashcroft the thumbs up sign as he gulped the coffee down, though he made a mental note to remind him he was on sweeteners now. His phone, set to silent, was charging on his desk. He was about to check it when DC Whitehead called over. 'No joy on the schools, Sarge, childminder and nurseries have drawn a blank too.'

'Could have moved out of the area,' Coupland suggested, heading over to the bank of desks the detectives were working from, 'could hardly blame her I suppose. Widen it out to Greater Manchester.' He turned to Krispy to include him in the instruction. 'She might have been rehoused but stayed close enough to be near relatives.'

Krispy nodded, writing the new search criterion onto a pad. 'Bright kid,' Ashcroft murmured as he moved beside Coupland, 'knows his way around a computer alright.'

'Thank Christ someone does.' Coupland was all too aware of his own shortcomings in that area.

'What's going to happen to Sandford, you reckon?'

Coupland's mouth turned down at the edges as he mulled it over. 'He was a serving officer at the time of the incident. Mallender reckons Professional Standards will want to take a look at this first, but there's no doubt he'll be in prison this time next year.'

'What goes around...' Ashcroft muttered into the space between them. Yet Coupland felt no satisfaction in this. Sandford deserved to go to prison but his wife didn't deserve to be left bringing up their daughter's children single handed, for he had little faith in her son-in-law stepping up to the mark. Nathaniel Mathers was another casualty of Sandford's misdirection. He'd lost his daughter for no other reason than trusting what his colleagues told him to be true. Coupland closed his eyes; hoped to Christ they made a breakthrough soon.

'I've found her, Sarge!' Krispy called out, his face reddening at the sound of his own voice. 'The housing manager at the council called me back to say a *Pat* Doyle had moved to Davyhulme with a new partner. I've spoken to the housing association who owns the flat she lives in and they've given me her contact details.'

'Halle-bloody-lujah.' Coupland only just resisted the urge to ruffle Krispy's hair. 'You go for it, son,' he instructed, watching Krispy dial the number, holding his breath while he waited for it to pick up. The phone rang out. The young DC tried once more but the outcome was the same.

'I'll go round there,' Ashcroft offered, writing Patsy's address and postcode down on a post-it-note.

'Take Turnbull with you,' Coupland instructed, 'he's due time off checking through archives for good behaviour. Remember, no heroics,' he added firmly, 'call for back up the moment you think you need it. I'll speak to DCI Mallender, get some cars on standby.'

The address Krispy had given them was a nondescript housing association flat on the outskirts of Davyhulme within easy reach of a primary school. Ashcroft pulled up outside, climbed out of the car quickly and rang the buzzer.

Turnbull preferred to take his time, checking out the area around him. 'There's no one home,' he said after Ashcroft's third attempt went unanswered.

'I can see that,' Ashcroft replied irritably; some part of him was hoping to reel in the killer without DS Coupland by his side. He returned to the car, drumming his fingers on the steering wheel while Turnbull meandered to the end of the street. When the pavement gave way to road he turned, slowing his pace as he returned to the car.

Ashcroft lowered the driver's window: 'In your own time,' he called out, turning on the ignition to show his impatience.

'I think you'll find,' Turnbull said, his voice low and undulating, 'that school has just finished for the day. Maybe if we wait a few minutes longer we'll be in luck.'

Ashcroft narrowed his eyes but he was more annoyed at himself for not working that out than anything else. 'Smartarse,' he muttered, switching the engine off before leaning back in his seat to see if Know All was right.

After a moment or two a couple of women with small children in tow came into view as they entered the street. One woman was in her twenties and of Asian origin; she held the hand of a small boy as she crossed the road, waving to her companion as she let herself into one of the properties opposite. The other woman was white, early forties, accompanying a girl who was walking in front, already embarrassed about being seen with a parent. The woman glanced at Turnbull who by now was leaning against the car door as though shooting the breeze with its occupant. He nodded, waited while she made her way her way to the main door Ashcroft had tried ten minutes earlier before slapping his hand on the car's roof and saying 'we're on,' with just a touch more smugness than Ashcroft thought it deserved.

Turnbull reached the front door just as the woman tried closing it behind her. Startled, she looked from him to Ashcroft, who held his warrant card aloft. 'What is it?' she gasped. The child had moved to her side during this exchange, happy to engage now something strange was afoot.

'Pat Doyle?'

The woman nodded, her arm snaking around the girl's shoulders.

'We need to speak to your son, love, do you know where he is?'

The woman blinked. 'I don't have a son,' she squeezed the girl's shoulders, 'there must be some mistake.'

'No mistake love.' Turnbull reached for his mobile then scrolled down for the email Krispy had circulated earlier with the newspaper article reporting on Lee Dawson's trial attached as a scanned copy. The photograph was grainy, but when he zoomed in on the pregnant woman leaving court after the verdict there was no mistaking it was her. He held it out for Pat to see. There were lines around her eyes now, and her hair may have been thinner than the woman's in the photo, but the glare she gave the camera back then was the same glare she gave the detectives now.

'Let me see,' the little girl said, but the woman held her back. 'Please Mum,' the girl begged. Sighing the woman reached into her bag for her purse, pulling out two fifty pence pieces. 'Go and get yourself some sweets from the corner shop, but mind you don't speak to anyone on the way. Straight back, you hear?' The girl didn't need telling twice; she snatched the money, running down the path before her mother had time to change her mind. 'You'd better come in,' Pat said, climbing the stairs to her flat on the first floor.

The place was sparsely furnished; the only photographs were the cardboard framed school photos charting the growth of her daughter every year since nursery. In the open plan living room/kitchen there was a small television and a wooden framed settee, a crocheted blanket over the back of it. Pat followed Turnbull's gaze. 'I brought him home in that shawl,' she said, 'couldn't bear to be parted with it… afterwards.' Ashcroft leaned against the breakfast bar where a radio was perched. A jute shopping bag lay on its side, beside it shopping yet to be put away: an unsliced loaf in a paper bag, a carton of eggs, a tub of supermarket own brand margarine beside it. The place smelled ever so slightly of damp. Pat turned to face them. 'You've got until she gets back.'

'Fair enough,' Turnbull agreed.

'How did you find me?'

'Wasn't difficult,' Ashcroft shrugged. 'Look, I know this isn't easy for you, but we're only interested in the boy.'

'Why?'

'Slow walker, is she, your daughter?' Turnbull countered.

The corners of the woman's mouth turned up in a smile, albeit an awkward one that didn't make it to her eyes. 'Fine,' she shrugged, moving to the window which looked out on the street below. 'You know about his dad then?' She kept her back to them as she asked this.

'We do.'

'He was innocent,' she told them, half turning. 'I knew Lee better than anyone, back then anyway, and if he'd killed Eddie Garside he would have told me. Even if that meant asking me to keep it a secret afterwards.'

'You didn't wait for him though?'

'We were going through a rough patch when he was arrested, we wouldn't have stayed together even if they'd let him go.'

'And the boy?'

A pause. 'I called him Lee after his dad. I gave him up when he was six months old. What choice did I have? I didn't have two pennies to rub together back then, my parents had their hands full with my younger brothers and sisters. There were times when I couldn't even feed him.'

Ashcroft looked at her hard. 'Couldn't you get help?'

She looked away. 'I'd started drinking, wouldn't have accepted help even if it had been offered. You've seen this place, I know it's not much but it's a palace compared to where I used to live.'

'And you've the girl now?'

Her face lit up at the mention of her daughter. 'Still with her father, too.'

Ashcroft's gaze swept over the counter top, the cheap cans of supermarket beer waiting to be put into the fridge. 'They're for him, not me,' she said sharply.

'I take it your partner doesn't know about your son?'

She shook her head. 'What was the point? It would have meant dredging up the past.'

'And you wouldn't have come out of it looking too well.'

A sour look passed over her face. 'I suppose if you put it like that, no.'

Ashcroft stepped out into the hallway. 'I need to make a call,' was all he said.

Pat waited until he was out of earshot. 'What's eating him?'

'We need to track down your son urgently. He might be in a lot of trouble.'

She regarded the older DC shrewdly. 'What kind of trouble?'

'The worst kind.'

There was a pause. Through the window her daughter could be seen walking back along the street, a slim bar of chocolate already open and half demolished. Pat hesitated as though making her mind up about something. She turned to face the detective full on. 'Then you'll want to hear this,' she said gravely.

Coupland was long enough in the tooth to know that the more you wanted something to run smoothly the less chance there was of it happening that way. The likelihood of Ashcroft returning with an address for Lee Dawson's son never mind turning up with the killer himself was always going to be a long shot; he was probably hiding out somewhere plotting to go on the run – or his next murder. But the call he'd just taken from Ashcroft – telling him that the boy, named Lee after his father, had gone into care as a baby meant the investigation had taken a huge step back while they relied on social services to help them track him down. Mallender had already made a call to the head of Salford Council's Children and Families department requesting that full cooperation be given to the investigation, reminding them that now wasn't the time to obstruct any enquiries by referencing client confidentiality and data protection. Mallender had insisted that he make that call himself, reminding Coupland that while his strengths were many, diplomacy wasn't one of them. Coupland had put up no resistance, conceding that on this the DCI was right. The incident room was full to capacity with call handlers and officers – both uniformed and CID, working through actions that made Coupland hope they got a result soon, for the sake of morale. An uneasiness settled on his shoulders.

Ashcroft and Turnbull said they'd be back by now, he found himself thinking.

CHAPTER 17

He was surprised at the pressure he needed to exert to pierce her flesh. He'd used a kitchen knife, made for cutting through skin and bone but even so it stalled on entry, and she'd looked at him then like he was a loser, that even in the process of killing he hadn't got what it took. That's what he thought her look meant anyway, it could have been fear. He'd got it right in the end though, and he'd stood back fascinated, watching blood pool around her as her face took on an entirely different look.

Ashcroft frowned when Turnbull put his head round Pat's front door, calling him back into her flat. 'We need to go.'

He raised his hands palm upwards as though saying, *What the fuck?*

Turnbull stood his ground. 'You need to see this.' He widened his eyes in response. There was something in his tone that put Ashcroft on alert. Curious, he followed Turnbull back into Pat's living room. There was a shoebox on the breakfast bar, an old one by the look of it, *Dolcis* in large letters across the lid.

'Tell him what you told me,' Turnbull prompted. Pat's mouth became downturned once more. 'My son came to see me not long ago.' She swiped a strand of hair that fell across her face behind her ear. 'It hadn't taken him long to find me, it's not like I was hiding from him – more the press and the members of Eddie Garside's family who thought it was okay to put dog shit through my door. I just wanted a quiet life…'

'And then he showed up.'

'Yeah, but it wasn't the shock you're imagining. I suppose I'd always hoped he'd come find me… only it didn't quite work out the way I'd pictured in my head all these years.'

'What do you mean?'

'He wasn't really interested in me, just his dad.'

'What did he want to know?'

'He'd found out from his adopted father that his dad was in jail. The selfish bastard hadn't bothered telling him much else and understandably he was distressed. He came looking for me to get answers.'

Something she said jarred with Ashcroft. 'Help me out here, you called his adopted father a selfish bastard, why would you say that?'

'Because he knew Lee's dad swore blind he was innocent yet he chose not to mention that when he told him about his past.'

'You're very informed about a complete stranger,' Ashcroft observed.

A sigh, 'It was a private adoption, okay? I knew the couple I'd left him with.'

'Right,' Ashcroft said urgently, 'you really do need to start at the beginning…' He was thinking of the call he'd made to Sergeant Coupland, wondered whether he'd sent him on a wild goose chase. Unable to stand still, he paced around the room as he listened to Pat.

'I worked a couple of days a week in the local newsagents close to where Lee and I lived. The owners had a daughter, Karen, a couple of years older than me, married. We hadn't been friends as such at school but when I started working for her parents we started to chat when she came into the shop and she'd confided that she and her husband had been trying for a baby only he must've been firing blanks or something because nothing had happened. She'd been a little put out when I fell pregnant by accident – I hadn't been with Lee all that long but she got over it and everything was fine.'

'Until your boyfriend was sent down for murder and you turned to drink,' Ashcroft added for her.

'Pretty much,' Pat agreed. 'By then I was struggling on my own in a run-down flat and I think we both came to the same conclusion round about the same time: Karen and her husband could provide a far better home for a baby than I ever could. She was very good to me, didn't judge me or anything. She knew how hard it was for me to give my baby up – I agreed I would move away so they could raise him with a free hand on the condition she and I kept in touch.'

Behind them the living room door opened to reveal the little girl standing in the doorway. 'What you got there, Mum?' she enquired, her eyes locked onto the shoebox.

'Mind your own beeswax,' the woman snapped before relenting when she saw the girl's stricken face. 'Why don't you go to your room and play on your computer for half an hour?'

'I've not done my homework yet,' the girl objected, keeping her smile in check before retreating in case her mother had time to change her mind. 'Thanks Mum!' she called out, padding down the hall. Pat waited for the sound of a bedroom door closing before she continued.

'The only thing was Karen didn't want her husband finding out that we were still in contact, he'd felt it would

280

be better for everyone concerned if we cut all ties, so we came to an agreement that once a year she would write to me and update me on Lee's progress. She kept her word, every once in a while a card would arrive in the post from her – she used my sister's address – stopped any unwanted questions from this end.' She inclined her head in the direction of the hallway and the sound of music coming from her daughter's room. 'I kept them in here.' She pointed to the shoebox.

Ashcroft moved towards the breakfast bar and peered into it. There were a number of greeting cards inside, most with no message on the front, just a picture of a flower or a sunset. He was about to reach for one when his hand brushed against a laminated pink card with tiny baby footprints on it. He picked the card up to read the message beneath the image: *Danielle, Too precious to stay, 3 September 1992.* Ashcroft frowned.

'I was pregnant with twins,' Pat explained, her voice low, arms wrapped around her middle, 'The girl was stillborn, nothing could be done for her… it's what tipped me over the edge I think.'

She wasn't the only one, Ashcroft thought. 'Did your son know this?'

Patsy became defensive. 'Not till he came to see me, but I was hardly going to hide it from him, he'd had enough secrets to stomach over the years…'

Ashcroft looked at Turnbull but he was already reaching for his phone. 'I'll let the boss know,' he said, turning his back on them as he hit the call button. Ashcroft sifted through the other cards in the box, lifting them out one by one. Inside the first one, the brief message said, *My first birthday*, accompanied by a photograph of a chubby baby sitting in his high chair, laughing for the camera.

'Robbed of his dad and then of his sister, hardly the best start in life, was it?' Pat went on. Ashcroft said nothing as he lifted another card, this time the photograph was of a small boy with a rucksack on his back that was far too big for him, the handwritten message said: *First day at school.* Pat's voice became anxious. 'Maybe you can't change the course of events, no matter how hard you try.'

Ashcroft selected another card as he glanced up at her. 'How did he react when you told him about his sister?'

'How do you think? Though it was nothing compared to his reaction when I told him about his father. Can you imagine, finding out your old man had been released from jail only to discover he'd died while you were serving your own prison sentence? How messed up is that?' Ashcroft opened the card he was holding and slid out the photo. His breath caught in his throat. 'You don't know the half of it,' he said quietly.

CHAPTER 18

Krispy rolled his eyes at Coupland as he relayed his phone call to the council's social services team whilst waiting on hold for the person dealing with this request to come back to him. 'Says her computer system's down at the moment which means she'll need to requisition paper copies.'

Coupland could feel his blood surging through his veins. 'Tell her to—' he stopped mid-sentence; one look at Ashcroft as he hurried into the incident room told him they had a serious problem. 'You took your time,' he barked, 'I saw Turnbull's missed call, tried ringing you back but...' Already something inside him was pulsing.

Ashcroft moved towards him, pulling a photograph out of his pocket. He thrust it under Coupland's nose as he drew level, Turnbull behind him grim faced. 'It's a picture of Pat Doyle's son.'

Coupland's brow creased as he regarded both men but took the photograph anyway, conscious of Quinlan's team looking over in his direction. Many had started to pull on jackets, catching each other's eye before leaving the room. Ashcroft was speaking, but his words were drowned out by a noise inside Coupland's head that resembled radio static. 'You need to look at the photo, Sarge.' He held the photo steady for Coupland to see. There was something familiar about the teenage boy grinning for the camera. He was dressed for a wedding yet he seemed too young to be the groom, or the best man for that matter, Coupland studied the boy's face, turning the photo over to see if anything had been written on the reverse: *Vinny's school dance, 2009*.

His hands began to shake.

He was staring at Amy's boyfriend.

'Vinny's his adopted name,' Turnbull added as Coupland tried to steady himself. He could no longer feel the floor beneath his feet. He opened his mouth to object but Turnbull was ahead of him. 'He's Pat's son alright, there's no mistake. The couple who adopted him didn't want any reminders of his past so they changed his name.' Coupland continued to stare at the picture, his hand moving instinctively to his neck to loosen a tie that wasn't there.

'I arrested him following a brawl he had in a bar. He got sent down because of me,' his voice came out like a croak. Something occurred to him. 'When was he released?' Yet already he knew the answer.

'Not until after his dad had died,' Ashcroft responded.

The room seemed smaller now. Like it had run out of air.

Ashcroft's voice was urgent. 'We phoned ahead to DCI Mallender, he's despatched units to Amy's college and Vinny's flat in case he's still there.' Coupland tried to nod but it didn't feel right. He felt detached from his body, as though he was looking down on himself from above. He could see his stunned face, could hear his heart thudding beneath his shirt. So that's where Quinlan's men were going, to pick up Vincent Underwood because they knew Coupland would be in no fit state to. Or rather he couldn't be trusted when he did catch up with him.

He doubted he'd be much use to anyone right now; his legs felt leaden, his breath came in gasps, he could barely string two thoughts together in his head, but he uttered one word.

'Amy…'

Reaching for his mobile he dialled her number, all too aware of the bad terms on which they'd parted.

'Come on, love, pick up pick up pick up…'

No answer.

He spoke into the phone: 'Amy love, it's Dad, call me. Please.'

'She can't be a target,' Turnbull attempted, oblivious to the warning look Ashcroft sent in his direction. 'If she'd been a target she'd have been dead by now…' It was like standing in a vacuum, Coupland's life force was being sucked right out of him.

'He was avenging his father's imprisonment,' Ashcroft told him. 'If it hadn't been for the cop who stitched Dawson up, Vinny would have got to know his Dad. You played no part in that.'

His words seem to galvanise Coupland. 'You're wrong! He got sent down because of me, remember? And while he was in jail his father died. Of course he blames me. I'm just another cop who kept him apart from his old man.' All the sly glances and the goading he'd sent Coupland's way when he'd been round to the house, he'd been planning his revenge from the moment of his release. Seeking Amy out and what? Saving her until last?

'I need to find my daughter…'

'A patrol car will be at college any minute,' Ashcroft reassured him. 'Best thing you can do is wait for them to radio in that she's safe.'

Just then Mallender appeared in the doorway, his face grey like a corpse. As Coupland watched the DCI move purposefully in his direction he was aware that Ashcroft and Turnbull had positioned themselves either side of him. Fear washed over him like an incoming tide. He'd felt the same way that very first time waiting outside the consultant's room with Lynn. Like his world was about to fork in two.

'There's no sign of anyone at Vincent Underwood's flat,' Mallender told them, 'nor at the college,' a pause, 'he hasn't been in work today—'

'—and Amy?'

Another pause. 'Amy phoned in sick.' Mallender looked uneasy.

'WHAT?' Coupland yelled, lunging towards him. 'For Christ's sake spit it out!'

'There were signs of a struggle at the flat.'

Coupland felt his colon contract. He looked across the incident room into CID. 'What are you not telling me?' He grabbed Mallender by the jacket, his fist curling around his lapel,

'Easy now, Sarge,' Ashcroft cautioned, reaching for Coupland's arm and signalling for Turnbull to do the same. Coupland's head was level with the DCI.

'Why did you despatch so many officers to do a location check, what's going on?'

Mallender wouldn't look at him. 'The body of a young woman has been found by the canal…there's no ID…' Coupland became aware of two things at that point: the static in his head went up several notches, and the only thing keeping him off the floor were the two pairs of hands gripping onto him.

CHAPTER 19

Police vehicles threaded their way along Worsley Road, following the flashing blue and whites of the lead car. Ashcroft was at the wheel. Turnbull was in the passenger seat beside him, casting worried looks in Coupland's direction. Coupland, sat in the back with Mallender, stared out of the car window as traffic parted like the Red Sea for the convoy of police cars racing through the town. The patrol cars were doing that for his benefit, he knew that; blues and twos were intended for rescue, not recovery.

Several police cars were already parked along Bridgewater Way. As he approached them Ashcroft took a sharp left, drove along the path as far as he could. A police van had been deliberately parked across it, blocking further access. Something visceral rose up in Coupland, an urgency borne of fear as he unbuckled his seat belt and threw the car door open.

'Kevin, wait!' Mallender called after him. 'Do you have a recent photo of Amy we can use?' His voice had a tremor in it, didn't carry as far as it normally would but Coupland wasn't listening, was already out of the patrol car, pushing through the uniformed officers positioned at the foot of the canal path. There was a rushing noise in his head, like his radio frequency button had been turned to crazy. He was aware that Ashcroft was behind him, calling out his name, but they both knew even if he caught up with him he wouldn't be able to hold him back.

Amy. Dead.

The two words he feared most in the world. Coupland's heart hammered in his chest as he propelled himself forward. At the far end of the canal bank a tent had been erected to shield the body from prying eyes. He moved towards it. Above him a helicopter circled overhead. Coupland stopped short. 'Please don't let it be her,' he whispered, before stepping inside.

The forensic team milling about inside the tent did a double take upon his arrival. The low hum of forensic procedure, the scraping, clipping and bagging turned to awkward silence. Those who didn't know Coupland knew something was afoot, took one look at the fat angry detective standing in their midst and followed the lead from their colleagues, keeping heads low, focussing on the task in front of them. Quinlan had been speaking to one of his team but when he clapped eyes on Coupland he moved away sharply, stepping towards him intending to bar his entry. His CSI suit rustled as he approached, his hand already out to block Coupland's path. 'You can't be here,' he hissed, his eyes darting behind him as though seeking reinforcements. 'For the love of God, man, let someone else do this.'

Without slowing his pace Coupland shoved him out of the way. Time seemed to stop around him. The only thing blocking his view of the victim was Benson, who had moved from his crouching position beside the body when he sensed the tension behind him. He turned to face Coupland. His overshoes were slick with blood. His bodysuit had smears where he'd knelt by the victim's head. He shifted his position to shield Coupland from the worst of it. Coupland held up a finger which he pointed in Benson's direction. 'Not a word,' he threatened, waiting until the pathologist stepped aside. Several pairs of eyes turned in his direction as he moved towards the body.

Slowly.

One heavy step at a time.

And then when he saw what the victim was wearing something inside him shattered. That's when it dawned on him. The reason everyone was staring was the sound he was making.

Amy had pestered him to buy her a designer top on holiday. 'Think of the money you're saving if you buy it me here,' she'd wheedled, 'it can be my birthday present.'

'You've just had your birthday,' he reminded her.

'Next year's then,' she'd grinned. He'd given in. The top was black and silver with some daft logo that showed it was expensive. She wore it with leggings that Coupland said looked like tights and ballet style pumps from Primark.

The same as the victim was wearing.

Coupland hauled in a breath. Mallender and Ashcroft appeared by his side, regarding him warily. His breathing was shallow and he clutched at his chest.

'Is it Amy, Kevin?'

Coupland dragged his gaze up to the victim's face, then lurched outside the tent to be sick.

CHAPTER 20

Relief washed over him in waves. His arms and chest pulsated. Ashcroft had followed him outside, waiting for a reaction he could relay back to the others; Coupland shook his head at him to let him know it wasn't Amy. Ashcroft closed his eyes, letting out a long breath before returning to the tent, his voice carrying though the thin material, 'It isn't her…'

Coupland's breathing was irregular; he gulped for air like a drowning man. Reaching for his cigarettes he moved to beyond the crime scene tape and lit up, hitting the speed dial number for Amy as he did so. Still no answer. Where the hell was she?

Ashcroft stepped out of the tent once more, glancing up and down the canal as though looking for someone. He spotted Coupland by the cordon, made a beeline straight to him. 'You OK?'

'I've been better,' Coupland grunted. 'I need to find her.'

Ashcroft nodded. 'Forensics are fast tracking the DNA samples taken but it has to be our guy – only what's his motive this time?'

Unable to process anything beyond the location of his daughter Coupland turned away. 'She's wearing Amy's clothes, I'm certain of it. Why would he make her do that?'

Ashcroft didn't hesitate: 'To scare the shit out of you.'

It worked then. 'I'm needed back inside.' Ashcroft turned to make his way back to the tent when his phone rang making them both jump. The control room. He glanced at Coupland before putting the call onto loud speaker after hitting the answer button.

'We checked out Vince Underwood's place like you asked. Although we couldn't find the Sarge's girl we did find a woman's bag with photo ID belonging to a Vanessa Millar... I've scanned it and sent it over in a text.' Ashcroft ended the call. A moment later his phone pinged. He tapped the screen to open the photo.

'It's her.' He inclined his head in the direction of the tent while holding up his screen towards Coupland but he declined to look, her features already seared onto his brain. 'But what I don't get is how the hell she fits into this?'

Coupland reared back his head. 'I think I know,' he said, his pulse quickening as he recalled the conversation they'd had with Harry Sandford. 'Get back onto control,' he instructed Ashcroft, backing away, 'tell them Vince's flat needs preserving as a crime scene, there'll be a laptop there, get it over to DC Bateman. Amy said Vince was studying online, I reckon instead of course notes we'll find an email account on there with a thread of conversations with Kathleen Williams.' Coupland remembered the night he'd put Vinny under surveillance, the night of the college burglary – and Kathleen Williams' murder. Vinny said he'd met the men who'd accompanied him on the robbery in prison, he never did say what he was getting in return for getting them into the college – the loan of their van perhaps, to follow Maria Wellbeck and 'accidentally' bump into Kathleen Williams' car? Maybe he'd used it to follow them all, what's more anonymous than a grimy white van? And to think they had him on camera speaking to Sharon Mathers outside the Dog and Duck. Amy hadn't helped matters, claiming to have been with him, but then if she'd been asleep, or thought he was in another room working...

'Make sure the back of his property is secured as well,' he added.

'You reckon he slipped out the back way while I was parked out front the other night?' Ashcroft was on the same wavelength.

'I wouldn't put anything past him,' Coupland said gravely.

Ashcroft reached for his phone. 'What do you want me to do?'

'Go speak to Vince's adoptive parents, see if they know where he might have gone to ground.' His hand reached out for the patrol car's keys.

Ashcroft looked up at him in surprise. 'Where are you going?'

'I'm going to deliver the death message to Vanessa Millar's parents, find out how the hell they fit into this.'

Ashcroft regarded him warily. 'Fine,' he said, reaching into his pocket, 'but when I've finished up I'll come find you.'

*

Vince Underwood's adoptive parents lived in a detached house on a cul-de-sac in Boothstown. A double-fronted property with a covered porch and a painted white bench beneath one of the large downstairs windows. Ashcroft wondered what they made of Vinny's current digs. 'Mrs

Underwood?'

The woman who answered the door called out for her husband when Ashcroft showed her his warrant card. 'It's okay,' he attempted, 'I just need to ask you a few questions.' He wanted to reassure her but didn't want to lie, let her believe there was nothing to worry about when their world was about to be turned upside down, only not in the way they were imagining, given the stricken look on the woman's face.

She was joined in the hallway by a slim built man, a V-neck jumper over a checked shirt. 'What is it?' He addressed the question to his wife as though it wasn't his job to deal with strangers who came calling.

The woman's hand's flew to her throat. 'Police.'

*

Coupland pulled into the parking bay opposite Swinton shopping precinct and checked the address control had texted over to him. 'If I'm right it's the one above the estate agents,' he said to the female police constable Mallender had insisted accompany him when he informed Vanessa Millar's parents of the reason she didn't come home last night. They lived in a two bedroomed flat above a row of shops. She'd been reported missing in the last hour; it wasn't unusual for her to stay over at a mate's but she'd normally text and let her mum know, only this time she hadn't heard a word from her. 'Probably hoped she'd turn up in her own sweet time,' Coupland muttered as he rang the doorbell, 'not like they'd be in any hurry to engage our services.'

The WPC considered this. 'Because he's been inside?'

Coupland only had time to nod as the door was flung

open by a woman who looked as though she hadn't slept. The woman was small with bird-like features and a nose just a smidgeon out of proportion to her face. She wore a thigh length tunic over skinny jeans and a long chain around her neck which she began to fiddle with. One look at Coupland's face had her yelling for her husband.

*

Ashcroft stood his ground on the doorstep, resisting the urge to put his foot over the threshold before they invited him in. 'I think it's better if I speak to you inside,' he repeated. A look passed between the couple before stepping back to grant him entry.

'I wanted to speak to you about your son,' he began.

'Adopted son,' the man corrected. His tone was clipped, his eyes narrowing at the reference to Vince. 'What's he done now?' he sighed.

Ashcroft turned his back to him, addressing the woman instead: 'When did you see him last, Mrs Underwood?'

A pause. 'We haven't seen him since he was released,' she said meekly, her fingers running back and forth over the links of a small pendant around her neck.

'He's not welcome,' came the sour voice behind him.

'How so?'

The man regarded Ashcroft as though he were simple. 'The shame he's brought on us, going to prison.'

The woman's hands flew to her mouth as though holding back her response, claims and accusations better left unsaid. 'Come through, please.' She led the way into a large kitchen, modern units with gadgets on top that Ashcroft had seen in department stores though he'd never quite fathomed their use. 'Can I get you a drink?'

She moved towards a coffee machine already on, placed a mug beneath its nozzle.

'For God's sake, Karen, can't you see he needs to get on?'

'I'm fine, honestly.' Ashcroft waved away her offer. 'We just need to find your son.'

Karen stopped fussing and turned to face the DC, all trace of hospitality gone. 'What's he done?'

Her husband slapped his hand down hard on the counter top. 'Jesus wept! Can't you see it's serious, woman? You don't get plain-clothed officers turning up for joy riding!'

'He's not done that for years!' she snapped, fixing him with a look. 'He managed to stay out of trouble—'

'—Yeah, go and ask the bloke eating his meals through a straw, I'm sure he'll vouch for his good behaviour!'

Ashcroft's head moved from one side to the other as the pair parried words. 'Is it any wonder he reacted the way he did!' Karen cried, rounding on her husband. 'We should have told him about his father years ago but no, we had to do it your way, had to keep his past a secret. Was it any wonder he got himself arrested?'

Ashcroft raised his hand to silence them, before turning to the husband. 'Did something happen at home the night he attacked his victim?'

Karen's husband harrumphed into his chest, 'Nothing of any consequence,' he said, avoiding his wife's eye. Karen's eyebrows shot into her hairline. 'Okay, finding out about his dad out of the blue like that was probably a shock but to react the way he did—'

'—What, going out and getting bladdered as a way of solving problems? I wonder where he gets that from…'

'There you go again, any excuse to have a dig at me.'

The woman put her hands to her face and sighed. 'It isn't all about you, Jerry.' She blinked then, as though remembering Ashcroft was still there. 'What do you want to know?' she asked eventually.

'I'd like it if you could show me his old room.'

'Manage that on your own, can you?' Jerry shot at his wife, while reaching for an anorak from a peg by the front door, then turning to the DC, 'unless you think I can help you with anything?'

Ashcroft shoved his hands deep into his pockets lest they found themselves around the pompous prick's neck. 'I'd very much doubt it, sir,' he muttered.

Vince's old bedroom was on the first floor at the back of the house, looking onto the play area of a family restaurant over the road. The single bed had been stripped, an off-white duvet folded on top of it. Karen stared out of the window, indicating the driveway below where a car door slammed shut. 'He wanted to redecorate this room while Vinny was in prison, as though he could paint him out of our lives but I put my foot down on that.'

There was a backbone there, hidden beneath the downtrodden doormat. This got him thinking. 'When did you really last see Vinny?'

Karen dropped her gaze for a couple of beats but when she looked up there was a challenge in her eye. 'He's got himself a place close to where he works, up at the college. I go round once a week to give the place a tidy, take him a bit of shopping, that's all. No harm is there? Though better my husband doesn't know.'

Ashcroft nodded. 'You mentioned an argument before he went into town that night and got arrested, what was it about?'

'He and his dad hadn't been getting on for a while; it was though Vinny couldn't put a foot right. Truth was his dad had never been as keen on the idea of adoption as I'd been, he never said it out loud, but over the years he's made his position clear. Put-downs, snide comments, like he was jealous of any attention I gave him. Vinny going off the rails gave him an excuse to stay on his back. Then one night they were going at it again when out of the blue Jerry drops the bombshell. 'Glad you're not mine,' he shouts, 'the way you're going you'll end up inside like your old man.'

'Vinny thought he was joking at first, he looked at me to see if there was any truth in it,' her voice began to wobble, 'and I suppose my face gave it away, next thing he slammed out.' Off on a bender and a run in with a stranger as angry as he was, next thing he's up on a charge of GBH.

'When he came out of jail he wanted to come back here but his dad wouldn't entertain it. I helped him find the place that he's in now.' She looked at Ashcroft steadily. 'I'm helping out with the rent too.'

'Did he ask you about his father's past?'

Karen nodded. 'I told him what little I remembered. He asked me if I knew where his real mum was and I didn't want to lie anymore; there'd been enough secrets to last a lifetime, so I told him where she'd moved to.'

'When was this?'

'About a month ago.'

'He isn't at work today, any idea where he might be?'

A shrug. 'He's seeing some girl, I got that much out of him last time we spoke, maybe he's with her…' That was what Ashcroft feared. Karen hesitated, 'You might want these…' she sighed; opening the built-in wardrobe she lifted a manila file from the top shelf which she handed to him. 'He asked me to look after them the last time I was round at his place.'

Ashcroft peered inside before moving to the stripped bed and upending the contents of the file onto the mattress. Newspaper cuttings and printouts of online articles about his father's trial fanned out before them.

'He said his birth mother had given him the original cuttings and it got him thinking about a conversation he'd had with a fellow prisoner while he'd been in jail.'

'Did he say what?'

Karen shook her head. 'Said he didn't want to worry me. He was adamant his dad was telling the truth though, about his innocence, "Without a shadow of doubt," he said it just like that, as though he was party to something the rest of us were in the dark about.'

Ashcroft pulled out his phone. 'I need to make a call,' he told her.

CHAPTER 21

While Jonny Millar paced the living room floor like a caged animal, his wife's screams could be heard through the paper-thin walls. There was no ebb and flow to the sound, just a constant wail, like an animal in distress. She'd cried out for her sister when Coupland had broken the news, the WPC making the call that ten minutes later had a bottle blonde banging on the front door to be let in. The women were together in the main bedroom, the sister working her way through the couple's address book while the WPC made tea no one wanted. Coupland watched Millar fight emotions he had wrestled with himself less than an hour before. Whereas he'd had a reprieve, Millar's worst fear had just come true. 'I'm sorry for your loss, Jonny,' he began, 'but I do need to ask you some questions—'

Millar's head jerked back as he glared at Coupland, '—NO WAY!' he stormed, 'You're never going to ask me what I was doing when she was killed are you?' Foamed spit gathered in the corners of his mouth like a rabid dog. 'You can't go accusing me of this! Surely to God…'

'No, Jonny,' Coupland cut in quickly, 'but I do need to find out how you know Vince Underwood.'

Jonny's brows knotted together as he stared at Coupland in confusion. 'Vinny? He was in the nick the same time as me. What's this got to do wi—?'

'—What can you tell me about him?' Coupland cut in

once more.

A shrug. 'He's no more than a kid, reminded me of myself twenty-odd years ago. He didn't get on with his old man but then neither did I. I felt sorry for him I suppose, took him under my wing a bit. Why? Do you think he had something to do with this?' Millar's confusion gave way to something else entirely. Without warning he punched the wall beside Coupland's head, his face a vicious mask, 'Because if he did…'

Coupland grabbed Millar's arm, holding it at bay until the tension eased out of it. 'I don't have time for this Jonny,' he warned, just as his phone rang. He yanked it out of his pocket with his free hand. It was Ashcroft. 'What?' he spat. '*Vince's adopted mother says he met someone in prison who proved his dad was inno—*' Coupland terminated the call, grinding his teeth together as he tightened his grip on Millar's arm.

'Now shut up and listen, I need to know exactly what you said to Vince Underwood to make him want to get back at you this way.'

Millar stared at Coupland as he thought through the implication of his words. Coupland released his grip but stayed within grabbing distance in case he made a run for it, the last thing he needed was a vigilante on his hands.

'I didn't say anything to upset him…' Millar shook his head slowly as he spoke. 'I told you, we got on well together. I took him under my wing! You know what old lags are like, boasting about our past to the next generation, well he was wet behind the ears, and more than willing to listen. I was an armed robber getting to the end of my first sentence behind bars after a lifetime as a career criminal. I'd not done so badly, all told. I used to laugh with him about the crimes I'd got away with.' His face drained of colour as something occurred to him.

'Sweet Jesus,' he whispered, before collapsing into a chair.

The Millars' GP arrived to find Coupland leaning over Jonny, one hand resting on the man's shoulder as though offering reassurance. 'Does he need a sedative too?' the GP asked, looking around the room for Millar's wife.

'She's through here,' the bottle blonde called out as she stepped into the hallway, black streaks down her face where her mascara had run.

'Don't worry about him, Doc,' Coupland said, nodding at his charge, 'the duty doc'll give him something to take the edge off once we take him down to the station. Now if you don't mind…' he said pointedly, ' I'm about to take down a confession, or have I got the wrong end of the stick here, Jonny?'

Millar bowed his head, rubbing his hands over the stubble on his chin. 'Fine.' He puffed out a breath, waited for his sister-in-law to escort the doctor through to his wife.

'I was a football casual,' he began once he was sure they were alone, 'you know, back in the day like. I went around with a local gang, we all dressed a certain way, followed the same team, basically beat the shit out of anyone who wasn't just like us. It was all about showing how far we were prepared to go to prove our loyalty, and it was always about the violence. I'd been a lucky little so 'n so, never got caught shoplifting, got away with breaking and entering in my teens, always came away better off during our weekly match day punch ups. I wanted to move up the ranks, though, but to do that you had to prove yourself. I was too impatient for that, I wanted the top spot.'

'Eddie Garside's spot?'

A nod. From the hallway came the sound of a toilet flushing and moments later the WPC entered the room. She was about to say something but the look on Coupland's face silenced her. 'So what did you do?' Coupland prompted.

'We'd had a run in before a derby game with one of the local United crews, our paths crossed again when we were being escorted from the stadium. I saw a chance to get rid of Garside and at the same time stir up a bit of trouble with the opposition. Like I said, there was nothing like a good ruck after a game, get the old adrenaline going. It couldn't have gone any sweeter, the crowd surged and before the cops realised what was happening we'd broken through their barrier and were going at it hammer and tongs with this firm. I signalled to Eddie to leg it into this multi-storey car park on Oldham Street to get away from the cops. They'd sent reinforcements by that time but we managed to slip away. I kept a knife in the lining of my coat; I pulled it out and stabbed him.' On a nod from Coupland the WPC stepped into the hallway to radio for another unit to come and take Millar to the station. 'The weirdest thing happened, though,' he continued, 'when I'd done the deed I turned and ran and almost collided with one of your lot, only he didn't seem to give a toss that I had a knife in my hand. He was limping, he looked like he'd been given a doing himself and I guess he was trying to find somewhere to lay low; either way I seemed to be the least of his problems.'

'What did you do?'

'I got out of the way sharpish, kept on running until I

joined the crowd as it surged by the car park. Ten minutes later there's an ambulance trying to make its way through with motorbike cops riding shotgun. I reckoned it was only a matter of time before the law came knocking for me – I mean, the copper had taken a damn good look at me, yet next thing this other kid gets lifted for the murder and before you know it he's banged up. I could hardly say anything in his defence without implicating myself, so…'

'So you thought you'd leave the poor sap to rot in jail while you lived the life that should have been his.'

'Just the luck of the draw,' Millar shrugged. 'Been lucky all my life, me.'

Until now.

The knock on the door was loud, insistent, followed by heavy footfall in the hallway as the WPC let in the officers that had come to transport Millar to the station to make his statement. 'Who was he then?' Millar demanded as an officer pulled him to his feet, moving his arms behind his back to cuff him. Coupland had already read him his rights. 'What was Vinny to the bloke who got the blame?'

'His son.'

Millar folded in on himself, 'He saw my wife and daughter come visit me inside.' He righted himself but his legs were weak; the officers either side of him did their best to keep him upright. 'I told him how chuffed I was when Vicky got a job at the local kid's nursery!' His face screwed up as though in pain. 'You know, she'd started getting friendly with some fella she bumped into after work a couple of weeks ago. He'd been giving her lifts home when the weather was bad, never came in though. We didn't think any more about it, she's – was – a good looking girl, a sensible one, wouldn't have taken any risks.'

303

Coupland took a step towards him, dipped his head to Millar's height. 'She probably didn't, Jonny, whatever he'd learned about her from you he'd have been able to put to his advantage, making out he liked the same things, knew the same people, it was bound to reassure her.'

Millar opened his eyes. His body started to tremble as the truth of it set in. He stopped at the doorway, looked back at Coupland one last time. 'I handed her to him on a plate, didn't I?'

Coupland didn't reply, instead he turned to the WPC. 'How's his wife?'

'Out of it, for the moment.'

'You stay here,' he ordered, 'when she comes round let her know the score, you may need to call the doctor back again before you do.'

'Understood, Sarge.'

Coupland stood in the flat's doorway, he was about to call Ashcroft on his mobile when the DC appeared on the balcony. 'Came to see if you needed a hand. A couple of uniforms doing house to house along Underwood's road have reported that a neighbour saw a girl resembling Vicky go into his flat with him around 11.30pm last night. Thought she looked a bit tipsy. They found discarded clothes in the bin outside which have been bagged for DNA testing, but we're guessing they belong to her.'

Coupland frowned. 'He probably drugged her so he could change her clothing, the PM will tell us for sure.' One thing baffled him. 'So where was Amy when this was going on?' Ashcroft wondered how much he could tell him, 'She could have been sleeping upstairs,' he ventured, testing his sergeant's reaction. 'Maybe she woke up and disturbed him.' Coupland's gaze burned into him. 'I'm just saying it might explain the signs of struggle uniforms found when they trawled through the place this morning,' he stammered.

A feeling of dread settled in Coupland's stomach. Amy may not be dead yet, but Vince Underwood had absconded with her.

It was only a matter of time.

The static of the officers' radios crackled as they led Millar out of his flat: *'Two people have been seen on top of the multi-storey car park on Oldham Street.'* Coupland's stomach lurched. It was the car park where Vinny's father had been set up for murder all those years ago; of course it would be the place where he'd want the final act of retribution to be carried out.

'Oh, God no.' It was as though someone had hold of Coupland's heart and kept on squeezing.

'Sarge?'

Tighter.

Coupland sprang into action, running down the stairwell towards the pool car as Ashcroft raced after him, only catching him up as he bleeped his fob to unlock it. 'Come on,' Ashcroft said, reaching out for the ignition keys. 'I'll drive.'

Coupland pushed him away, fixing him with a steely glare. 'Go near that steering wheel and I'll kill you.' His voice sounded different, as though several pebbles were stuck in his throat. He yanked open the driver's door and climbed in.

Ashcroft banged on the glass. 'What can I do?'

Coupland lowered the front passenger window. 'Shut the fuck up and get in.'

He started the engine, crunching through the gears

on auto pilot as he screeched into the oncoming traffic causing several cars to brake without warning. Ashcroft reached for the blues and twos. 'No.' Coupland instructed, 'We don't let him know we are coming.'

Ashcroft nodded, keeping his eye on the speedometer, holding onto the car's grab handle for dear life. 'If she's up on the roof at least we know she's alive,' he murmured, cursing himself for tempting fate.

Coupland said nothing. His heart battered against his chest. It felt odd, as though it had gone out of rhythm; an extra beat or a missing one he couldn't be sure. A voice in his head told him to stay calm. It sounded like Lynn but it couldn't be her because she didn't know Amy was in danger. 'Sweet Jesus, it'll kill her,' he whispered. Lynn would be at work right now. Oblivious. Soothing parents whose children were in peril. He should call her. No, better to wait. Find out the extent of it. A pain wrapped itself around his chest forcing him to suck in his breath. Ashcroft looked at him sharply as he overtook the car in front of him on the inside, the driver hogging the middle of the lane.

'GET OUT OF THE FUCKING WAY!' Coupland yelled. His palms were sweating; they were beginning to slip on the steering wheel. He gripped tighter. His head throbbed. The last time he saw Amy she had yelled at him to leave her alone. He'd yelled at his old man once. Before he'd learned to judge his mood. The bastard had dragged him to the kitchen sink, filled it with water, pushed his head underneath, holding it down till he'd played dead. That's how he felt now.

Like he was drowning.

Entering the multi-storey car park at speed, he crashed

through the barrier as he zig zagged up the ramps to the roof where he screeched to a halt. Vinny was standing close to the edge, holding onto a shivering Amy. The wail of a siren told him back up was on its way.

'Stay here,' he ordered Ashcroft, before stepping out of the car.

CHAPTER 22

14 March 1992

The chants can be heard half a mile away. Taunts, rising in the air, carrying across the city like a toxic gas. Threats and counter threats, pushing and shoving, a flick of a blade to show who means business. Greater Manchester Police has pulled out all the stops. The brief being to put a ring of steel around Old Trafford but even with beat cops drafted in from other areas the best they can do is focus on the hot spots, use the intelligence they've been given to swarm the likely battlegrounds, keep the opposing football firms apart. Several police Alsatians wait with their handlers on the canal towpath.

An army of men wearing Lacoste tracksuit tops over polo necks and baggy jeans are lined up against the exterior wall of a pub as they are searched one by one. Many wear thick overcoats even though the weather no longer merits it; it bulks them up, makes them look hard. Two uniformed officers carry out the searches; a dozen more stand guard, making sure none of the supporters break free from the line. Even so the officers carrying out this task have been chosen for their size; heavy built, bulky men, more able to stand their ground if needed. They take their time, checking pockets, lifting trouser legs to check for weapons strapped to ankles. Patting the groin area is the worse bit because of the catcalls and mickey taking, the complaints if they get too rough. Truth is if someone wanted to carry something into the ground they could, and nothing short of a cavity search would stop them. A youth, impatient at waiting his turn in the line, raises both his arms and starts singing:

'Uni-TED, Uni-TED are the team for me
With a nick nack paddy wack
Give the dog a bone,
Why don't city fuck off home.'

He wears a Pringle jumper over a Fred Perry shirt and Farah trousers. Adidas Three Stripe trainers. A Burberry scarf is wrapped around his neck several times, his baseball cap pulled down low over his face. He's not a ring leader, more a team mascot; the officer regards him evenly, already identifying him as a possible troublemaker. The other supporters join in the song and laugh when Burberry Man tries wriggling away as the officer starts patting him down. The officer's response is automatic, his face an angry snarl as he grabs Burberry Man, pushing him against the wall before telling him to shut the fuck up. The youth grins, tries to carry on singing but the cop drags him to the ground while shoving his arm up his back. Burberry Man is tall but slender, he squirms on the tarmac but the officer pinning him down is heavier and refuses to give him any purchase. He is hoisted to his feet and told if he steps out of line or opens his fucking mouth again it would be shut for him properly.

Burberry Man falls silent. Silent but unrepentant.

He and his fellow supporters are ushered out of the pub car park where a tag team of officers escort them to the football ground. As he passes by the cop who patted him down he mimes the wanker sign. 'Why, you little bast—' The officer makes as if to go after the boy but his colleague holds him back, tells him not to be so damned stupid. His colleague is a black man, a little older than the others with a care worn face, someone who's seen a lot worse in his time and knows it isn't worth fanning flames. The officer objects at first, doesn't take kindly to being told what to do but then something catches his eye. As the car park empties a familiar checked scarf can be seen on the tarmac. He makes sure no one is looking before stooping to retrieve it, then slips it inside his high-viz jacket.

CHAPTER 23

This is where it all began. Where Jonny Millar killed Eddie Garside and left Dad to take the blame. He'd laughed when he'd told me, and at the time I'd laughed too because I didn't know the whole story, didn't realise the 'poor sod' he was talking about was my old man. He won't be laughing now, and neither will Detective Sergeant Coupland when he scrapes his girl up from the pavement below. She's crying now, her face covered in blotches, not the babe I told her she was when I first sought her out. With a surname like that she was easy to track down, her Facebook page telling the world what college she attended. Her old man should have had a word with her about that; you never know who's going to look you up.

Too late now.

Amy's still crying, asking me to see sense, telling me that she knows I don't want to hurt her. How can she say that when she saw what I did to Millar's girl? She'd screamed when she walked in on us, when she saw me putting her clothes onto a comatose girl. I'd had no choice but to hit her, told her there was more where that came from if she made another sound. I'd had to tie her up then, while I got rid of Vicky. S'funny, afterwards I didn't get a peep out of her all the while we were in the car, and now we're on the roof it doesn't matter. She can scream her head off if she wants to. While she still can.

Not like it'll make any difference.

From the top of the building the city of Salford stretched out before them. Fluorescent strips in office block windows twinkled like stars on the horizon. Inside, cleaners would be making their way from room to room, earphones stuffed in to block out the monotonous hum. The tower block lights of Tattersall illuminated tribes of young men wearing hoodies and low rise jeans going about their drug dealing business, oblivious to what was occurring on a car park roof less than a mile away from their turf.

A low wall provided a barrier around the perimeter of the roof. A bitter wind hurtled across it. Leaning into the wind Coupland moved towards them carefully, hands in the air to show he was no threat. Easy now. He gazed out towards the city's landmarks, a city he'd protected for over twenty years. If something happened to Amy what would be the point of it? Heart pounding, he moved closer.

'I DIDN'T PUT YOUR DAD AWAY!' he shouted.

'No, you put ME away instead!'

'I didn't know who you were...'

'So it would have made a difference, would it?'

Coupland looked away. 'Just answer me this. Why kill their daughters?'

'Because of the sister I never had. The one that died because of the stress Mum was under during the trial. The men that caused this went on to have happy families yet my dad was left with nothing. Then you came along and robbed me of ever getting to know him.'

The final nail in the coffin.

Coupland tried a different tack. 'I thought you loved Amy.'

The wind whipped around them. 'I do. At first she was a way to get to you.' Vinny's voice faltered. 'I didn't expect to fall for her.'

The sound of sirens echoed up from the street below. The wailing ended abruptly, followed by the sound of car doors slamming and boots pounding on tarmac. Amy cried out in terror when Vinny leaned forward to look over the edge, pulling her forward with him. Every action was perilous; one wrong move could be fatal. Coupland prayed Ashcroft had the sense to tell the assembling tactical support team to stand down. If Vinny fell backward when the bullet hit him he'd be taking Amy with him. Vinny reached out to hold onto the low wall.

'So why hurt her?' Coupland demanded. 'You'll be losing someone else that you love.' A pause. Planes flew overhead, streaking the sky with their jet stream. And then it dawned on him.

Vinny was going to kill them both.

'Don't,' Coupland said, taking a step nearer. 'Don't hurt her.'

'What choice do I have? I don't want to live out the rest of my life in jail.'

All the while he was talking he was moving closer to the edge.

'Dad, I'm so sorry...' Amy whimpered.

'I'm sorry too,' Coupland shouted into the wind.

For what he was about to do.

Coupland lunged forward and wrapped his arms around Amy, clinging onto her with nothing but the metal barrier giving him purchase, stopping him from hurtling to the concrete floor below any second now. Vinny pulled Amy towards him but her arms were locked with Coupland's, resulting in a bizarre tug of love. Coupland pulled her one way. Vinny pulled her the other. In a rage Vinny pulled too hard; stumbling backwards he lost his footing before falling onto the pavement below. He didn't scream long for someone who knew what a mess he'd make when he landed.

'Don't let go of me, Dad!' Amy cried.

'Never,' he whispered into the air between them, hanging on for grim death until Ashcroft came running to his aid and helped to lift her over the barrier.

Coupland held Amy's shaking body close as they huddled together in the lift, murmuring that everything would be fine. It was when he took hold of her hand as they stepped out onto the ground floor that he felt it. The crushing sensation that felt like an elephant had settled on his chest. He turned to Amy in surprise, saw her mouth form an 'O' shape as he fell to his knees, heard Ashcroft yell 'We need some help here…' to the waiting paramedics.

EPILOGUE

'Is someone going to answer the door or what, then?' Lynn called out from the kitchen where she'd set about making sandwiches, spreading butter onto bread before scraping it off again. Ashcroft pushed himself up from his chair in the living room. 'Sit back down love, you're a guest,' Lynn ordered, looking pointedly at Amy who had assumed the position of lady of the manor, lying on the settee, picking at the chocolates Ashcroft had brought.

'The doctor told me to rest,' Amy reminded her, 'after all that I've been through.'

'I don't mind,' Ashcroft said, making his way to the front door where a woman stood waiting, one hand holding onto a mischievous looking boy and the other gripping onto a child's car seat containing a sleeping infant. 'You must be Alex.' Ashcroft stepped to one side to let the boy run in; the small car he clutched was driven along each wall as he made car chase noises.

Alex hurried in after him. 'He's had a sugar rush and it'll be this one's feeding time soon, with any luck this visit'll knacker them both out. Bliss! An hour in front of the telly eating my body weight in chocolate.'

Just then Coupland stepped out of the downstairs toilet carrying a newspaper. 'I'd give it five minutes, if I were you,' he warned them before wrapping his arms around Alex. 'I take it you've met Ashcroft then,' he checked when he finally let her go.

'We've not been formally introduced as such,' Alex smiled at the DC, 'but even with my baby brain I figured you're the guy trying to squeeze into my size five shoes.'

'Come on through, Alex,' Lynn called. 'I'm making up a spot of lunch; you'll join us, won't you?'

'Too right, it's a rare day that I get to feed myself anything that doesn't come out of a wrapper, I'll be glad when Carl gets back from his training course. Anyway, how are you, muffin?' Alex paused by Amy, placing a hand on her shoulder to give it a squeeze.

'The doctor says I've suffered a huge shock.' Amy moved her legs out of the way so that Alex could sit beside her.

'I'm not surprised,' Alex said, noticing the dark circles and sallow skin. 'Mind you, the sight of your dad in jogging bottoms is not for the faint hearted.'

She raised an eyebrow at Coupland. 'You do know that nobody over 40 should wear them, don't you? There should be some sort of health warning.'

'Ha bloody ha,' Coupland sighed, 'they're comfy.'

Lynn brought a large plate of sandwiches through, placing them on the coffee table along with a stack of smaller plates and paper towels folded into triangles.

'How are you bearing up?' Alex asked her quietly.

'Getting there,' she smiled, 'especially now this one's back home.' She glanced at Coupland, her eyes crinkling at the corners. 'You taken your tablets?'

'Yup.' He hunkered down to put a ham triangle on a plate for Ben. 'You're lucky,' he whispered, ruffling the boy's hair, 'I have to have salad on mine.'

'Stop moaning,' Lynn scolded. 'I've put the butter on

you like.'

Coupland lifted the lid of a cheese salad triangle and peered at its underbelly. 'Only just,' he sniffed.

Alex's face fell serious as she regarded her old partner. 'So what did the hospital say?'

'High blood pressure,' Coupland tutted, 'they asked whether I'd been under any undue stress recently.' They both grinned.

'I thought you'd be on sick leave; when I called at the station and they said you were on a rest day I thought I was hearing things.'

'I'm not ill, the chest pain was just a wakeup call, the sooner we get back to normal the better.' Coupland tried to catch Amy's eye as he said this but she was too busy reading the chocolate assortment menu. He knew the brave face was for his benefit; he'd heard her crying in her room most nights but by morning the shutters came down. She'd refused the counselling offered to her, refused to let anyone mention Vinny in her presence. She was hurting, and there seemed precious little he could do to make it better. 'And there was me thinking you'd come specially to see me.'

Alex rolled her eyes. 'It's taken me two hours to get us out the front door. There's less planning needed for an armed raid. Once I've got us out it makes sense to cram in as many visits in the day as is feasible.'

Lynn peered at Todd asleep in his car seat. 'Nice having a baby about the place again,' she clucked, causing Coupland to scowl.

'Don't go getting any bloody ideas,' he warned her, his scowl softening as he looked over at Amy. His heart would surely burst if there was another one to run around after; better to count their blessings.

Amy looked up from the chocolate box and smiled, distracted. She chewed on her lip as she glanced away, too busy worrying about the positive pregnancy test hidden in her underwear drawer to pay much attention to the conversation going on around her.

THE END

ABOUT THE AUTHOR

Born in Salford Emma moved to the Peak District as a child, commuting into Manchester's financial district as a consultant for HSBC. Spells in Brummie beckoned (Selly Oak then Solihull) after winning a bank scholarship to Birmingham University before working out of bank branches in Castle Bromwich, Coleshill and Shirley.

Emma loved English Literature at school but studied Business and Finance in order to secure a 'proper' job. Other jobs have included selling ladies knickers at Grey Mare Lane Market and packing boiler suits in a clothing factory. After moving to Scotland Emma worked for a housing association supporting socially excluded young men into employment before setting up her own training company.

Widowed with two sons Emma writes from her home in East Lothian which they share with their rescue dog, Star.

Find out more about the author and her other books at: https://www.emmasalisbury.com

The first chapter of the next book in this series, ABSENT, is over the page…

CHAPTER ONE

He is running towards his target yelling every profanity under the sun. The sound of helicopter blades overhead wipes out his threats but his enemy gets the gist of it, can already tell what is coming.

Fear is not an option.

He is a killing machine.

His mind is his greatest weapon.

He will not be defeated.

He tightens the grip on his gun before dropping onto one knee to take aim. He shoots at them indiscriminately, enjoying the sound of metal ripping through skin, the thud as each victim hits the ground. He sits back on his heels to survey his work and smiles. He's good at this and each day he gets better. He just needs to keep up the practice. He leans forward on his haunches, takes aim once more.

'For God's sake, there you are!'

Startled, Jason smiled at the young woman standing in the doorway balancing a packing box on her hips. 'I've only just picked up the controls, honest!' he said, dropping them as he got to his feet hastily, like a teenager caught watching porn. He still had his headset on, which meant he'd been playing long enough to check in with his on-line pals.

'We've still got boxes to unpack, Jase,' she sighed, 'masses of them, if you haven't noticed; can't the X-box wait a while?'

'Just taking a bit of downtime, Ali,' he grinned in the way that stopped her getting angry with him. Or at least it had until now.

'That only makes sense if you've actually done something this morning, hun,' Ali pouted, her eyes giving lie to the scowl on her lips. Fair enough he'd driven them across town that morning and lugged the heaviest boxes up the steep flight of stairs, but since then he'd avoided actually opening any of them.

'I want this place to look good by the time Mum and Dad get here,' she reminded him. Frown lines creased his brow as he shook his head.

'They're coming to help us move in, Ali, what's the point of getting everything unpacked before they get here? I thought the general idea of people coming to help was that they actually pitched in.' The look on Ali's face told him his opinion was superfluous. He spoke into the mouthpiece of his headset: 'Talk to you later buddy,' he said to his online team mate before taking it off, dropping it onto the bean bag he'd been slouched against before following her out of the room.

'Grab one of those boxes and bring it through to the bedroom,' Ali instructed, pointing to a stack of cardboard boxes in the narrow hallway. Nudging the door open with her hip she placed the box she was carrying on top of an unmade double bed. 'Christ, this room stinks!' She moved over to the sash window and opened it wide, wafting the stale air out with her hand.

'What's up now?' he sighed as he carried two boxes into the room, one balanced on top of the other preventing him from seeing where he was going.

She moved towards him, taking the top box from him and placing it on the bed beside the one she'd just put down. 'There's glass in this one, be careful!' she scolded, before opening a large built-in wardrobe and nodding to the box he held in his hands. 'Your clothes are in that one, still on the hangers, thought I'd make life easy for you.'

'Nice one!' he beamed, opening the box and lifting out several creased shirts before placing them straight onto the wardrobe rails. The creases would drop out in time, if he left them long enough.

Ali pointed to a large sports bag in the bottom of the cupboard, her nose wrinkling at the smell coming from it. 'Don't tell me you've got your rugby kit in there! You could at least have washed it before you moved out, or got your mum to do it.' His mother was a soft touch when it came to her son, ran round after him all day long; if he'd asked her she would have held onto it, brought it over once his kit had been washed and ironed. Not for the first time Ali slid a worrying look at Jason, if he thought she was going to provide the same level of devoted service as his mother he was going to be woefully disappointed.

'It's not mine,' he shrugged.

'Well it's not mine either,' she retorted. 'Don't tell me we've inherited junk from the previous tenant, the landlord promised he'd shift all their stuff when I paid him the deposit. I'm going to ring him now…' She headed towards the bedroom door, pulling her mobile phone from the pocket of her skinny jeans.

'Just chuck it out, Ali, what's the point of stressing yourself over a dirty sports kit? It's not ours, the flat's been empty for a while, whoever it belongs to doesn't want it. I say let's throw it out and get on with the rest of the day.'

Ali was already shaking her head. 'There's a couple of things I wanted to tell him though,' she insisted, 'he promised he'd refresh all the paintwork and he hasn't, and there are marks on the settee in the lounge that I don't want us getting the blame for.' Their combined budget had got them something not much bigger than a garage as it was.

'So take a photo and email it to him,' Jason cajoled. Moving towards her he slipped his arms around her waist. 'I can think of far better ways to spend the morning…'

Ali's mouth curled into a smile. 'Fine,' she conceded, as he pulled her closer, 'but we'll need to be quick, Mum and Dad will be here at 12…' The grin on his face got wider as he homed in for a kiss.

'Not so fast buster,' she persisted, her nose wrinkling as she pushed him away, 'you need to shift that stinking kit first. While you're doing that I'll go take photos of the repairs he needs to do on my phone and send them across.'

Eager to please now his luck was in, Jason laughed as he reached for the sports bag to hoist it over his shoulder. Then he stopped in his tracks. The bag was heavier than expected, though that wasn't what worried him.

It was the greasy liquid seeping through the canvas base into the carpet below that made his stomach heave.

The slow drip of something viscous and foul.

Printed in Great Britain
by Amazon